They Call Me Sherlock

Triplets: Three Aren't One Book Five

By USA Today Bestselling Author

Dani Haviland

Copyright

Book Description

Life gets exciting for the rich and clever 'butler' when his sweetheart from 1969's Woodstock shows up looking younger than possible. What was her secret? And did she still care about him as much as he did her?

Praise and Awards

USA Today Bestselling Author

Kindle Top 100 Bestselling Author

Amazon Top 100 Historical fiction Author

Amazon Top 100 Biographies and Memoirs Author

Amazon Top 100 Short Story Anthologies and Collections

Amazon Top 100 History of Women in the American Civil War

Amazon Top 100 United States Drama and Plays

Amazon Top 100 LGBT Mysteries Author

Amazon Top 100 Weddings

Amazon Top 100 Satire

"There wasn't a heartstring this one didn't pull at! And, no spoilers, but that's one of the nicest endings I could have imagined – all round, proving redemption's possible, some things will last forever, and …. Karma. This isn't just a story of Jose and Loren; it's so much more.   Amazon reader on *Too Fast for You* (http://bit.ly/2fast4YOU)

"From the picturesque descriptions of the Alaskan wilderness, to weaving a beautiful love story, the author's writing style is both serious and quirky. A perfect, relaxing read!"
   Amazon review of *One Arctic Summer* (http://bit.ly/2OneArcticSummer)

Dedicated

This story is dedicated to my great friend Mary Kelley. She wasn't born of my mother, but like the many others in this story, she has become 'kin' and an important part of my family. Thanks for being there for me, sister!

Chapter 1: Woodstock

Thursday, August 14, 1969
near Middletown, New York

"I'm sure this is the way," Silas said to himself, clutching the straps of his backpack. He pulled out the map he'd picked up at the gas station before he left home in Plymouth, Massachusetts. Yup, walking away from the sun in the morning and towards it in the afternoon would keep him on the right heading.

"An Aquarian Exposition." He looked at his ticket for the hundredth time since waking at dawn. "Ugh. It'll never catch on. They should call it Woodstock like the deejays do. Easy to remember. Solid and earthy but still groovy."

The sput-sputter of a vehicle with a hole in its muffler caught his attention. He tucked the map under his arm and stuck out his thumb.

The VW microbus covered in brilliantly colored peace signs and flowers slowed to a stop a couple hundred feet in front of him. A ginger-haired male with a picked-out afro hairdo stuck his head out the window. "Headed to Woodstock?"

"Yes, I am!" Silas hollered as he ran toward him.

The side door opened and marijuana smoke roiled out. He coughed and waved it aside, then saw the inside of the van was packed with at least a dozen people. He bit off the question, 'Are you sure you have room?' and stepped in. He grabbed the window frame as the van lurched onto the highway while he stood, looking for an open spot.

"You can sit on my lap," a young man with pouty lips said, his eyes blinking in unabashed flirtation.

"Or mine," an ebony young woman offered. "I don't bite." She nodded to pretty boy. "He might."

"No contest." Silas twisted in place, trying to find a way to sit down without putting his body parts in someone else's face.

"Take off the pack first," the friendly female said. "Then hold it in your lap. We're less than an hour away. I'm sure we'll manage for that long."

He did as told and lowered himself as gracefully as he could. The cramped quarters were packed with knees, heads, and elbows, a reefer being passed back and forth between them. Pretty Boy reached out and greeted Silas with a heavily costume-jeweled hand. "Pleased to meet you. I'm Eros. And you are?"

"Arrows?" Silas asked, the last syllable ending as a squeak, surprised by the young woman grasping him by the hips to pull him the rest of the way onto her lap. "Like bows and arrows?" he added, stifling a laugh.

"Eros! You know, like the Greek god of love? It's the name I chose. So, who are you?"

Silas chewed back his chuckle, then realized that although he'd been in the van less than a minute, the marijuana-charged atmosphere was getting to him. Or it was simply the lack of oxygen. "Me?"

Eros scoffed but didn't take his eyes from him.

Silas could feel the young woman sink her face into his back, the tremors of her laugh stifled by his body, hidden from Eros. He cleared his throat and said, "They call me Sherlock."

"Oh," Eros responded dryly. "That's John F. driving, and that's Buttercup from Boston – you can tell when she talks – Sunshine the blonde, Raven with the black hair, Levi in the ripped denims, Luther the botanist, Rapunzel with the long hair, Angel from L.A., Semen from Hard Rock…"

Silas felt a new wave of giggles get buried in his back, then heard nothing else Eros said. That is until the angry young man's voice raised loud enough that everyone in the van stopped talking.

"You have to have a name, woman, so spill. It's the cost of the trip."

"No, it's not," John. F. from the driver's seat called back brightly. "It's right on the bumper sticker: Ass, Grass, or Gas – Nobody rides for Free."

"I got a few bucks," Silas whispered to her over his shoulder.

"Dorothy from Oz is in the house… I mean, in the van!" she called out boldly.

Cheers erupted from everyone but Eros who had sunk back into his cramped corner and was sulking. He looked up at 'Sherlock' one more time with his best doe-eyed pout of innocence, but it was futile. The tall Adonis with long dark hair was now half-turned around on the Amazon's lap, his face radiant with enchantment and flirtation. Definitely hetero. Not even a chance he was curious.

"Wow!" John F. said, slowing down to pull over to the side of the road. "Come on out, everyone. You gotta see this."

The dozen dazed youths rolled out of the van, backs arching, arms and legs stretching at reclaiming the ability to move freely, clearing their smoke-filled lungs with fresh air.

"Wow, is right," Silas said, staring at how long the line of vehicles was ahead of them. "And we're a day early. I wonder what it's going to be like tomorrow."

"Worse," his warm-bodied chair replied tersely.

He turned around and saw her again for the first time. She was huge! Not fat but a giantess. She was half a head taller than he was, with broad shoulders and a commanding presence that made him want to shelter in place with her for a lifetime.

"Dorothy?" he squeaked.

She chuckled. She was used to people's first reaction to her height and used humor to deal with it. "Not my real name," she said dryly. "Do you want to go through the gate or try and sneak in with the others?"

Silas patted his backpack. "I already bought my ticket. I don't think it's right to steal. There are costs involved with renting the venue, providing electricity…"

3

'Dorothy' rolled her eyes. "I'll catch you later then," she said. "I'm short of cash. At least what they're using here. This was sort of last-minute deal for me."

"What? You got a pocket full of pesos or something?

She smiled broadly. "Yeah, something like that. *Adios!"*

And then she was gone, her long-legged stride catching up to the others before he realized the two of them hadn't decided on a hookup spot. He turned around and saw the hundreds of cars already slowing down to join the queue. There would be thousands, maybe even hundreds of thousands, of visitors to this event. How would he find her? "Shit!"

***

The agent at the gate was polite even if a bit harried. "Yeah, if you can find a flat spot, go ahead and set up your tent for tonight. Don't get carried away, though. Make sure you can strike it in a hurry. Once the music starts, folks will stomp over everything to get to the stage. Next!"

Silas took off for the side of the hayfield his microbus group had been headed toward when they had parted company. He grinned to himself. He didn't know much – actually knew nothing – about her. But, she was very, very tall. As long as she was upright and not standing in a hole, he'd find her, her stunning smile beaming bright above the crowds.

After four hours, he still hadn't found her. He went back to the site he had chosen for his tent and picked up the official-looking 'Keep Back: Unexploded Grenade' sign he had made before leaving home and returned it to his backpack.

Click!

Silas looked up and saw Rapunzel, Luther at her side. "Cool trick," Luther said, then looked away, scanning the area through his camera lens for more shots of interest.

Noticing the stares from the crowd around him, Silas suppressed his smirk and waved a two-fingered peace sign to those who were either scowling and flipping him off, or grinning and

4

giving him a thumbs-up reaction.

"That was clever, Sherlock," she said.

"Oh, hi." He dropped the bag and some of its contents spilled out. "You found me!" His smile of happiness was even more brilliant with the added shine of sweat, both from the heat of the August afternoon and the exertion of looking for her.

She nodded to his backpack and the tent pieces sticking out. "Looks like you came prepared."

He picked up a tent peg and hammer, shrugging with a mixture of embarrassment and modesty. "I do my research and try to anticipate any situation."

"Even rain?"

Looking up, he saw the dark clouds gathering, just like the forecast had predicted. "Yes, ma'am," then bent to work.

"Ma'am! I'm not anyone's ma'am. I'm not even seventeen."

Thwack!

Silas gasped at the pain, his thumb throbbing from the missed strike. "Sixteen?" he squeaked, his injured hand now stuck under his armpit.

"Here, let me," she said, picking up the dropped hammer. "I'm pretty good at this sort of thing. I grew up on a farm. My da was always building something, and I'd do anything to keep out of the kitchen."

"So, are you from around here then?" Silas asked, letting her take the lead on the shelter project.

She paused to think of a clever answer but went back to her initial reply. "Oz."

"All right, *Dorothy*. Did you come on a tornado?"

She snickered and shook her head. "Why do you ask so many questions?"

He inspected his injured thumb, thought about putting it in his mouth to ease the fiery pain, then realized it was filthy. He blew on it briefly. "Questions? Me? It's just who I am, I guess. Inquiring minds want to know... Hey, that's kind of catchy."

"Yeah. Right. Here, use your good hand to hold this. I want it taut to make sure I have the pegs in the right spot."

Silas did as told, letting his smile of appreciation bloom free as he watched her work, tight milk-chocolate brown curls pulled back at the nape of her neck with a leather thong.

"So, since I'm doing all the work, or at least most of it, are you going to share your spot with me, *sir*?" she asked sassily, looking up to feel the first drops of rain on her face.

"Sir? I'm not even eighteen yet," he said.

She laughed out loud. "Gee, I knew there was something else about you I liked."

"Else?"

She wiped her hand on her skirt, looked at it to make sure it was relatively clean, then ran her fingers through one side of his long hair, bringing a wayward strand back behind his ear. "You have very nice hair."

"Thank you. And yes, I'd be honored to share my meager accommodations. Who knows? You might have other valuable skills."

"I might…"

***

"It's too early to go to sleep," he said, looking up at the drab olive-green nylon ceiling.

"And there's not enough room for *some* of us to sit up, even if we had a deck of cards." She paused a moment, then asked, "Don't tell me you brought cards…"

"Yes, I did but that's only because they were already in my bag from my last trip. Do you want to build a castle?"

"Do you mean a house of cards?" she asked.

"I don't aim low," he said wryly and leaned close to look her in the eyes. "A castle."

"Is that a tall person joke," she asked, a shiver of attraction running up her arms despite the sultry temperature.

"No. I aspire." He wiped his upper lip with the side of his hand.

"And perspire. Dang. I didn't bring a razor."

"Really? All this craziness that's going to happen, and you worry about being clean-shaven?"

"Going to happen?" he asked, one eyebrow raised. "Do you know something I don't know?"

She gulped, coughed slightly to buy some time, then replied, "With half a million people, of course, it's going to be crazy."

"Where did you hear half a million? Last I heard, the high estimate was two hundred thousand?"

Tempted to cough again, this time she went with the catch-all lame excuse that always worked at home. "Really? I guess I got confused."

"You know, if it wasn't so cloudy, it would be a perfect night for watching the stars." Silas pointed up. "See, there's the Big Dipper, Orion's Belt..."

She scooted head-to-head and pointed out an imaginary constellation. "That's Leo, right. Oh," she pointed through the tent opening to the east. "And we should be able to see Venus and Mars in the morning. Last bright lights in the sky."

"No," Silas said and turned to face her.

"No?" she shifted to her side and lifted onto her elbow, scowling.

He copied her movement and neared her, as close as he could get without his eyes crossing. "No."

"Yes!" she said, a frown of playfulness almost breaking into a laugh.

"No, because by morning, the sun – the last bright light – will be out."

"No. The sun will be the first bright light out."

Silas sighed in defeat and leaned closer. "First and last in a continuing cycle. It's all relative."

"I don't know about relative but it's not important."

"The argument of the ages: which came first," he said and paused, waiting for her to finish the thought.

"The dinosaur or the egg?" she said.

"You're so funny." Then he leaned in three inches and kissed her gently on the mouth, paused to appreciate the softness, then pulled back. "Umm."

"That one, we can agree on," she said, then leaned to meet his mouth again. "Umm."

***

They awoke the next morning to the sounds of shouts and footsteps. "Over here's a good spot!" and "No, someone's claimed it already."

"Day One begins," she whispered. "Are you ready?"

Silas smiled broadly, then shifted the front of his jeans as inconspicuously as possible. "I will be. Let's take this down and find the porta-potties. They should still be clean."

"Let's go together, though. I don't think I could find you again. At least with the *great number* of attendees that are supposed to show up," she said, teasing him.

He felt so complete. Fulfilled. The empty spots in his emotions were now warm and cuddly. They hadn't got carried away last night but they had perfected kissing. Three more days and nights with her. And she didn't want to get separated again, either!

The two quickly struck the tent, packed it, and spotted the johns in the distance. "Over there," he said.

She nodded but didn't speak, preoccupied. *She has to be here. Mali always said she wanted to come.*

Silas watched as she searched the grounds as if she was looking for someone. *Maybe she's trying to spot one of the headliners. Don't say anything to make her feel self-conscious.*

They both used the facilities then came out, pinched-faced and scowling.

"If this is the first day, I don't think I want to eat or drink the rest of the time I'm here. Yuck!" Silas said.

"What do you mean? At least you're a guy. Then again, why do you think I wore a full skirt?" she said, bowing her knees and

8

bending into a half-squat.

"What? I mean, you'd do that?"

"Hey, that's what the women did in the old days and still do in some areas of the world."

Silas gulped as he realized that meant she probably wasn't wearing underwear. A thrill went down his belly then crept lower, thoughts bubbling of lying with her for three more nights sans undergarments. He glanced back at the portable bathrooms, the grossest thing he could think of on such short notice to turn his stomach and stifle his surging stiffy. *She's sixteen, she's sixteen. Even if you're only seventeen, she's only sixteen!*

Chapter Two: The Wedding Party

January 30, 2010
After Vickie's Wedding
Near Plymouth, Massachusetts

Silas noticed the tall dark woman sitting alone, isolated from the rest of the rambunctious wedding party. It couldn't be her, could it? She looked too young. Without thinking, he found himself walking toward her, holding his breath in anticipation. In hope.

He paused at her table, but before he could get the nerve for an introduction, she spoke. "It's you, it really is you…isn't it?" she asked.

With a smile so wide, his cheeks hurt and his eyes teared, Silas sputtered, "I was going to ask you the same thing. Woodstock '69?"

"Ah, a very good year."

"Good and wet," he agreed with a chuckle. "But the music was fantastic. May I join you?"

"Might as well. You never did tell me your real name. It really isn't Sherlock, is it?"

He shook his head, his grin still wide. "My name is Silas Priest, but yes, they call me Sherlock. You're truly not Dorothy from Oz, though…"

Silas watched her twinkle of delight fade into embarrassment. "I was trying to find a clever name, too. Actually, I did feel like I was in the land of Oz. Everything was so strange there. So primitive."

"Yes, positively the most unsanitary place I've ever seen. A hut in equatorial Africa would be the Hilton compared to that mess of mud and ponchos. Where did you go? As I recall, it was Monday morning and Jimi Hendrix was supposed to come out for the finale. I went to get our milk bottles refilled with water. When I returned, you were gone. You'll have to forgive me for not getting back to you, but without so much as a real name or even a hint of where you were from, I wasn't able to track you down."

"You looked for me?"

Silas nodded, his smile now a smirk of irony. "For two long years."

Her wide-eyed reaction was worth the search, questioning stoned hippies and frustrated farmers in the neighborhood, following false leads, and hoped-for fantasies. Maybe she hadn't been trying to hide from him.

"Don't worry about it. I may not have found you, but I did stumble into a great career and made some fabulous connections. Now, please tell me your real name before, *poof,* you disappear again," he said, his hands tickling the air to emphasize his statement.

"I shouldn't be too hard to find now. At least, I'll be in the states. It looks like my son has found the girl he's been pining over since last summer. I doubt he'll want to return to France with me. He's over there with her now, trying to make things right." She nodded at Oscar, the handsome young man with fair skin and dark hair who was awash with emotions, frustrated at trying to get his point across to the fireball with short blond hair who was dressed for shoveling snow rather than a wedding.

"He's had girlfriends before," she continued, "but this is the first time he's been infatuated. He and Tori had a spat before he came to see me. I thought he'd have a meltdown not being able to see or talk to her for months. It looks like they're communicating now, though."

She sighed, watching their courting from afar, Oscar stepping in, then backing away. The girl doing the same, both of them uncertain of what to do next. "I sure hope she doesn't break his heart."

Silas turned to watch, too. The young couple's initial confrontation had been chilly but was quickly warming up to a pensive touch, then a hug, and now an awkward nose-crunching kiss. "You do know she – Tori – is my granddaughter, right?"

The woman's jaw dropped open then shut with a *hmph* of realization. "I knew there was something else I liked about that girl.

She's so perceptive and open-minded…must be a family trait."

Silas put his hand on the table, then catching her eye to watch her reaction, moved it on top of hers. "If it is, it's a recessive gene. She and her triplet sisters may look alike, but those three are not one. Definitely. Actually, I think the one trait they all have in common is they're all dynamic – forces to be reckoned with – but all in different fields. Now, what do you mean by something *else* you liked about her? What was the first thing?"

She rolled her eyes, trying to think of what to say that wouldn't be a lie nor would be telling him too much about her. She didn't want to scare him away.

Lifting her chin, she decided to invest it all. "She's quite brilliant, you know. She and I were discussing time travel. She offered a few very interesting observations on it."

"Oh, okay," he said, nodding, waiting for the rest of her comment. When she didn't say more, Silas picked up the thread, hoping to erase the awkward pause. "I take it you both believe in it. I mean, most people don't, so if you two were of one accord, it must be because she's not closed-minded."

"No. I mean, yes. I mean…" She took a deep breath to search for the words.

Seeing that he had made her uncomfortable, Silas changed the subject. Sort of.

"You know, if I'm not being too bold, I'd rather have the answer to another question or two. First, how do you stay so young? I mean, it was forty-one years ago that we were together. We were only a year apart. Sixteen, you said. So, did you have a drop or two of Fountain of Youth water or did you…" Silas bent forward across the table, waiting for her to lean closer.

She saw the glimmer in his eye and fell for his charm again. "Yes," she drawled as she bent near his lips, those full, soft portals to pleasure that had given her her first tantalizing kiss so many, many years ago.

He blinked twice at her nearness, then realized she was waiting for him to speak. "Or did you slip forward through time twenty-five years," he whispered with a wink.

Still focused on his mouth, she felt rather than saw his playfulness. Instead of making a joke out of his words, she took the teasing torch and ran with it. "The latter," she said dryly, then added, "but it was only twenty. A woman still needs to take care of herself, you know. I moisturize, eat my greens, and try to find something positive about every sour situation."

"Really?" Silas said, pulling back to examine her expression. Faces didn't lie.

"Oh, yes. You'd be amazed at how stress, hate, anger – all those negative emotions – not only age you but also tear your body apart. They literally eat up your immune system, so it attacks itself."

Julianna watched as he closed his mouth and swallowed. Emboldened by his shock, she leaned forward again, waving at him minimally for him to come back. "I don't believe there's such a thing as a Fountain of Youth, though" she whispered, intentionally avoiding the topic of time travel. "I think it's just a fairy tale."

Silas's head shook back and forth slowly as he realized who she was. Or rather, what her age secret had to be. "No, there really is a Fountain of Youth. Or there was. At least, I know there are a few little blue vials of its water scattered around the world." He took a deep breath, hoping to inhale two day's worth of confidence so he could share his secret with her. "I know it's real because I actually held a bottle of it once."

Julianna scoffed but didn't say a word. He was making fun of her. So much for having a happy ever after.

Silas reached out and held her hand. She tried to pull it away, but he grasped it harder, hoping he wasn't hurting her but eager to keep her in his life.

"I know it's real because I really did have it in my hands. It was years ago. I was tracking it down with an old – very old – acquaintance. Have you ever heard of a man called Master Simon?"

She blinked, fluttering her eyes as if she was trying to rid herself of a wayward lash, wondering where she had heard that name. She remembered and her eyes widened. "The time traveler?"

"He calls himself Simon, the master of dimensional transportation with an emphasis on acquiring rare and exotic specimens of nature and man for the benefit of furthering our understanding of life on earth," Silas said in one breath, then inhaled deeply and huffed to recuperate.

"That's a mouthful," she said, laughing. "My dad used to call us fairies. I mean, call them fairies," she stammered. "I mean, he called time travelers fairies. Not the ones with lacy wings that were killed by disbelief like Tinkerball or…or…"

"Tinkerbell," Silas corrected. He picked up her hand and kissed it. "I guess I should have asked Simon for a drop or two when I had the opportunity. When you and I first met, we were only months apart. Now you look young enough to be my daughter."

"Huh? Wait! You mean, there really is a liquid you can drink that will make you younger?"

He grinned and answered, "You mean, you really can go back – or forward – in time?" one eyebrow lifted, his sincerity obvious.

She sighed and brought their joined hands to her face and kissed the ball of his thumb, noticing the faint scent of bay rum.

"Wow," he whispered. "It takes a lot to shock me, but I think a minor earthquake just rumbled through this old man's body. I still have one question, though."

"Anything. You already know my biggest secret."

"What's your name?"

"Julianna. So, do you think we can pick up where we left off? I'm over eighteen now?"

He chuckled. "I'm *well* over eighteen and although I didn't skip a couple of decades or drink a magic elixir, I'm not ready for a pine box, either. Remember how we spoke of exploring North Carolina?" he asked.

Julianna's eyes dimmed then brightened, the whole gamut of emotions zipping through her body in a moment. "Call it a leap of faith, but I think I'd follow you to the ends of the earth... Unless you're some sort of creeper that just got out of prison or..."

"No, not a creeper or miscreant of any kind," he said. "And I'd follow you to the end of *time*. Even if you are a creeper!"

"Deal!" she said, then leaned forward and gave him a gentle kiss, the first sincere one in decades. She pulled back minimally. "And I'm not a creeper, either. But I think we'd better not get started kissing or we'll make a scene."

He moved in for one more, then pulled back. "I hate to say it, but I think you're right. To be continued elsewhere."

"Absolutely!"

Chapter Three: Eighteen and Legal

"Speaking of eighteen now," Silas said, sitting tall in the chair. He looked over at the boisterous young couple – her son and his granddaughter – becoming the center of attention at the wedding party. He stood up to make sure trouble wasn't brewing. "It's hard to believe we were younger than they are now when we first got involved."

"Hmm. Speaking of involved…" Julianna mused, watching the physical interaction between the two. "Looks like they're getting a little *too* carried away. I think it's time for me to step in."

"Eighteen long years. That's how long it took me to find Tori and her adoptive parents. I only met her less than an hour ago, yet I feel as if I've known her all my life. Oh, I'm sorry. You said you wanted to check on them? I'm sure they'll be fine, but if that's what you want."

"Well, one thing is obvious, she's very fond of Oscar. Do you want to have some fun? Let's shake up the kids. You know, mess with them a little."

"Okay, and then let's find someplace private that's warm and dry…and with indoor plumbing," Silas said, then whispered, "This hound dog's getting too old for pup tents."

As they weaved their way through the tables and chairs. Silas placed his hand gently on Julianna's upper back. He knew she didn't need guiding but couldn't resist touching her. Tingles of his adolescent crush echoed through his body as he held onto her, making sure he didn't lose her again.

"That's enough, granddaughter," he said in a mock stern voice.

Tori quickly pulled out of the elevated hug and kiss as the red-faced Oscar released his embrace, letting her slide to the floor in a controlled drop.

"I didn't mean to startle you," Silas said with a sly grin.

"Yes, you did," Tori replied sassily, then rolled her eyes and added, "Grandpa."

"Actually, it was my idea to come over to talk to you," Julianna said, smiling at Tori, patting her shoulder with reassurance. "At first, it looked like you two were having a serious but angry discussion. We were going to wait until you had it sorted, but then your method of conversation changed in a hurry. I didn't want you to get too carried away using body language instead of words."

Oscar looked back and forth between his two favorite females. "You and Tori? You're buddies now? I mean, Tori has never been a very social person. So, that must mean you two found something in common."

"Oh, she and I get along famously," Julianna said. She reached out and pulled Silas close. "I wanted to talk to you, Oscar, before you and your lady friend made too many plans for your future." She winked at Tori with the word 'future' and continued. "Silas and I have been chatting, too. It seems we have a lot in common. I have a mystery and he's a bit of a sleuth. I think we're going to North Carolina to do a little exploring and research soon, very soon."

Julianna furtively grabbed Silas by the hand and looked at him, sending him a silent 'Just trust me' with her fervent clutch and deep gaze. He winked and squeezed back in reply. 'Message received.'

She swallowed hard and turned back to the young couple. "In other words, you won't need to come back to France with me, son."

"You're leaving? With him? But…but…you just met!"

"Actually, we knew each other a long time ago. I recognized him right away, but I think you two understand taking advantage of a situation when the *time* is right, yes?"

"Mom…" Oscar asked, his concern obvious with the tone of that single word. His eyes narrowed, "*Are you talking about that time travel nonsense again?*"

Julianna saw his inferred question and said, "Don't worry about me. I'll be in good hands. I'll make sure to keep in contact." She held up her phone and grinned.

"Just make sure you have the right *device* for the job," Tori said with an exaggerated wink, referring to their initial conversation about with the right mechanism, time travel would be possible.

"Absolutely!" Silas and Julianna said at the same time. On saying the same word at the same time, they smiled at each other, hands clutching in adolescent excitement.

"That's my granddaughter," Silas said. "She figured it out before I did."

"Mom…" Oscar grumbled, his voice just a half-tone above a growl.

"I'm okay, son," she said. "Really, I am. You have the keys to the car and the hotel. I'm going to make up for lost time with Silas."

"Whoa. Wait," Tori said, her face pinched as she tried to figure out what was going on. She turned to Oscar. "You mean my grandpa and your mother are dating?"

"Yeah, it looks like it," Oscar said, not even trying to hide his frown.

"Yes, we are!" Julianna crowed. "Wasn't it just a few hours ago, Oscar, that you told me to get a life? Maybe I'd meet someone here in the US?"

"Yeah, but…" Oscar looked Silas up, down, and back up again to stare at his gray hair. "But…"

"Don't worry about it…" Silas bit off the term of endearment 'son.' "We're taking our time with getting reacquainted," he said primly, adding a nod.

"Doubling up on relatives?" Tori said dryly. "That should make sending out Christmas cards easier. Oh, and Grandpa…"

"Yes, dear…"

"Don't lose her again, alright?" Tori said with a wink.

"I promise."

***

Julianna and Silas headed toward the cloakroom, eager to leave the wedding venue. They stopped and gave farewells to Julianna's nephew Rich and his new bride, Vickie – another one of Silas's newly acknowledged triplet granddaughters; Ria the third triplet and her beau, Evan; and the rush of others they encountered on their way

18

to what turned out to be a not-too-discreet exit.

The pair stepped into the parking lot and the brisk winter night's air. "So, where to now…?" Julianna asked, then faltered, suddenly ill at ease.

"Are you okay? You look gray…I mean…you don't look like you feel too good." Silas put his hand on her arm as she pulled her cashmere jacket close.

She chuckled at his discomfort. "A black woman gray? Is that a racist joke?"

"No, it's an 'I care about your health' question."

Julianna closed her eyes and shook her head, refusing to give in to insecurity. Her stomach relaxed with the conscious effort. "Don't take this wrong, but we have to be brutally honest from the get-go. Because if not, I'll go right back in and leave with my son."

"Good Lord, yes! By all means, be honest. However, I don't think either one of us needs to be brutal. I mean, we've both just shared deep secrets that anyone else would take as proof that we belonged in a nuthouse."

"Silas, I've been in a nuthouse," she said, her eyes half-closed with the pain of recalling the shame and humiliation.

"It wasn't like Bedlam, was it?" he asked gently. "I meant no disrespect. And for the record, just from what I know of you this evening and of our weekend in August of '69, I'd say your committal to an institution was an accident. You're not crazy. Just…how about we say you're *overly experienced*?"

Julianna's discomfort and anxiety evaporated, and hope and joy replaced it. "I never thought of it like that! How could I possibly explain a concept if the psychiatrist had no reference point? I'm sorry I doubted the veracity of you and your experience with the Fountain of Youth. I had no reference point, so treated you just like those overpriced shrinks my husband sicced on me." She rolled her eyes and said, "God rest Hugh's soul wherever he is."

"I thought you were divorced," Silas said. "I'm sorry. I guess it doesn't make a difference whether you're a widow or divorcee." He

19

squeezed her close. "You're mine now."

Julianna let him hold her tight, glad that between their position and the darkness, he couldn't see the fear in her face. *I don't know which I am either.*

Chapter 4: Rude Awakening

"Where to now?" Silas asked, opening the door to his classic Cadillac for her. "Do you have a preference? Find a hotel or head to my place?"

She waited for him to get comfortable then laid her head on his shoulder. "Which is closest?" she asked then giggled. Before he could answer, she suddenly sat up. "Crap."

"Excuse me?"

"I forgot my wallet. It has my ID. I don't know if they let you rent a room without it."

"I'll tell you what," Silas said, patting her leg in reassurance. "Since I don't know this town, and don't want to chance having an issue checking in without the proper identification, how about a twenty-minute drive to my place? I'm pretty sure my roommates will still be busy with the wedding fête for at least a couple more hours."

"You have roommates? At your age?" Julianna asked, her voice rising at the end. She scoffed. "You're messing with me, right?"

"Nope. Two of the other grandpas to the triplets and I share Doc Armstrong's place. It's a convenient arrangement for all of us. However, if you don't mind waiting for an extra five minutes, I can guarantee complete solitude. No need to hang a sock on the doorknob."

"A sock on the doorknob? What does that mean?"

Silas chuckled. "It was an old college trick. If a roommate had a girl in the room and didn't want to be disturbed, he hung a sock on the door. The guys and I haven't had to resort to that old ploy, though."

"No socks or no girls?" Julianna asked, not sure whether he was teasing or not.

"Lots of socks, but none of us ever met a woman worthy of bringing back. We're pretty much three confirmed old bachelors."

"Twenty-five minutes," she said, squirming with a coy chuckle.

"Beats the hell out of forty years."

She put her head back on his shoulder and sighed as he pulled out of the parking lot. "I agree. However, if I sit still for very long, the meds I'm on make me drowsy." She yawned and covered her mouth. "Excuse me! I think I'll take a nap now so I'm perky later…"

And then she was out, emitting soft little snores between sighs of 'mmm…'

Twenty minutes later – the speed limit severely bent but not too badly broken – Silas pulled in front of his twenty-acre estate. He pushed in his security code, the chain and gear mechanism groaning and screeching as the front gate swung open.

The unfamiliar noise startled Julianna, rousing her from deep sleep to a half-lucid panic, her arms flailing, batting at Silas. She clutched at the seatbelt as if fighting off unseen assailants, her head thrashed back and forth.

"Whoa! It's okay, Julianna," Silas said, foot on the brake. He tried to restrain her hands – both to protect her from herself and to avoid another blow to his face, but that enraged her even more. Cowered beneath his elbow, he put the Cadillac in park, grabbed the key, and got out.

He rushed to the passenger side and opened her door. She lurched out, enraged. "You're fine, sweetheart," he said soothingly, standing out of reach, his hands behind his back. "No one's going to hurt you. You can wake up now."

As quickly as she'd erupted into a Class Five tizzy, Julianna snapped out of it. Her eyes wide, she looked around at the unfamiliar terrain and gated yard, at the mansion at the end of the long driveway. She blanched, trying to orient herself. Swallowing hard, she closed her mouth, and turned around in place, taking it in, hoping something would be familiar.

And then she saw him.

"Silas?" she asked. "It is you, isn't it?"

"Yes, it is." He bit off the question, 'Are you okay,' not wanting her to be more flustered than she already was. "I guess arriving early threw you off a little."

"Where are we?"

"At the bottom of my driveway. If you'd like to get back in the car, I'll take you to my home."

Julianna gawked at the brightly lit mansion, a mini-version of the White House. "That…that's your house? No, I'm sorry. Of course, it's not. Are you the caretaker?"

"Oh, it's my home, all right. Lock, block, and cellar stocked with wine barrels. Don't tell anyone, though. A lot of folks still think I'm the butler. I get fewer requests for charity donations that way."

Dazed, Julianna walked to the car, Silas's hand gently touching her back. She let him guide her into the front seat, then saw his face. A long scratch shone bright red with fresh blood. "Did I…?"

Silas could feel the burn of the fresh wound but didn't reach up or acknowledge its presence. "Let's get inside. It's cold out here."

A long, eerily quiet minute later, he pulled into the below ground level garage. He started humming Janice Joplin's 'Take another piece of my heart' as he pulled in beside an orange and white restored VW microbus –1959 Westfalia camper special – accented with colorful vinyl decals of pop art flowers and peace signs.

"That's not the same version we rode in," Julianna began.

"No…" he agreed and waited.

"I think it's better." Julianna let herself out of the Cadillac and moved to the classic camper special, her hand hovering above the window as she looked inside. "Oh, my…"

"That's what I thought, too. It's too cold to take you for a spin, but as soon as the roads are clear and dry – or at least all the ice and snow are gone – we can take this baby over the mountains and plains, to all the rivers, lakes and oceans, campgrounds and wide spots from here to the ends of the earth."

She turned and looked at him, embarrassed. "I'm sorry I…" She stared at the fresh scratch and started to cry.

"Sorry for falling asleep? Or for being confused when you woke up with an old man you didn't recognize driving a car you'd never been in before? Either one would have been a good reason to be startled. Now, this is just the basement. It's a bit chilly in here, so let's go in the house. How about a hot toddy or a cup of cocoa?"

"Cocoa," she said, a smile rising. "With marshmallows, if you have them."

"I think I can make that happen."

Silas led the way into the kitchen, grabbed the remote from the wall, and with three taps, the mood was set in the den: lights on dim, gas fireplace lit, and the stereo playing sitar music by Ravi Shankar.

"What's that?" Julianna asked, nodding to the device he was returning to its home on the wall.

"*My* butler," he said, chuckling. He turned the kitchen light to bright and investigated the contents of the cupboard and the refrigerator. "Hmm. Only half and half – no milk. That ought to do. Would you like Mexican or American cocoa?"

"What's the difference? Is Mexican made out of *jumping* cocoa beans?"

The unexpected joke almost made Silas drop the carton. "No, the Mexican kind has cinnamon and a dash of cayenne. You can still have marshmallows, though."

"I'll try the Mexican," she said, then sidled up to him while he pulled the ingredients from the cabinet. Her hand hovered above the scrape, then moved behind his ear as if pushing long hair back.

"I cut it right after Woodstock," he said to her unspoken question. "This is about as long as it ever gets."

"Why?" she asked and tucked her hand under her arm.

"My father said it was time to get a job, pay my way in the world. Long hair wasn't conducive to high-paying employment. I worked my way through three years of college. I couldn't afford the luxury of being the hippie stoner war protester who was the inner me."

24

"You? A stoner? While everyone else at Woodstock was getting high, you were holding your breath!" Julianna laughed in recall. "I remember how you got ticked when some of the others were blowing smoke up that little dog's nose."

"And I'd still get riled about that." Silas took his set of measuring spoons out of the drawer and measured out the cocoa and sugar and added them to the small saucepan. "That poor pup had about one-fiftieth of a person's body mass. Who knew what it would do to him?"

Julianna's laughter stopped. "I never thought of that... I guess you do that a lot though, huh?"

"What?"

"Think," she said softly. "Sometimes I don't do that enough." She pointed to his scratch. "I react."

"You were sixteen when I met you and from what I could tell, living on your own, right?"

"Well, yeah..."

"You weren't done growing emotionally or intellectually. I don't know anything about your parent or parents, but whether they were saints or serving life sentences on Alcatraz, they never had a chance to finish your education in life. Or whatever you want to call it."

"Oh, I had both parents. They were more in the saint category, but you're right. I left before I completed the finishing school of life." She sighed deeply. "That's why I made sure no matter how much I wanted to take off and find..." Julianna gulped, stopping herself from telling too much. "Take off and find the meaning of life," she said and rolled her eyes, hoping he thought that's what she had meant to say.

Silas's eyes narrowed as he inspected her for signs of fibbing. Most definitely hiding but no overt lies. "So, you weren't necessarily happily married to Oscar's father, but you stayed with him for the boy's sake, correct?"

"Spot on, Sherlock. I'd ask how you knew, but it doesn't

25

matter. When a situation like that happens, the kids are the ones who suffer. Suffer from mountains of guilt because they see how miserable their parents are. Guilty because if they weren't around, the parents could be living separate lives, either with or without a new partner. Either way, Mom and Dad would be free from their imprisoned lives of co-parenting."

"And people wonder why I never married…"

"Hugh wasn't a bad man. He couldn't sire a child, though. We liked each other enough – we both volunteered at the shelter where I used to live. One day, a lady came in off the streets very pregnant. She made me promise that if something happened to her, I'd take care of the baby. Well, five days after Oscar was born, she was gone. *Pfft!*

"So, there I was with a baby and an heir-craving co-worker who'd been helping take care of Oscar since the day he was born. Well, getting married was the easiest way to legalize the adoption of a child with no mother available to sign away her rights. So, we made it work. Mostly. I mean, Oscar's a good kid, never been in trouble, and I think he turned out just fine."

Julianna beamed with classic maternal pride. "He finished college early. He's a talented botanist who has a major crush on your granddaughter."

"And Tori was adopted by one of the most gifted botanists in the world and his loving wife. A fine match, for sure. But you're wrong on one point."

"What?" she asked, then stuck her finger into the powdery concoction of cocoa, sugar, and spices, then licked it. "Yum!"

"He's not a kid; he's a young man. I can see it in his eyes. He's wise beyond his years; skeptical and analytical, yet passionate. I like him," he said with a broad smile and nod of endorsement.

Julianna laughed, then bent to kiss Silas on the cheek close to the scratch. "It sounds as if you just described yourself. Let's get the cocoa started, then I want to clean up that long-nailed sleepwalker's mishap."

Silas scooted the saucepan of dry ingredients to the back of the counter. "How about a little first aid then cocoa? I have a medicine cabinet in my room."

"Just make sure you have everything you need in there. I am still fertile, you know…"

Silas looked at the clock and groaned softly, his eyes half-closed in frustration. There wasn't a market or pharmacy open within an hour's drive. "Maybe a Band-Aid, and then a few hours of foreplay?"

"Ah, every woman's dream. Except for the Band-Aid part."

He grabbed her hand and brought it to his lips. "Maybe this time you'll let me bring out my stethoscope…"

Julianna stepped into his arms. "Lead the way, Doc!"

Chapter 5: The Red Room

"Which one is your room?" Julianna asked, her hand softly touching the polished carved oak handrail as they ascended the broad swirling staircase to the second floor.

"All of them," he said.

"But you said you had roommates…"

"I do, but not here. I usually live with my friends. Life changed for them. They were used to having family around. I wasn't, but I did enjoy their company. I was the best cook of the three, so they bribed me, and I moved in with them. We became a happily unmarried trio."

"Bribed you? With what?"

"I'll tell you later."

"If I'm a good girl?" she asked coyly, her eyes shining with mischief.

Now at the top of the stairs, Silas slipped his arm around her waist and spun her around to look down at the view of the entryway and sitting rooms, polished marble floors gleaming, classic antique furniture upholstered in deep roses and burgundies accented with lamps and sconces of polished brass.

"Maybe being a bad girl would be better…" he cooed as he kissed her below the ear.

"And all this is yours?" she squeaked at his tickle, taking in the magnificence.

He pulled back and grinned. "Does it make a difference? Let's just say none of this is stolen nor is it in danger of being repossessed."

Julianna pursed her lips and squinted, trying to figure him out. "I thought you were a butler."

"I was." He stepped closer and rubbed his nose on hers. "Great retirement plan and benefits program. Oh, and dental, too."

"You're silly," she said and gave him a quick kiss.

"And you're out of practice. I remember kisses that lasted for hours…"

"And made you squirm," she said, squatting down a little so she was rubbing up against him, belly to belly.

"Damn! I should have taken Hal's advice to keep a box of condoms on hand 'just in case.'"

"Hal? Who's he? Your butler?"

"No, one of my roomies at the other house."

"You own two homes like this?"

"No." Silas brought her fingers to his mouth again and kissed them gently, glad to have the opportunity to divert her attention so he could rearrange himself with his other hand. "Do you want to pick a room or should I?"

"Which was the last room you used for a liaison?" she asked.

"What? I mean, really? What kind of question is that?"

"I don't want you to be thinking of another woman while we're – how should I say – getting reacquainted?"

"Julianna, you can take your pick of any or every room in this house and not rouse any romantic memories or leftover vibes from another female. Or male. At least, as it pertains to me. Over the years, there have been other residents here, and I can't speak for them or the ghosts they may have left behind. There are twelve bedrooms plus assorted offices, parlors, game rooms, and a library, not to mention the bathrooms, kitchens, and the guest house. All are, shall we say, chaste, devoid of any sexual experiences of mine."

"Any?" she asked, one eyebrow raised.

"Well, solo doesn't count," he replied, quickly kissing her again to hide his blush. "Come on. If you don't pick a room, I will."

"Which is the room you slept in last?"

"This way," he said, arm around her waist. "The red room as I call it." He opened the door to a large suite with a huge dark European oak desk as the focal point. A picture window at the far right of the room provided a view for the king-sized bed, smothered in oversized red pillows.

"A guy's room…with pillows?" she asked, a giggle in her

voice.

"Pillows aren't just for decorations, you know. They're great for propping up in bed to read or for back support after a rough day of…of whatever."

"Ditch digging or tennis?" Julianna teased.

Silas bent his head and answered, "Gardening. I'm a closet farmer, I suppose. You should see the tomatoes I get at Hal's place. We have a competition every year – Doc, Hal, and me."

"Hmm," Julianna mused, feigning interest as she slowly started unbuttoning his shirt.

"Hmm?" he replied as a question.

"I want to see that farmer's tan."

Goose pimples raced up his arms at her touch, her long delicate fingers pulling off the shirt across his shoulders. "Danged undershirt," she whispered, tugging it out of his slacks.

"Let me help," he said softly and unfastened his belt and the top closure of his trousers.

She tugged again, freeing the tee. He crossed his arms and pulled it off over his head.

"My silver Adonis," she said, her fingers stroking his shimmering chest hair. "Oh, my!" She lightly brushed his abs. "Not an ounce of fat on you."

"It's dark in here," he said, nuzzling her hair, still bashful about touching the rest of her. "I have more than a bit of…ahem…insulation, but if you don't see it, I won't point it out to you."

She stroked the front of his slacks familiarly, ending at his waistband. "Looks like you're trying to point something out to me."

"He remembers you."

"Oh, does my puppy want to come out and play?" she asked coyly, tugging at the zipper tab.

"I may be an old dog, but the spirit is still there."

"And the muscle," she said, unzipping his pants. "Oh, and the question is answered…"

Silas pulled her chin up to look at him. "What question?"

She giggled and kissed him. "Boxers, briefs, or commando. I guess you gave up freestyling, eh?"

"Knit boxers definitely have their benefits. Comfortable and discreet. Now, how about you?" he asked.

"Nope, neither boxers nor briefs."

"Commando?"

She lifted the side of her skirt and guided his hand up her thigh. "Thong underwear, a late-twentieth-century creation that, although not necessarily comfortable, does help establish a sleek line under today's form-fitting garments."

Silas gasped as she led his hand to her bared fanny. He cupped her ass cheek and sighed deeply, hoping it didn't sound like the desperate groan it was. "Would you allow me?"

"Go for it," she cooed into his ear. "I've been yearning for you for decades." She looked up at the ceiling. "And zero chance of precipitation in here."

"Lath and plaster interspersed with drywall," he replied, fumbling with the zipper at the back of her dress with his free hand. "Much better than a Yellow Front emergency shelter."

She shoved his pants past his hips. "Still, these are easier to take off than button-fly 501s."

He laughed at the memory as he stepped out of his loafers and kicked them aside. "They were hard for everyone unless they were so old, they'd become flannel-soft and pliable."

She stroked him again. "Still hard, not flannel-soft," she said and giggled. "If you take too much longer getting me out of this dress, though, I'm going to rip it off!"

Zip!

"Got it. I'll say one thing about me, I am tenacious."

"And determined," she said, then wriggled out of her dress. "And they're not the same thing." She let go of him, then bent to tug his slacks off the rest of the way, pulling them away as he stepped out. She hastily folded them and threw them on the chair beside the bed, then tossed her dress on top. "Phew! I guess we're out of practice. Hopefully, next time it won't take so long."

"Gawd, you're gorgeous. Still. No, wait. Even more so. I never saw so much of you at once."

Julianna stuck her thumbs under the straps of her lacy push-up bra. "And there's even more to see."

Silas stepped backward, almost tripping on his shoes before he regained his balance. He threw all but two of the pillows off to the side of the bed, then pulled back the bedspread and covers, exposing vibrant red satin sheets. "Join me?"

Julianna kicked off her shoes one at a time, her eyes fixed on his as she moved toward him seductively, her hands rising to her breasts with an unspoken invitation. "All night foreplay?" she asked.

Feeling himself throb in anticipation, Silas winced, remembering the trick he'd learned from an old Elvis Presley movie. *Just recite your multiplication tables.*

She kissed him softly, then pulled away. "Can we get under the covers first? My feet are cold."

"Whatever the lady desires." He held back the covers for her, then picked up the remote from his side of the bed and clicked a few buttons. The sound of ocean waves crashing on the surf resounded from the hidden speakers in the ceiling, the lights dimmed to moonlight brightness, and the foot portion of the warming as the heating pad kicked in. Ideal.

Bra and panties still on, Julianna climbed into bed, a sudden flare of uncertainty searing hot as Hugh's last hurtful words screamed at her. *You're nothing but a slut!* She did as the last psychiatrist had told her and ordered her demons to leave her alone. "Shut up! You're a liar!" she mouthed, barely breathing as she spoke. No sound came out, but the emotional rebuff worked.

Silas watched the long-legged beauty ease onto the silky sheets, her milk-chocolate hued body as perfect as any man – or woman - could ever want. He glanced up just in time to see her lips move in a silent admonition. Uncertainty. Conflict.

32

He slid in, pulled the blankets up, and rearranged the pillows, opening one arm out to her. "Come over here and let me hold you. I'm not going anywhere, and I hope you aren't either. We don't need to rush things. It's been a long time. Let's get to know a little about each other. I mean, even if we could erase the last forty years and skip to the day after Woodstock, we probably wouldn't have wound up in bed with each other. We were still minors, after all."

"Why are you so smart?" she asked and sidled over to him. She lay her head on his shoulder and rearranged her hair so it wasn't in his face.

He kissed her forehead. "I read a lot. Plus I watch and listen to what's going on around me. It's not intelligence, per se – although I hope I have at least an average amount – but it's what you do with what's out there that solves problems or gets answers."

"Observe and interpret?" she suggested.

"See, you have it, too. Like right now. We were so wrapped up with each other, the past we lost and the present we were suddenly gifted, that we were about to head full speed into... Well, I don't know, but I was ready to go all the way, as we used to say."

"Me, too."

"Yes, and I'm pretty sure it would have felt fantastic, but it's the aftereffects, the residual emotions, that are left with us forever. It's better to prepare ourselves, like a garden. We can't go slinging seeds before we clear out the stones and weeds, break down the clumps, and level the ground so it – we – will thrive."

Silas shifted sideways so he could look at her, see her eyes. "Julianna, I've been a single man my whole life. I've never met a woman I wanted to share..." He waved his hand around the room, stopping at the huge picture window. "I never met a woman I wanted to share my world with. Except you. I had to wonder if my infatuation with you was all a fantasy. I could have had others. I've met a few worthy women who would have been quite satisfied to have me as an escort, a partner in business or travel, but they didn't give me that zing.

"When we met at the wedding, rather when you recognized me there – and I realized you were real and still gave me that zing – I knew I'd been right to hold off on settling for second best."

"That's a lot to live up to," Julianna said, frowning.

"Yes, and that's why we're talking and not eh hem…"

"Well, that and you don't have any condoms…"

Silas rolled his eyes and sighed. "True. I think if I had a drawerful of them, we'd be after-glowing instead of lying here, semi-clothed, introspecting, frustrated. Damn it."

"How about a little hybrid farming? We can toss out a few rocks and weeds, but do a little prodding and kneading, too."

Silas reached over and grabbed her bare bottom, his thumb under the hip of her thong. "Just don't leave me again. I don't think my heart could stand it."

She closed her eyes and came in close. "You're my everything," she whispered, and kissed him, ignoring his comment. "My everything," she repeated and rolled over on top of him, holding him tight between her legs, ready to be in charge of the wildest dry hump ever.

***

Silas reached over, terrified she was gone.

Something was wrong. Julianna was still here, asleep next to him, her soft snores the same as they were when they shared a tent forty years ago. He relaxed back onto his pillow, then realized what was odd and sat up straight. He looked around the room and saw he was right. The power was off. The soft music had stopped, the hum of the heater was silent, and the only light was the glow of the moon, reflecting off low clouds through the curtainless window.

Kerthunk!

And there it was. The backup generator kicked in. The music and lights were still off, but the heater and battery-operated light in the hall were on now.

Julianna startled at the mechanical noise, her snores now whimpers of fretful sleep.

He patted the side of her hip. "It's all right. I'm here with you," he said softly.

She moaned sweetly in reply. "Silas?" and rolled over to face him. "It is you, isn't it? I wasn't dreaming."

"Well, I don't know what you were dreaming, but yes, it's really me. I don't ever want to lose you again."

"Now, isn't that sweet," a woman's gruff voice called from the doorway.

Silas started to reach for the gun in the top drawer of his nightstand, then changed his mind and grabbed his discarded undershirt. He pulled it on over his head, using the time to try and figure out who could have bypassed his security systems.

"Who's she?" Julianna asked harshly, pulling the sheet over her bare bosom.

"I have no idea," he growled, then reached over and patted her leg in reassurance, then left it there. "But she certainly doesn't belong here."

Julianna squeezed his hand in a silent response of trust.

"Oh, sweet, sweet Silas. How soon you forget," the woman said as she walked into the room, stopping in front of the desk. "I'm the woman who gave you a child. You must have figured that out by now, surely. I mean, isn't that why they call you Sherlock?"

A deep breath, almost a growl, came from Silas. He wanted to speak but decided to give Victoria the Viper, his buddy Hal's ex-wife, the rope she would certainly give him to bind her with.

"Who's the floozie?" Victoria asked, nodding to Julianna. "Aren't you going to introduce us? No, wait. She's just an escort and you never remembered her name if you even bothered to ask it. As if she'd give you a real one."

"Can I deck her?" Julianna asked Silas coolly. "She did break and enter, right?"

"No and yes. I mean, wait. Yes, you're correct – she did not have permission to enter. But no, don't hit her. I don't think she's worth the legal hassle if you hurt her."

"*When* I hurt her," Julianna corrected.

"Oh, she's such a cute little tart. And obedient, too. Are you into chocolate now, Silas dear?"

"Oh, go ahead," Silas said. "She's in the country illegally, I'm sure. ICE won't care if she's bruised up a bit."

Julianna jumped out of bed, even though Victoria had a gun pointed at her.

Whoosh!

The pillow Silas had thrown when Julianna leaped out took the viper off guard, her pistol firing harmlessly into the ceiling.

Julianna's elbow flew up in an offensive move, sending the intruder stumbling against the desk.

One-two, one-two, right cross, uppercut!

Bare-assed Julianna stepped back, letting the pummeled female drop to the floor.

"Have I told you lately how hot you are?" Silas asked, standing beside the bed. "There's nothing sexier than a naked woman taking down a thief and blackmailer except..."

Julianna wiped the hair off her forehead and looked back at him. "Except?" she asked.

"Except when that sexy naked woman is mine," he said and came to stand next to her.

Julianna stared down at the front of him and giggled. "That shirt doesn't quite come low enough for decency, but it does prove you're telling the truth. You look pretty sexy yourself."

Silas followed her gaze then reacted quickly, his hands automatically covering his aroused privates in embarrassment.

"Still got it, eh?" the awakening voice mumbled from the floor.

Julianna picked up the tossed pillow and covered the woman's face, securing it with her foot. "You get dressed first. It's time to take out the trash."

***

"Now what?" Julianna asked.

Silas finished tying Victoria to the snowboard, verifying the shop-rag gag was secured and he wouldn't have to hear any more of her curses.

"I'll make a call and let Hal decide what to do."

"No! No!" Victoria protested through the gag, twisting and turning so hard to escape that she knocked her improvised fiberglass stockade sideways.

Clunk!

Now on the concrete floor, face down, her pleas continued.

Silas touched Julianna's arm. "Let's go upstairs. It's too noisy here in the garage."

She nodded and followed, turning around at the last minute to stick her tongue out at her nemesis.

"Grrr! Bitch!" Victoria mumbled, then kicked furiously.

"Hello, Hal? Yeah, sorry to wake you so early after the wedding and all, but we have a major problem. She's back. Yeah, *her!* She broke into my place an hour ago. She's neutralized, but I don't know what to do with her. Are you sure? I was just joking when I said I'd drop her off at the immigration office. All right. I'm pretty sure it's still in the federal complex. Well, here's hoping she doesn't bullshit them and get right back out. Really? I didn't know she had outstanding warrants. Oh, that's right. I forgot about the assault with a deadly weapon. I was just glad Grace was okay. Shooting her only child ought to impress a judge enough that he keeps her locked up without bail. Okay, I'll keep you informed. Hush! Tell Doc I never kiss and tell. Bye."

Silas clicked end on the phone call and smiled at Julianna. "I take it you got the gist of what's going on?"

"I got the chapter headings, but you can fill me in on the details while we're in transit. Or for the next week, if needed. She shot her daughter – your daughter?"

"Thanks for not alluding that she and I ever were a couple, because we weren't. Short version, she got me drunk and I woke up cuffed to a bed in a seedy sex hotel, bare-assed naked and with the hangover from hell."

"That sounds awful!"

"The worst part was waiting for someone to come get me. Those maids were used to all sorts of strange stuff, so my situation wasn't anything out of the ordinary for them."

Julianna stifled a giggle. "Oh, I'm so sorry." She suddenly sobered up, thinking of how she'd feel if it had been her instead of him. "That bitch! She should be tarred and feathered for that. She…she…"

Silas put his hand on her shoulder. "I got over it. No one even knew for sure that I had sired a child that roofie-hazed night until Tori pointed it out at the wedding. Hal and I suspected it for a long time, especially since he could never sire another child and tested sterile, but we never spoke of it. I've been close to Grace through him. Although I missed the day-to-day events of her life, I was around for many of the major events. Plus, now I have three granddaughters I can acknowledge. That's how Hal bribed me into moving in with him and Doc. Full access to the daughter and granddaughters I couldn't acknowledge without raising a ruckus."

"Triplets?"

"Super fertility runs in the family," Silas said. "Now you know why I was extra careful last night." He kissed her softly, then moved in and finished with a sigh-inducing finale. "Don't ever think I don't want you because I do." He looked in her eyes and saw fear begin, so didn't add the, 'And always will,' he'd been thinking.

Julianna put her head on his shoulder, tears starting to well at those unsaid words she was glad he hadn't spoken. She'd never wanted anyone so much in her life. Would he be her undoing, though? Her desires always seemed to attract disasters. "I'm sorry, you were saying?"

"It's cold outside. All I can offer you are some of my gym clothes. I don't have women's clothing here."

"Well, that makes me feel better," Julianna said. "I can't imagine you in a Dior gown." She squinted and tried to visualize him in a strapless, white floor-length dress. "Nah."

"What? Why not? I may be missing the bust, but I do have decent legs. Put me in something split up to here," he said, touching the outside of his thigh, "and I'd be a real head-turner."

"Come on, Sweet Meat," Julianna said, laughing. "You're going to get me all turned on and we still don't have any condoms."

"Really?"

She shrugged and frowned. "I don't know. If we run out of things to do, we'll try it. But first, let's take out the trash."

"Oh, yeah…" Silas feigned gagging. "You take one end of the snowboard, and I'll take the other. She should fit in the backseat of the Caddie."

"If not, we can force her a little, maybe stick her in upside down and sideways."

"Or cut her in half…" Silas said. "Nah, too messy. I like that old car. I've had other Cadillacs but that '89 DeVille has a special place in my heart."

"Your first?"

"Yup. Come on, partner. Work first, then I'll make us a fantastic breakfast."

"Good, because I never got my cocoa last night." Julianna saw him smile at her remark. "Yes, I know, but you got yours, right?"

"Just like you, I'm still waiting for the cream to be added," he said with a wink.

Chapter 6: Disappearing Act

"Where'd she go?" Julianna asked, tugging at the crotch of the borrowed sweatpants which were too short for her long legs. She bent down and looked under the Cadillac while Silas did the same, looking under all of the other vehicles.

"Damned if I know." He turned around and winked at Julianna. "All right. She'll either show up or is gone for good. In the meantime, let's go play around a little."

Julianna squinted at him dubiously. "Sounds like a great idea to me, my Adonis. Come send me to paradise with your majestic member!"

Silas's hand flew to his mouth just in time to stifle his laugh.

Julianna saw that she had probably gone too far with her joke and he couldn't reply. When she realized her words would probably be wrapped in giggles, too, she hummed loudly and grabbed onto him as they beat a hasty exit.

As soon as they were out of the garage, Silas opened the electrical panel on the wall, flipped a switch, and secured the area. "Come on," he whispered. "If she hasn't already left, she won't get out. Let's go check the security footage."

Silas led her to the annex just off the kitchen. He noticed the saucepan with cocoa ingredients was right where they left it and sighed.

"Work first," Julianna said, noticing his focus. "If she's truly vicious and unpredictable, I don't want her on the loose." She paused and added, "Even if I can kick her butt."

"That's my woman." He pulled up a stool and offered her the desk chair in front of the monitor. Cordless keyboard in hand, he tapped and swiped, bringing up the last half hour of the garage footage. "There she is," he said, pointing.

"And there she goes. What is that? A garbage chute?"

"Yes. Too bad I never use it. It's clean. I guess I could set off that old pest exterminator bomb that's been on the shelf for at least a decade, but if she's still inside, I don't want to kill her."

Julianna turned to him with an eyebrow raised.

"Just because I hate her and want her out of my life doesn't mean I want to kill her."

"And she is the mother of your daughter and grandmother to your granddaughters?" she said as a question, shaking her head in disbelief.

"Giving birth doesn't make you a mother any more than having similar DNA makes you a grandparent. Hal and the nanny are the reasons Grace survived that bitch. As far as I know, Victoria doesn't know anything about the triplets. We did a pretty good job of isolating Grace from her. I'm sure she knew she was pregnant, but not that she had a multiple birth. She'd have to be pretty clever to find out who the adoptive parents were, so the girls are safe."

"Unless Victoria found out Hal was going to a wedding and she showed up, saw all those young women who looked like Grace, and sorted it out herself? It wouldn't take a genius. The girls look more like quadruplets than triplets and a mother."

"Shit! So much for me being a Sherlock. Now what, Miss Marple?"

"Hey! I get that one! If you pay me a nickel, I won't be an amateur sleuth anymore."

Silas reached in his pocket and pulled out a coin. "No, not that one," he said, holding it up to the light, then put it back.

"Wait! Let me see that," Julianna said, suddenly panicked.

"That's just my lucky coin," Silas said, leaving it in his pocket. "Let's not get distracted." He rewound the video and saw Victoria had managed to get into the trash chute with the snowboard still attached to her back. He tapped on the keyboard and brought up an exterior camera.

"And there she goes…" Julianna said, then looked back at Silas.

"She either has an accomplice who's going to pick her up or she's going to get stopped by the locked gate. I doubt she can make it through there, even as skinny as she is, but if she does, the community watch group will grab her."

"So, you're saying let nature take its course?" Julianna asked.

"Yes, I am. However..." Silas tapped a few keys and hit enter. "Now the fence is electrified. It has enough juice going through it to stun a buck."

"Or a doe," Julianna said wryly, fidgeting in the chair. "Are we done here then?"

"Don't you want to watch her do the spaz dance when she gets zapped?"

"I'll catch it on reruns."

Silas set the keyboard back on the counter. "Are you all right?"

She winced at the familiar words she'd heard for years, the phrase that meant she was acting squirrelly and an increase in medication was on the way.

By her reaction, Silas realized he had just used negative trigger words. "I'm sorry," he said, ignoring what he had just asked. "You have to be ravenous. A big breakfast always makes the world brighter. Especially after kicking a major witch's butt."

Despite her insecurity, Julianna giggled. "Witch with a capital B. Did anyone ever tell you that you were a sweetheart?"

"Yes, but I told him that I was saving myself." He stood up and offered his hand. "Would you like to come with me? I'd ask if you'd like to supervise, but I know the way around my kitchen. However, I have no idea what kind of food you prefer. Sorry, I don't have any Twinkies, Oreos, or any of the other junk food we used to eat. I gave it up for Lent..." He squinted and tipped his head back and pretended to calculate, his fingers writing numbers, mumbling, "Carry the one, take away five..." before looking back at her. "Lent 1970. And since the computer's in the other room and my mental calculator doesn't work before breakfast, 'a long time' will have to be the accepted answer."

Julianna shook her head and moved close to him, holding his expressive hands in hers. "Are you for real? I feel as if I'm still asleep or in a drug-induced dream. Why hasn't someone come along and grabbed you up."

Silas looked down at their intertwined hands. "She just did."

Her tears were back. What would he do if he saw them? She took a deep breath and sighed. Probably nothing but try to make her feel better. "Breakfast. Eggs with any kind of cheese and or vegetables you have on hand. Skip the bread but coffee and some of that half and half would be very much appreciated. I think you're right. I have low blood sugar."

Silas kissed her on the cheek. "Some of us are more susceptible to it than others. Don't let anyone make you feel bad about it. We *all* have frailties. It's just some of them are more noticeable than others."

That did it. The tears started pouring out, followed by shoulder heaves and hiccups. "Why are you so nice?" she wept.

He grabbed a double-fistful of tissues and handed them to her, then gave her the whole box. "Did you ever hear the phrase, 'Treat others as you would like to be treated?'"

"The Golden Rule? Yes… But…"

"Did you know that pretty much all the major religions of the world have a variation of that same quote as a mantra or standard or law or whatever you want to call it?"

"Credo?"

"Yes, that, too. If I was shaky from hunger, in a strange house, had just battled an attempted murderess before she struck again, and was trying to make sure I didn't look…" Silas stalled, looking for a word that didn't mean crazy. "Trying to make sure I wasn't *unappealing*, good Lord, woman. That's enough stress to cause a major zit."

Julianna's sobs had been drying up with his consoling, but at his last remark, she started laughing. "Oh, my God! I forgot about that. Right before a big dance or photo day, I'd always get a huge pimple."

"Stress just takes different forms as we age. From what you told me last night, I have about twenty more years of life experience than you have. Would you let me help solve some of your problems? I mean, the easy ones for sure. Like making breakfast. We'll tackle clothes next, and then…" He shrugged.

"Finding condoms?"

"That's not what I was going to say. We need to get 'close' before we get 'close.' I don't care what you've done, I'll always want you. That's not going to change. But I don't want you for a one-night stand. I know it makes you uncomfortable when I get all sappy, so I won't."

Julianna's face skewed up and she snorted.

"I'll *try* not to get all sappy…" He sighed. "Let's just get through breakfast. I think I'm a bit hypoglycemic, too."

"Battling an attempted murderess rapist before six will do that to you," Julianna said. "Point me to the coffee and coffee maker. That much I should be able to handle."

***

"That was probably the best mushroom omelet I've ever had! What's your secret?" Julianna asked.

"The company I keep."

Julianna scoffed before drinking the last of her coffee. Her face scrunched up in distaste. "Maybe I was wrong. I think I'll let you make coffee next time, too."

"I like your positive attitude."

"Huh?"

"You're already looking forward to another morning with me. See, all we needed was food and to be rid of The Viper." Silas looked at the clock. "Oh, shoot! I should have called Hal right away to let him know she's on the loose again. Dang! Where is my brain?"

Julianna pointed to herself with her thumb. "Somewhere between ground zero and six-four," she said.

He smiled back at her and picked up his phone. "I thought you grew. I did, too. Back in '69, I was only five-ten. By the time I was twenty, I'd squeezed out another couple inches." He pushed and held a button, speed-dialing Hal.

"From what I recall, both horizontal and vertical."

His eyes widened and he sputtered into the phone just as the call connected. "Sorry about that, Hal. Something got to me. Hey, I'm sorry I didn't call right away; I got distracted. The Viper escaped. *Poof!* We had her all tied up to my old snowboard, but she managed to wiggle her way over to the garbage chute. No, dang it. It was clean. It hadn't been used in twenty years, at least. Yeah, well we can hope a raccoon was living in there. It'd serve her right, coming out covered in vermin turds. I'll run back and review the surveillance videos and see if she has an accomplice. Well, you know how it is. Or maybe you don't remember. Yes, I got distracted. Hush. Be nice. I can't commit to dinner because we have some shopping to do plus anything I do, I'd like to get her okay on, too. Well, if this is what having a ball and chain feels like, you can keep the key. I haven't smiled so much in years. Okay. I'll keep you posted on any news. Oh, and make sure Doc eats his banana every day. It doesn't count if he gives it to the dog. Bye."

"Ball and chain, eh?" Julianna asked.

"I was bragging, not complaining," Silas said. "Doc's been a widower for years, and Hal was miserable, married to Victoria until about eighteen years ago. We have a video of her making whoopie with her porn star gigolo. She'd do anything to get her hands on that. She ripped off all Hal's and Grace's bank accounts before he caught her. She's *persona non grata* from here to Costa Rico. Their prenup said infidelity would negate any alimony or settlement. He made sure it ran both ways. The screwing she got was the screwing she deserved."

"And you had sex with her when she was married? Couldn't he get out of the marriage with you testifying or whatever?"

"That happened a week before they were married. Plus, I wasn't the only one. She was a sneaky slut. But that doesn't make a difference now. Let's go look at the security footage and see if she has a sidekick."

"Or if she got zapped," Julianna said, eyes bright with anticipation.

"It would be worth the nickel cost of admission to see that," Silas said, watching Julianna's reaction closely.

Her smile dimmed into a frown of deep thought, then popped back but without the shine. "And since it's on tape, we can watch it over and over again," she said with forced enthusiasm.

"Come on. We'll pass on the popcorn this time."

Silas sat down with the keyboard. He punched keys and played with the mouse, rewinding and fast-forwarding, until he found it. "Look at that!"

"Who is that brute?" Julianna asked, remarking on body-builder hulk who was trying to pull Victoria off the charged fence. "Don't touch her, don't touch her, you idiot! Oh, man! Talk about getting knocked on your butt!"

The clueless muscleman with the thinning hair managed to loosen his hold from Victoria's shoulder and stumbled backward. He shook off the stunned aftereffect, then planted his feet firmly, and karate kicked the now frizzy-haired intruder off the fence and into the bushes.

"That's electrician's safety 101. When there's a live wire – or person with electricity running through her – use a stick or broom handle or anything that's non-conductive to break the contact."

"Fast forward a bit. Can you tell what kind of vehicle they're driving?"

Silas sped through the next ten minutes but nothing showed. "He must have parked in the blind spot. My neighbor doesn't believe in security cameras or I'd ask to see his footage."

"So, does that mean we lock up the place, go shopping for some *condom-ments*," she said, adding a wink, "and maybe drop by the hotel to pick up some clothes for me?"

"How about just locking up and then go shopping? If we go back and find Oscar and Tori, they might want to hang out with us."

Julianna shook her head emphatically. "You're right. Let's

hurry up and go so we can hurry up and get back to make up for lost time. As far as shopping goes, I don't know this part of the world, but you might want to see if there are any Big and Tall Women's clothing stores around. It's either that or I'm back to wearing men's sweats and tees."

"Gotcha," Silas said, opening a browser. Three clicks later, he'd found the store. "Ten minutes away. Whole Lotta Ladywear, coming up."

Chapter 7: The Card Game

"I don't have any experience shopping with women, but from the horror stories I've heard from men who were brave enough to go – or were blackmailed into going – shopping with the fairer sex was supposed to be miserable. This wasn't bad at all."

"First off, I think I'm not in any way the fairer sex," Julianna said, holding up her dark-skinned arm and smirking.

"I meant in a dainty way…"

She stood tall, shoulders back, her sly grin now wide.

Silas shook his head. "And you can handle yourself in a bare-knuckle boxing match better than any man I've ever seen. So, were all those men lying, or are you just that magnificent?"

"The latter. And you already know about the other stereotype I've been shattering my whole life."

"That is…"

"I can't cook. I can't even brew a cup of tea with a teabag and pot of boiling water much less a cup of coffee or espresso. I'm still waiting on my Mexican cocoa, by the way."

Silas pulled up to the gate, rolled the window down to punch in his security code, and stilled. "Oh, jeez…"

"What?" Julianna asked and leaned in front of him to look.

"Oh, jeez is right. Do you think they did it before or after she broke in the first time?" The panel looked like a bomb had been thrown at it, jagged tears through the metal shield, the plastic keypad melted into a Dali-surrealistic blob.

Silas put the car in park and got out to get a closer look. Although it was still the middle of winter, it was a sunny day and the driveway was clear. It hadn't snowed in two weeks, but he noticed the fresh breaks in the frozen hillocks along the fence line. The icecaps were too old and brittle to hold a footprint, but they had been stepped on. The tracks were on the side opposite of Victoria and her gigolo's earlier spaz dance.

"New tracks?" Julianna asked, now standing beside him,

watching his narrow-eyed gaze.

"I doubt they were here last night. Looks like they came back."

"Or they never left," she said.

He looked at her, curious. "True. We never heard or saw a vehicle leave."

"Your neighbor who doesn't believe in security cameras, is he here, or does he leave for the winter?"

"Gone until spring. You're right – they might have holed up there. Maybe I should call you Sherlock."

"Nah. The name isn't big enough for both of us. I'm just picking up stuff you'd probably see if you could take your eyes off of what's really intriguing you," she said, grinning and squeezing her breasts together.

"I hate to admit it, but that's very possible. Still, that's no excuse. It's our safety I have to consider."

"Do you know what she wants?"

Silas cleared his throat. "That, my dear, is the real mystery. Come on. Let's go inside. I'll call the cops and report a break-in next door, then make some cocoa. I'm not going to let her dictate my life."

"How are we going to get inside?"

Silas reached around the access panel to the other side of the brick and concrete pillar, moved his fingers about for a moment, then felt the notch and pushed hard. The gate swung open. "I try to always have a plan B."

"Good idea."

Once in the garage, Julianna grabbed the shopping bag and got out. "I'm going to put on some girly clothes while you make your phone calls," she said and dashed upstairs.

The little tingle that meant something was wrong raced up Silas's back. He shifted in his shirt, trying to rid himself of it, but he knew it was futile. That fifth sense was there to protect him. Once again, he felt that Julianna was hiding something. Part of him was glad they hadn't gotten closer. She had that same 'It's not you, it's me' aura that meant she was going to bolt soon. 'Let's enjoy each other while we can. I'm not worthy.'

"Damn it!" he said aloud, knowing she couldn't hear him. "You are worthy, woman! If you just wash away that stigma, you could enjoy life." He sighed. "And me," he added softly.

He took his phone out of his pocket and quickly dialed the police station, bypassing 9-1-1. "Hey, Sarge. This is Silas Priest. Well, just in case you didn't recognize my voice I thought I'd better identify myself. Hey, my neighbor John Rathmore is out of town for another couple of months but it appears someone's camping out over there. Yeah, I figured you'd want to check it out. Right. You, too. And give the missus a hug from me. Bye."

Silas stared at the phone. No need to tell anyone about the break-in at his place. He didn't want or need cops snooping around. If there were any clues here, he'd find them.

By the time Silas was done with the call, Julianna had changed clothes and was already in the kitchen, her head in the refrigerator. "Look what I found," she said, shaking the pint-sized container of half and half. "I'm still waiting on my cream…"

He walked over and kissed her gently. "Cocoa first?" he asked, taking it out of her hand and setting it on the counter.

"Or maybe *condom-ments*?" she asked, holding up the box of twelve condoms.

He gently nudged her hand down and kissed her more thoroughly. "I don't want to go too fast," he whispered.

"I don't care how fast you go the first time. I'm sure the second and third time you'll last longer."

Silas pulled out of the embrace and cleared his throat. "You insult me, woman. Only a dozen?"

"No, I bought three boxes of twelve. I figure they should last us for a day or two."

"Now you're flattering me," he said with a chuckle. He suddenly sobered. "But I was serious about my garden analogy. Clearing out our problems before jumping in and sowing seeds."

"Or deep plowing?" Julianna asked with a grin.

"Or deep plowing. I know it's going to be good. Even if we have a bit of awkwardness at first, we'll soon find perfection."

"At least sixty-nine forms of perfection," she joked.

"And if we run out of ideas, there's always the Kama Sutra. I'm sure I have a copy of it around here somewhere," Silas said, looking around the room as if searching. "But I want to know more about you and want you to know about me. What if you're a Democrat and I'm a Tea Party Republican? What then?"

"We won't discuss politics."

"What if I want children and you don't?" he asked, one eyebrow raised.

"Really? At your age? I mean, I know I'm young enough, but you? You're what, fifty-eight?"

"Good memory, woman. Don't worry about the number. Remember, I have a contact who has a little blue bottle of Fountain of Youth water. I might decide to ring him up and ask for a drop or two. You know, I could sire a child now, but I'd like to be around long enough to watch him or her grow into adulthood."

"How could you? I mean, with the way this world is going to hell…" Julianna saw his slight smile. "You did that on purpose, didn't you? You don't really want a child? Would you want to rejuvenate just to watch a child grow up in this mess?"

"We need to talk, Julianna. It doesn't have to be an interrogation. Let's make a game out of it. Loser has to answer a question. Honestly. No dancing around the truth or redirects, okay?"

Silas pulled open a drawer in the kitchen, rummaged through it, and found what he was looking for. "Remember these?" He took them out of the plastic bag and handed them to her.

"Oh, my God, Silas. Are these the same cards we played with at Woodstock?" She held them to her nose, sniffed, then wrinkled it.

"Yes, they are. That *eau de* marijuana and rain aroma stays as long as I keep them bagged up. I take a sniff every once in a while, just for the heck of it. I remind myself that I wasn't always a lonely old man. I had to bring them here because the guys accused me of snorting something illegal when I had them there."

"You keep them in the kitchen?"

"Nobody but me messes around in here. Can you imagine a thief ransacking pantry shelves for valuables? No, they'd look for a safe or would look in the desk. I believe in hide in plain sight."

"But those cards aren't valuable to anyone but you or me."

"Who says that's the only thing around here in plain sight?" he asked, watching for her reaction.

Fast blinking. Guilt. Or planning, conniving. *Crap! Start the honesty game. Now.*

"Isn't it too early or too late for cocoa?' he asked. "How about a wine cooler or mulled wine instead?" *Lower the resistance with alcohol...*

"How about a throwback to the sixties and seventies: sangria! I saw you have fresh oranges," she replied, eyes bright.

"Ah, a feast. How about a big bowl of crinkle-cut potato chips, French onion dip, and a pitcher of shortcut sangria: orange juice and Boone's Farm?"

"Now you're making me hungry."

"I won't shortcut on the sangria, and we'll have to use sliced cucumbers or baby carrots for the dip. I haven't had potato chips in years. I have to watch my figure, you know."

"Say, how come you have fresh food in the house? I thought you didn't live here?"

"I don't, but I do know how to text my personal shopper and have him bring over a few of the necessities for me while I'm out shopping with my lady friend."

"Well, 'him' must not have been Hal or he would have stocked you with another necessity."

Silas winked, kissed her on the cheek, and whispered, "Give me five minutes to slice, dice, and combine. In the meantime, take a look around the place. Pick a room to play cards in."

Julianna strolled through the house, her fingertips gliding across the polished surfaces. Nothing was dusty or out of place. It was ideal. She'd lived that life before, but this one didn't feel restricted. If she smudged a mirror or left a coat on a chair rather than hang it up, Silas wouldn't care. He'd never make her feel bad about a misspoken word or a few dollars spent on frivolities. She inhaled deeply. The scent of freedom. True, there was wealth here, too, but she'd rather be free of guilt or insecurities than have billions of dollars to share, spend, or burn.

"I have the sangria in the refrigerator chilling. We can drink a little now, but it is much better after letting the flavors blend for an hour or so." He handed her a wine glass with a slice of orange on the side, little triangles of various citrus and strawberries floating inside.

She took a cautious sip. "Ah, it's already the best I've ever had. Come on back to the kitchen. I think it's my favorite room so far. Except for 'the red room.' I'm pretty sure you don't want to go in there yet."

"Operative word there is yet. Let's see if we can cram forty years of life into a few hours of cards."

"It was only twenty for me, remember?" she asked.

"And that, dear women," he said, toasting her and clinking glasses, "is one of the more fascinating subjects I want to find out about."

Julianna smiled weakly, then realized it was a conditioned reflex. He wasn't a prying psychiatrist trying to figure out her psyche, or an angry husband who wanted to force her into his mold of the ideal woman. Silas really cared about her. *'Damn it!'*

Silas watched as a palette of emotions colored her face, ending with an ashen pallor at her silent lip-synched curse.

"Let's use the breakfast nook, then," he said, breaking her out of her last glazed-eyed mood. "The sun's still there. We can play cats and bask in the natural light."

He took her hand and led her to the bright yellow corner with a window seat. "You can't be sad when bathed in sunlight and buttercups, right?"

"And have a gentleman's gentleman at hand to see to my every need?"

"*Every* need," he stressed. "But in time. That's because I *truly* do care."

"So, what do you want to know?"

He handed her the cards. "Poker? Winner of each hand gets to ask a question."

She shuffled, then held them to her nose again, inhaling deeply. "They really do bring you back with the aroma, don't they? Okay. Five-card stud. Penny ante?" she asked, recalling the coin he had in his pocket.

"Sorry, not enough coins in this mostly cashless house. We'll have to do with toothpicks." He grabbed the little dispenser from the lazy susan and dumped out two piles. "No dollar value; these are just to make it fun."

"When you hear some of what I have to say, it's going to get very interesting, even without coins, cards, or toothpicks," she said. "Since I have the deck, I'll deal first."

"Yes, I was a gentleman's gentleman – a butler – for a few years. My employer was the former owner of this house. I, shall we say, saved his bacon and proved my worth as both a friend and an employee, and he gave me half interest in his estate, willing me the balance of everything on his death."

"So, you were partners?" Julianna asked.

"Yes, but that still isn't well known, so I'd appreciate it if you kept that confidential. Now, deal again. I have a few burning questions of my own."

Silas lost the next hand, too. "So, by partners, were you financial partners or lovers or both?"

"Really? I'll tell you what, let's say right now that we share any or all secrets *except* our sex lives."

"Why? Are you afraid you'll have a dirty little secret that will make me not want you? Because if that's the case, nothing you can say will change how I feel about you. It might get me a little turned on if you had a male lover, but I wouldn't think less of you."

Silas sighed and shook his head. "Right now, any sex partners we may have had or not had are not here to give their permission to share stories about intimacies. It just isn't right. Agreed?"

"Okay. Taboo subject."

"We were financial partners and friends. It wasn't well known because he did have a family. Giving away half a fortune to a butler who didn't have so much as a college degree would have had the dear man committed by his family. He would have lost it all, and they would have squandered it before a year was out."

"All this? They'd spend or lose all this in less than a year?"

Silas nodded. "Some people, right?" He reached for the cards. "Let me deal a few."

Julianna lost the next hand. "How did you do it?" he asked. "I mean, Tori alluded to having the right device for time travel. What do you need?"

"There are several ways to travel," she began then looked up.

Silas was scowling at her. "I can see an evasive answer brewing," he said. "I asked 'What do *you* need?'"

"I needed a coin. A special one. Plus you have to be in the right place."

"Does it have to be at the right time, too, like in those *Lost* novels?"

"You've read them?" she asked, wide-eyed and sitting up straight.

Taken aback by her concern, Silas nodded. "Yes, I told you I read a lot. Are they true? I mean, real?"

"You wouldn't believe me if I told you, so I'd better just wait until I lose another hand. Can I try some of that mellowed sangria now? If you could, add an extra splash of wine."

Two more hands went by before Julianna lost again.

"You never answered, does it have to be at a special time?"

"To travel, no. You do have to focus on where you're going, though. Otherwise, you could wind up in the middle of a tree."

"A tree?"

"You go through trees, like between them," she said, her eyes half-closed. She poured more wine in her cup, sloshing a little over the edge with her unsteady hand. "The trees are the markers to magnetic portals. You know, like the Bermuda Triangle and The House of Mystery? There are lots of places like that all over the world – magnetic vortexes. Some folks are more sensitive to finding them, but anyone can go through the portals with the right coin and focus. *Poof!* That's the easy way to go."

She lifted her glass to him in toast, tears filling her eyes. "But if you get stuck in a wrong time, without a coin, you're screwed. Or you'll have to do unsavory things to live."

"Like marry someone for convenience?" Silas offered, his hand gentle on her arm.

"No sex stories, remember?" she said, a gleam of disgust in her eye.

"How about some of those veggies and dip?" Silas asked. "The flavors and the sour cream should have blended by now. I think your tummy is a bit too empty to handle that much wine."

"But you did that on purpose, right? Got me drunk so I'd tell you more. Take away my inhibitions?"

"You didn't win a hand of cards, but I'll answer. Yes. I wanted to know why you were so interested in that coin I pulled out of my pocket earlier. It's the right one, isn't it?" He took the ancient Greek drachma out of his pocket and set it on the table in front of her.

She didn't have to say a word. The glow on her face answered for her. "Yes, it is. Do you know how long I've looked for one of these?" she asked, holding the silver coin up to the daylight to peer through the holes.

"Oh, I'd say about twenty years. You disappeared from Woodstock on that Monday morning in 1969 and jumped to 1989, right? That's where you lost your twenty years."

"Uh-huh." She set the coin down and looked up at him, tears now rolling down her cheeks. "And now that I have one, or at least know where one is, I don't want to use it."

"Why?" Silas asked, his face devoid of emotion.

"Because I don't want to screw up again and leave you."

"Oh, shit, woman!" he said, scooping her up from the breakfast nook, holding her in his arms like a lost child he'd just found. "It would take a lot of work to get rid of me. I've been looking for you for forty years."

She suddenly pulled back from the embrace. "Say! Where did you get it? And I don't think we need to play cards for answers anymore. We're beyond that."

"Amen on that. Oh, and that guy Simon I told you about? That master time traveler with the yard-long title?"

"The fairy king?"

Silas chuckled. "Yeah, something like that. He gave me that in exchange for the bottle of Fountain of Youth water I found for him. I'm sort of serious about getting younger, though. I mean, I'm not infirm or anything. I think you saw last night that all my parts work just fine…"

"Like I said, finer than when you were seventeen!"

"Yeah, well, my desire is greater, too."

"Does that mean we can go upstairs and use at least one of those condoms?" Julianna asked.

"At least two or three," Silas said and kissed her again.

Chapter 8: Like Riding a Bike

"Phew! You may be an old man, but you wore me out."

"Please tell me we can eat before going for fourths," Silas said, panting and grinning at the same time.

Julianna took the robe from the back of the chair and threw it at him. "Hide that thing from me for a while. It's addicting!"

"There's another robe in the closet on the left side. Oh, and back at you about covering up." He looked down at his belly. "Again? You have to be kidding. No, I'm cutting you off from Jules for at least an hour."

She looked and saw his excitement returning. "Really?"

"No, not really," he said. "I mean, *it* thinks so, but I don't. Hurry up and put on some clothes. It's all your fault."

Julianna faced him, one hand in front of her crotch, the other across her breasts. "This side?" She turned around and ran her hands up her fanny, bending over slightly and giving him an encouraging smile.

"Both, either, any part of you!" Silas covered his eyes with one hand, his cock with the other. "Don't look, either of you."

"Your dick doesn't have eyes," she chuckled.

"You and I know that but it doesn't. Down boy. Don't give me a heart attack. I have a lot of time to make up for, but I don't have to do it all today. Or even this week."

Julianna slipped the robe on and wrapped it closed, then knelt on the bed and gave Silas a long kiss. "How could I ever think of leaving you? Even if it wasn't the best loving I've ever had, it's you, the man with the sense of humor and compassion that I…"

She took a deep breath, then changed positions and cuddled up beside him. "I almost said it again, didn't I?"

"Is that why you left before?" he asked gently.

"Yes, and no. I mean, when I almost said it before, I realized I was falling for you. I had a mission. I couldn't let others get in my way."

"Mission?" he asked.

Her stomach grumbled in reply.

"Wait! Hold that answer," he said. "We're not doing that low blood sugar thing again. Come on. Help this old man up."

She looked at the terrycloth tent on his belly.

"Not him. Me. He really does have a mind of his own." He picked up the robe covering his cock. "Sorry I've neglected you for so long, dude. She's here to stay. I hope. Either way, if you don't pace yourself, you might break off. And unlike a gecko tail, you won't grow back."

He looked over at Julianna. "I think he'll listen now." He patted himself, already softer. "I scared him."

"Don't worry. I'm sure he'll come out of it. Yes, let's have at least a light dinner. Then I'll tell you about the mission. I promise."

Silas's tummy grumbled in reply. "Ah, the other hungry beast awakens."

***

Julianna swiped the cucumber slice through the French onion dip. "Um. It's even better than with potato chips." She put it in her mouth and chewed.

"And better for us, too." He copied her gesture with a carrot stick. "Eh, what's up, Doc?" he joked, then crunched it comically.

"Are you always like this? Lighthearted, whimsical...you know?"

"With whom? I have to be inspired. True, the guys and I kid around a lot. That's one reason for our odd little family over there. No drama or grumbling allowed. I'd like to think that's how we'll be, too."

"As long as you don't bitch about my housekeeping, cooking, what books I read, or how I spend my money," Julianna said, her forehead wrinkled with memories. She picked up a carrot and ate it without dip, realizing he hadn't said anything. "You're not even going to comment about my known shortcomings?"

"Maybe I will if you bring up any. So far, you haven't

mentioned drunken orgies with strangers, stealing me blind, arson, or serial murders. Cooking and cleaning can either be done by me or hired out, and what you read and spend your own money on isn't for me to dictate. You wouldn't do that to me, would you?"

"No… We're back to that Golden Rule, aren't we?"

"It never left, sweetheart," he said and put his hand on hers. "Now, don't fill up on veggies and dip because I have a light dessert. I was able to get fresh figs."

"Really? You are a wonder, aren't you?"

He shrugged then grinned. "They're *Mission* figs," he said dryly, one eyebrow raised.

"Oh, yeah. I was supposed to tell you about my mission after I had a bite to eat. Well, in a manner consistent with full disclosure, here goes. My elder sister ran away. I was trying to find her. Pretty simple, huh?"

"I take it she knows how to travel through time, too?"

"Yes, she does. It's a family tradition." She leaned forward, invigorated by his attention, glad there wasn't any skepticism in his voice. "Do you want to know more or go play?"

Silas wriggled in place, cleared his throat, and gave her a half-grin. "I think we ought to let our dinner settle. Hold on and I'll get those figs."

He brought out a china platter lined with golden-green fruit, ruby-red grapes, and slices of white cheese.

"Hey, you tricked me! Those aren't Missions or they'd be purple-black. Those are Kadotas. I may not know much, but I do know my figs."

"Yes, you're right, but you have to admit, it was a decent segue."

"True." Julianna leaned over the dish, inspecting the array. "We had both varieties at our place in North Carolina. It was years before we had enough to dry for winter. We kids would eat them as they ripened." She picked one off the platter, pulled off the stem, and bit into it. "Oh, man. The only way this could be better is if it was still sun-warmed." She sniffed it. "I miss the smell of green things growing. Some people think fig trees stink, but I don't. They remind me of stability, continuity, the sweetness of things to come."

"Maybe I should call you Shakespeare." He picked up one of the fruits, looked at it, then smelled it and copied her style of eating, pulling off the stem, biting into it like an apple. "You're right. Sweetness worthy of an Elizabethan ode."

She took another one and chose a slice of cheese. "Havarti?"

"My favorite."

"Mine, too! Oh, and I guess you want to know about the mission and the family tradition. Which first?"

"Your choice. I'm not going anywhere."

"Okay. So, my da was born in North Carolina of an American mother and a Scottish father." She paused and smirked devilishly. "In 1771."

"Really? I mean, go on. I'm intrigued."

"They came back to the twentieth century when he was about five or six. They moved to Scotland and that's where he picked up the accent. And attitude, but I digress. When he grew up, he decided he wanted to go back and see his grandparents."

"In the eighteenth century?" Silas asked.

"Yup. He made it with minor difficulties but wound up buying a slave."

Silas nodded, taking another fig and piece of cheese.

"He did it to spare her another flogging but fell in love with her."

"Your mother?"

"You got it, Sherlock. He couldn't marry her in eighteenth-century North Carolina, so brought her back here. They married, had lots of kids – biological, adopted, and foster – and lived happily ever after until my seventeen-year-old sister ran away with a psychotic Swede."

Silas coughed, nearly choking. "A minor? Gone? I bet they were horrified."

"You don't know the half of it. The world then is not what it is now. It's going to get crazy in about ten years. You're right to be a gardener. You might want to plow a few more acres or at least stockpile shelf-stable food, meds, and paper products. Oh, and cleaners and sanitizers. But I'm getting off topic again.

"Because there were so many kids involved, plus travel restrictions and the need to keep our farm going – and Da being held under a microscope by some government creepers – he couldn't go anywhere. I overheard him and Mom talking about it one night. He was going to risk it all, pretty much put the family farm and all he owned in jeopardy, and leave to find my sister. So, I took one for the team, so to speak. I left a note, told them to stay put, I'd find her, and that if they truly loved us, Da would let me do it. I sort of hinted I'd jumped forward in time and saw it all turned out okay if I left and he stayed."

"You lied."

"I assumed heavily. Or predicted with prejudice…"

Silas squinted at her and shook his head.

"Okay. I lied. I did it to save everyone and everything. Even if I never got her back, the rest of the family would be safe and not homeless. That wasn't too much of an assumption."

"But you never found her, did you?"

"Nope. Almost, though. Her name is Mali, like the country where our mother was born. You see, Mali and I were close. Very close. We'd bicker like any other sisters eighteen months apart, but we'd also finish each other's sentences, anticipate what we wanted to do next. Or where to go. She had a kind heart for hard-luck cases. I guess we both got that from our parents. At one point, there were fifteen kids in our family counting all the foster kids and strays.

"I knew she'd been researching the Valdez oil spill for her class report. We were homeschooled via distance learning – the internet – but still had projects to do. She was passionate about ecology. She used to fantasize that if someone could have been there and made sure that wreck didn't occur, all those birds and animals – the

62

thousands of fish and seals – and the economy of the whole area would have been spared."

Silas offered her another fig and she accepted it, eating it eagerly. She swallowed and continued.

"We shared everything, including secrets. I knew she'd been hanging out after basketball practice at the community center with this tall, redheaded guy. I never saw him, but she said he reminded her of Da. That's why I knew he had red hair and was about six-foot-seven."

"Wow! Is that why you're so tall?"

"Mom was the same height as I am now: six-four. I don't think there was a chance any of us could have been short unless dwarfism showed up. So, Mali had a major crush on the guy. She said his name was Storm and he was a Viking descendent."

Julianna leaned close to the table and Silas followed. "He told her Erik the Red was his grandfather and he was a time traveler. He wanted her to be his consort."

Silas sputtered. "But how? I mean, I don't want to interrupt you, but why did your father believe you could go on a time travel rescue mission? Did you have a coin?"

"Nope, but he did. I took it. Actually, it was the only one. He and Mom were able to share it. He couldn't follow me because I had the coin."

"Oh, crap. That poor man. He lost both his daughters and had no way to chase them down."

"Yeah, well, I didn't think about that until much later. That's a whole 'nother kind of guilt I have to deal with. And that's why I was so interested in your coin. I want to go back and tell him I'm sorry. I'm not sure when to go and make sure I catch him, though. Plus, now there's that other thing."

"What? What other thing?"

"You. I don't want to go anywhere without you. Mom and Da managed with one coin, but I don't want to take that chance. Do you think you could find another one?"

"Wow. I don't know how to get in touch with Simon. When he compensated me for my detective work with this, I thought he was being cheap. I didn't know what it was, but he said I'd find out when the time was right. Meanwhile, I should never let it out of my sight. 'Just consider it a good luck charm,' he said."

Silas handed her the coin. "I guess there are other ancient Greek drachmas in the world. I'm sure I can find one. Somewhere."

"With this as a pattern, you can drill holes the right size and in the right spot. I think that's been a problem in the past; holes in the wrong places." She handed it back to him. "Care for a little time traveling holiday, dear?"

"I'll grab my hat and sunblock whenever you say go, but I think I'd like to do a little research first. It might be there's a coin available at one of the antiquities shops. We can still travel wherever you'd like, though."

"How about whenever? I think I just figured out the date."

Chapter 9: Dropping In

"When?" Silas shook his head minimally, his lips pulled tight as he reflected on his one-word question. "I guess I mean that both ways. When do you want to leave and what time?"

"Well, there's no rush to leave. I want to go to the summer of 2015. It's a short hop forward – only five years. We don't have to worry about learning new idioms or slang, and we won't need new driver's licenses if we time it right."

"So you can mess with the year but not the day of the year or season, right?"

"Yup. Unless you're Simon. I guess he can slip in and out of any era. No one's figured a way to pop into different locations, though. You still have to be at the portal closest to your destination. No starting in Oregon and winding up in Orlando."

"So, where do you want to go?"

"Back to the old MacKay Manse in North Carolina. I know the date my folks bought the property and a little about what went on soon thereafter. I'm pretty sure they'll be there. And since that's where I was born and spent my first sixteen years, I could probably find the place blindfolded."

"Whoa, whoa, wait a second," Silas said, shifting in his chair. "You want to go to the future but to a time and place *before* you were born?"

She nodded and took another fig.

"But won't that scare the dickens out of your parents? I mean, will they even know who you are? Shoot! Would they even believe you if you told them?"

"Well, since both Mali and I look like paler versions of Mom, I'm pretty sure at least Da will believe me. Plus, Mom's only been through time once that I know of, but Da's popped back and forth a few times. He's more likely to accept me. They didn't talk about time travel much. It only came up once and we had to swear not to mention it to anyone outside the family. Still, they wanted us to know our heritage. That was the only way to explain Mom being born as a slave in 18th century Africa."

"Hush and keep it in the family? I don't blame them. They probably regret saying anything." Silas shook his head. "Do you realize your parents lost two daughters because they shared their history with you? If they had never said a word, you'd never have taken that coin. And Mali would never have believed there was such a thing as time travel and wouldn't have left with that slimy Swede."

"Actually, he's Norwegian," Julianna said sniffing, tears welling. "But psychotic Swede sounds better."

Silas looked up and saw her eyes getting red and realized he'd blown it. It was too late to take back his words, though. "I'm sorry. I should have kept my big mouth shut. I mean, I'm sure you came to the same conclusion a long time ago. It's just a lot for me to process and sometimes I think out loud." He reached over and held her hand. "I can't believe you've had to live with this for twenty years…and with someone who wouldn't believe you. I don't know how you survived."

"I had a son to bring up." She sighed and wiped her nose on her napkin. "I guess the more he needed me, the easier it was to ignore my past screw-ups. When he got older and had his own interests, I tried to find a way back home. I never mentioned time travel around Hugh, but he tracked my internet searches, and the books and articles I read. He knew what I was up to. I had confided in him right after we took on the responsibility of rearing Oscar together. I told him I thought Ciara – Oscar's birth mother – was a time traveler and that she either went 'sometime' else or she was kidnapped by the baby's father.

"Hugh ignored my first suggestion of what had happened to her and told me, 'Well, if she was kidnapped, she can be found.' I didn't pursue either option any further. The next day, he told me he hired a private detective to find her. Neither of us wanted to report it to the officials because we wanted to keep Oscar. I didn't think he'd harm Ciara if he found her. Offer her a million bucks to stay out of our lives, maybe, but he wouldn't hurt her."

"So, he knew but doubted you."

Julianna scoffed. "Being told and knowing are not the same thing. He trusted his detective to find any trace of her. Of course, all he had was her first name. Not even a photo. If she cut and dyed her hair, she could be anyone, especially after losing her baby belly. After two weeks of looking, he gave up. Or so he told me. It didn't make a difference. By then, neither of us wanted to find her."

"What about the baby's father? I mean, the man who got Ciara pregnant? Wouldn't he want the child if he knew about him?"

"Pbbt. No. Can we talk about something else?" She looked at the fig still in her hand and set it back on the plate. "Content with a full belly," she said with a wry smile. "Isn't it time for a nap?"

Silas took a deep breath and pushed the platter aside. "Do you always have such great ideas?"

"Hey, I'm bound to stumble on a good one now and then. I'd say race you to bed, but I don't have that much energy. Plus, I don't want to leave a mess here." She stood up and reached for his empty plate.

The two cleared the table together. "This much I can do," she joked, rinsing the glasses and setting them in the dishwasher as he finished putting the fruit and cheese away.

When they were done, they went upstairs to the red room, the mussed sheets and pillows blissfully reminding them how the bed got in such disarray. "The two spooned together on the big mattress, her belly to his bottom, a new sensation for Silas. A woman not only caring for him but protecting him, too. He could get used to it. He looked forward to it. A whole new volume of emotions had just been unsealed. And she was the perfect partner to share it with.

***

Silas awoke to the sound of Lionel Richie singing the refrain, 'You are my everything.' He reached over and no one was there. Startled, he threw back the covers, looked under the bed and in the closet, and even checked behind the curtains.

"Julianna? Julianna? Don't scare me like this…" He grabbed his robe and started to run to the kitchen, then realized how stupid he must look. He turned back, found his slippers, and made his way down the stairs as if he had all the time in the world. At least, he hoped he looked that way on the outside. His gut felt like he'd dined on broken glass and sulfuric acid. "Julianna?" he called again, forcing his voice to sound calm.

You told her to check out the other rooms in the house earlier. She probably couldn't sleep and now she's taking you up on the offer. Chill out, nervous Norman. Where would she go? Or how?

Silas checked everywhere, alternately calling out and whimsically singing 'Oh, where, oh where has my little girl gone,' making certain she would hear him one way or the other.

Twenty minutes of searching the house, plus a thorough inspection of the garage later, she still was missing.

'You are my everything…'

Silas was back in the bedroom changing into his street clothes when he heard it again. He hadn't been dreaming when he heard it the first time. On the bedstand was her cell phone. He picked it up and a picture of Julianna and Oscar making silly faces flashed, then disappeared. "Hello, hello?" he called into the phone. "Damn!"

He quickly hit call back and Oscar answered. "Mom? Where are you? Why…" Oscar stopped. "Who's this?"

"It's me, Silas Priest," he said. "You called and your mother didn't pick up, so I answered it."

"Duh! I called fifteen times, at least! What have you done to her, Silas? She always answers my calls on the first ring. Well, maybe two…"

"Um, she's not available right now. Would you like me to take a message?"

"No. I want to talk to her."

"As I said…"

"I know what you said and I don't trust you. Were you two having sex?"

"Wha…What? I mean, that's none of your business."

"That means you were. She hasn't had anyone *pay attention* to her in a long time. You did something to upset her, I know you did."

"I promise you, I did not."

"Then let me talk to her."

"Oscar, how can I make it any clearer, she is not available right now. Here, let me try again. Julianna!" he called out, holding the phone to his chest so he didn't blast the young man's eardrums. "It's Oscar and he wants to talk to you." He put the phone back to his ear. "See? She didn't reply. She's busy."

"No, she's not there. I can hear the fear in your voice. You did something to upset her. Were you two talking about that time travel nonsense? You may not know it, but that's what got her sent to the in-sanitarium. Twice. They messed her up with drugs. It took me months to get her out of there and off those psychotropic pills and herbs."

"Whoa. Wait. You got her out? Wasn't your father the one who put her in?"

"That's family business and you're not family." Oscar paused and snorted. "Yes, but he disappeared, I was the one they contacted when the automatic payments were canceled."

"So, your father is missing and now your mother is, too?"

"Aha! So, you don't know where she is, do you?"

"Actually, we were…um…resting when you called the first time. I awoke to music and she was gone. However, I didn't know the song was her ring tone. I thought I had been dreaming. I didn't hear your other calls because I was checking every room in this house plus the garage for her. Nothing. Zip."

"You must have a lot of rooms for it to take that long to look."

"Nineteen plus the garage."

"What? Couldn't afford twenty?" Oscar asked snidely.

"You can be rude, or if you'd like, you can help me look. I just realized I didn't check the guest house."

"Ring me in, then," Oscar said. "I'm at the front gate. By the way, it looks like someone was having target practice on this thing. I hope it still works."

"Target practice? Not a cherry bomb?"

"I'm no cop," Oscar said, "but these sure look like bullet holes to me."

"Hold on." Silas took his spare remote from the bedside table and pressed a button. "Is it opening?"

"It's trying… Nope."

"Okay. Back up. I'll see if I can get it to swing the other way."

Silas tried a different series of numbers, then heard, "You got it. Where do I go now?"

"I'll meet you out front," Silas said, the phone on speaker as he hurriedly dressed. He tucked his snowboots under his arm and rushed barefoot down the stairs.

He heard the thumping at the door as he leaned against it, slipping his feet into the boots. "Impatient kid!" he huffed, then took a calming breath. One excited male was one too many when looking for a missing person, especially a loved one.

The door swung open as soon as he unbolted it. "Grandpa!" Tori shouted, rushing into his unsuspecting arms. "Do you know how long I've been waiting for a grandparent? Either one, a grandma or a grandpa. Hey, are you going to marry Julianna? Because if you do, then Oscar will be my stepbrother. Ew. That'd be weird, huh, Oscar?"

"Grr! Tori, you promised you'd help look but not get in the way."

Tori pulled her dark knit cap over her short, flyaway blonde hair and huffed, pouting precociously, her eyes sparkling with mischief.

Silas reached out and pulled her inside, letting Oscar follow. "Let me grab my coat. And please, let me lead the way. There was a ruckus earlier. I want to take point in case there are any footprints or clues."

"A ruckus? Was my mom hurt? Why didn't you protect her? What kind of man are you?" Oscar's face turned red as he blurted out his questions, and it wasn't just the winter cold that caused it.

Tori opened her mouth, ready to tell him to chill out, but her boyfriend gave her the look. She brought her hand up and rubbed underneath her nose. She ignored her gut. She'd speak up when and if she saw something they didn't. Oscar wasn't the most observant person and she wasn't sure about her grandfather, but she saw and remembered everything. She'd wait.

Silas groaned and shook his head, knowing there was no calming the young man with words. The only solution was to find his mother. "This way," he said and took off toward the guest house.

"Is this place yours?" Oscar asked as they walked around the mansion. He gazed up at the second story and all the windows. "Nah, couldn't be. You're just the butler, right?"

"What difference does it make," Silas said, jaw clenched as he bent down to pick up a ponytail elastic. He brought it to his nose, sniffed, then held it away, frowning.

"Do you recognize the smell?" Tori asked. "Although by the face you made, I'd say you do."

"Here," he said, offering it to her.

She took a tentative whiff, then made the same sneer of disgust. "Ugh!"

"Let me," Oscar said, reaching for it.

Tori looked at Silas, smirking but staying silent.

"Ugh, is right! That is definitely *not* my mother's. Besides, she uses the fat ones. These skinny bands wouldn't hold her hair."

"That's Eau de Tigress," Silas said. "Some people find it appealing, others - meh. You're right, though. It isn't your mother's scent."

"Oh, God," Oscar said. "You've been sniffing my mother."

Tori whispered to him, "By his concern, I think they've been doing a lot more than sniffing."

"Not now, Tori," Oscar grumbled.

"What? You'd rather some icky man have the hots for her? Someone who wouldn't care if she *poof,* just disappeared? Hey, at least he cares for her and he's helping find her, so cut him some slack, all right?"

"Hey, if it wasn't for him, she wouldn't be missing. She'd be safe and…"

"Hush!" Silas said, then held his arms out to make sure they stopped. "There's someone up ahead."

Tori and Oscar moved around Silas, trying for a better vantage spot.

As soon as he saw what it was, Oscar jumped in front of Tori and pulled her to his chest. He covered her eyes, not saying a word. He looked back at the entanglement, stunned at what he was shielding her from. He looked over at Silas and shook his head. "What the hell?' he mimed.

Silas stepped forward, saw the action, then turned around and herded the young couple into the bushes. He put his finger to his lips, admonishing them to be still.

"Ahh…ahh…oh…" a husky male voice groaned.

Silas and Oscar snickered as Tori huffed, frustrated that they knew what was going on and she didn't. She opened her mouth but caught the look from both men and pursed her lips in anger.

Rustling and footsteps came from the site of activity. "Now can we leave?" a woman hissed.

Silas peeked out then popped back into the bushes. "Victoria," he whispered to himself.

Oscar's eyebrow raised in confusion as Tori's eyes widened in surprise.

Groaning softly, Silas fixed his granddaughter with a glare, shaking his head. "Not now," he whispered. *Not ever, I hope.*

Two people slushed through the yard, stomping on crunchy patches of crystallized snow, heedless of being seen. Atlas and Victoria made their way to the fence. The three watched as the man pulled back an evergreen cedar, allowing the skinny woman clad in a form-fitting black catsuit access to the outside world through a break in the wall.

"So, is anyone going to tell me what they were doing?" Tori huffed.

Oscar looked at Silas, more than happy to cede that explanation to him.

As Silas was trying to figure out how to explain fellatio to his innocent heir, she popped off another question.

"And who was that man? He looked like a wrestler or bodybuilder or something."

Grinning at being given a pass at answering her first question, Silas quickly replied. "That's André the Giant, and no, as far as the research I've done, he was never a wrestler and was only a bodybuilder for his own…ahem…diversion. He's an actor in a specialty movie genre and the…ahem…boyfriend of your grandmother."

"That was her grandmother?" Oscar asked, his voice squeaking out the designation.

Silas rolled his eyes in embarrassment. "Need I say there was a lot of alcohol and other factors involved in the procreation process."

"I know big words, too," Tori said. "Does that mean she drugged you then got you drunk and that's how Grace was conceived?"

Now it was time for Oscar to do the eye roll. Silas noticed and explained. "You might want to get used to Tori being brighter than you think." He cleared his throat. "That is, if you plan on keeping her in your life."

"He doesn't have a choice," Tori said, grabbing Oscar's arm. "And was Victoria giving him a blew job?"

Oscar and Silas both coughed and laughed at the same time, each one clinging onto delayed recovery so the other would have to offer Tori the correction. Eventually, it was Silas who explained. "That's blow, not blew. And thank you for calling her by her given name and not her genetic designation."

"Well, that's out of courtesy to you but from what I hear, she's a real piece of work…and not a good kind, either."

"So, she decided to come back," Julianna said, startling the trio.

"Mom! You're here! You scared the pee-waddles out of me. Don't do that!" Oscar screeched, hugging her tight.

Silas stood back and held the shivering Tori – now deprived of her boyfriend's warmth – and waited for his turn to speak.

"Oscar, I told you where I'd be. I'm fine." She looked up at Silas and smiled. "We're fine."

Relieved, Silas grinned back, holding in his fear-infused scolding, very similar to Oscar's. "You were here?" he asked calmly.

"I couldn't find a pen or paper to leave you a note. I...um...get insomnia, even if I'm bone-tired, content, and with a full belly. I decided to take you up on a tour of the house. It's beautiful. I was on the balcony – wondering if I should get dressed and check out the guest house – when I saw Victoria had returned. It looked like she brought her pet ape with her, too.

"I went inside to let you know, but you were gone. I figured you might be looking for me..." She looked at Silas and caught his half-smile and shrug.

"So, I went after you. I was upstairs when Oscar and Tori came to the door. I um...had to change clothes and get some shoes, and then I followed you out here."

"Can we find someplace warmer?" Tori asked. "I mean, if we're going to investigate, that's fine. Let's do it. I'm freezing my eyelashes off just standing here, though."

"Let's see what *else* they were up to," Silas said with a soft grunt of disgust as he tried to dislodge the mental image.

Silas punched in the code and opened the door. "This is your guest house?" Oscar asked, looking at the expansive living and dining room combination. He nodded to the other side of the room. "And that's the fanciest kitchen I ever saw."

"You haven't seen the one in the main house," Julianna said.

Oscar snorted. "All you'd ever need is a big microwave, Mom."

"Or..." she said, threading her arm through Silas's, "a huge

74

kitchen with a man who knows his way around it. Silas likes to cook."

"Me, too!" Tori popped in. She saw Oscar's scowl. "At least, I want to learn how."

"Stick around and we'll work on it," Silas said, arm out to welcome her to his other side.

"Are you taking all my women?" Oscar grumbled.

"She's my granddaughter and your mother is my girlfriend from many years ago. Are you wanting to deny either of them family or friendship? You know, the heart's capacity for love is limitless."

"Shakespeare," Julianna whispered, then giggled.

"No, it's not..." Tori said, then looked over and saw her smirk. "Oh, yeah. You're saying he puts words together well, huh?"

Julianna nodded then looked around the room. "Well, Silas, does it look like they got in?"

He pulled away from the women and checked the doors and windows for the short pieces of thread he left dangling. All were still in place except for the one that had fallen when he opened the back door to get in. "Let me check the bedrooms."

Oscar trailed behind him, Tori at his elbow. When they reached it, they all stopped and stared.

"They really tore this place up," Tori said. "And you better get a piece of plywood for that window or it's gonna freeze in here."

Julianna stood behind the shocked trio. "Oh, my," she gasped, observing the broken lamps, scattered bedding, and knifed pillows. Glass and down feathers covered the floor like ice and giant snowflakes "What were they looking for?" Oscar asked.

Silas shook his head back and forth, dazed. "Those stupid, stupid people. Did they really think I'd hide it in a pillow?"

"What is *it*?" Oscar asked.

"And why did they only look in one room?" Julianna added.

"And stop here? I mean, either they found it or they left without it," Tori said. "And if they didn't find it, why did they leave?"

Silas gave Tori a quick hug across the shoulders. "If I didn't know it already, I'd swear we were related. That's a great question. And the answer is, they found a decoy. However, I think they trashed the room and tore apart the pillows out of sheer orneriness. They broke the windows to get in but must have bypassed my alarms somehow."

Tori looked in the window track. "Bubblegum and tin foil," she said. "They messed with the electrical signal. Crude but clever."

"Just like them," Oscar said. "What now?"

"As Tori said, get some plywood and secure the room from the elements. And devise a new alarm system. They'll soon find out that videotape isn't the one they were after."

Chapter 10: The Insurance Policy

"What videotape were they after?" Julianna asked.

Silas cut his eyes over to Oscar and Tori, checking out the window frame. "Insurance," he said.

"What kind of insurance?" Tori asked, turning back to join them.

"Hey, we're all adults here," Oscar said, his arm now around Tori's shoulder. "You might as well let us know what we're getting into."

"Who said *we're* getting into anything?" Silas asked.

"You did. We're family now, right?" Oscar said, looking to his mother.

"So, you're all right with me dating Silas?"

"Yeah, well, he's going to be in my life one way or another with Tori. I might as well accept him. I might learn something. I saw he has a garden going fallow out there. He might be able to learn something from me, too."

"I wish there was a way I could do a mind meld or something so I could bypass any discussion, but since there isn't a way to do that…"

"Yet," Julianna whispered, then cleared her throat.

"Tori, that woman who was here earlier today made life miserable for Hal, my friend and your other grandfather."

"The man who brought up Grace, my biological mother. Right. Got it," Tori said, chin out. "I was told Victoria was a horrid person and don't ask about her, so I won't. No details necessary."

"Thank you. Hal had set a prenuptial agreement in place before he married her, so a divorce would have cost him everything. He was willing to do that, but we…ahem…found a way around it. You see, if she was unfaithful to him *while married*," Silas said. He stressed those two words to remind Julianna that he hadn't been intimate with Victoria when she was wed, whether he was drugged or sober, and to drop a hint to the other two that that's what had happened.

"If she was *caught* being unfaithful, he could divorce her and not owe a nickel of alimony, nor any share of their joint property. The prenup went both ways, but Hal wasn't – isn't – the cheating kind."

"So, you or someone else found her a boyfriend or caught her, right?" Tori asked. "Although if it had been me, I would have dangled a footlong carrot in front of her – set her up with cameras in place so I could film her when I was ready – rather than chase her all over town, trying to catch her in the act."

Oscar and Julianna looked at Tori with wide eyes, then at Silas, who had the same awed expression. He closed his mouth and swallowed. "Yes, one way is easier than the other, for sure. Anyhow, we – Hal and I – got the damning evidence, the divorce was rushed through, and the tape was to be held by me. It wasn't needed for the decree. Theirs was a no-contest dissolution so no embarrassment for her or loss of money for Hal. He shipped her off to Costa Rica with the admonition that if she came back, he'd share the video with the world. Her reputation would be ruined."

"But maybe now she wants the notoriety," Oscar said.

All eyes turned to him. "Hey, she'd be an instant celebrity, right? Vintage porn is the rage in some circles. Or so I've heard. But even if she didn't have a great backstory to go with it, she could put it out there to smear Grace and her granddaughters – you, Hal. Shoot, she could probably bring the American flag into the mix if she was clever enough."

"Talk about backfiring on you," Tori said, shaking her head. "Hey, could she just make another one and say it was the original?"

"Are you kidding?" Oscar asked. "There are so many amateur debunkers out there – no offense, Silas – who'd have it taken down in no time. If it was the real deal, though, it'd be as good as the Zapruder film."

"Huh?"

"The one that shows John Kennedy being assassinated, dear,"

Silas said, his hand on her shoulder. "Maybe they didn't talk about that in school."

"Yeah, huh. I would have remembered."

"I'd ask where the tape was, but I don't want to know," Julianna said. "Not that I'm curious, because I'm not. I just don't want to be asked and subconsciously glance at where it was or be tricked into telling."

"Or maybe someone could kidnap us," Tori said excitedly, "and demand the information or they'd kill us!"

"You've been watching too many movies," Julianna said.

"No, reading a lot of books," Tori replied, her rapid-fire supposition now slowed down to dejection. "But you're right. Sorry. Overactive imagination, I guess."

"No worries. The insurance is safe. Oscar, are you and Tori going to be all right? I mean, do you have a place to stay?" Silas asked, then suddenly paled. "Did your parents let you go with Oscar? By yourself? You'd better check in with them."

"Oh, they're cool," Tori said. "I guess they decided to do a little reminiscing while on the east coast. They haven't been here since I was born. Oscar promised to be respectful," she added with a giggle.

"You didn't hear what your dad told me," Oscar said, then gulped. "But you're right. I have an alert set on my watch to remind me to check in every evening."

Silas nodded, then frowned at the broken window. "Julianna, would you help me secure this? I have some hurricane season plywood we can use in the garage. I'd ask your son, but I think you have him bested in the height department."

Oscar stood next to her and stretched comically, tiptoeing in his boots and still four inches shy. "Yeah, she's every bit as strong as I am, too. Point us to the broom closet and Tori and I'll clean up the glass and feathers for you."

"Right over there," Silas said, nodding to the far side of the kitchen. "I don't know what I did to get such a great family, but I'm grateful."

"And if you need more help for anything, I have two sisters and their men to help. Plus a bonus mom and dad," Tori said.

"Sorry. It's just Mom and me," Oscar said with a shrug.

Silas clapped him on the shoulder. "And that's enough." He looked up at Julianna, smiling in pride at her son's acceptance of her boyfriend. "I take that back – that's plenty."

***

"I want to see it," André said. He grabbed for the videotape and caused Victoria to swerve on the road, barely missing a parked cop car.

"Not yet," she said, tucking it under her arm. She winced at the discomfort and handed it to him. "Just hold it. It's not like film. You can't hold it up to the light and see little images. We'll have to get a VHS player."

"But we don't have any money," André groused. "I could be making some big bucks on the beach as an escort if you hadn't talked me into coming to Boston in the winter."

"We're not in Boston…" Victoria said, biting off the word 'idiot.' "We're just a few miles from where the Pilgrims landed hundreds of years ago."

"Yeah, well, didn't they all freeze to death or something?"

Rather than agree with him, she said, "I didn't say we'd *buy* a tape player. There are other ways, you know."

André looked down at his crotch and rearranged himself. "I just hope it's a warm place. I don't like stripping in cold clubs."

"Not that!"

"Oh, I guess I could stand on the corner like the old days. I gotta watch it, though. Half the johns are gay."

"Not that, either," Victoria said, not even trying to hide her exasperation. "I told you, hooking is no longer allowed. I'm your one and only. Dancing doesn't count. You're not letting those old bitches do anything but stuff money down your G-string."

André swallowed hard and tried to keep his face stoic, but couldn't stop thinking of the sorority party where he'd been the

80

featured attraction. He was fond of Victoria – and put up with a lot of her nonsense about becoming instant millionaires because of that – but having his whole body stroked and oiled by a dozen unwrinkled women in one night was enough to keep him happy for a month. And what those six perky coeds had done for him…

He shifted in his seat and set the videotape on his lap, trying to calm his excitement. He looked out the window and stared at the icy gray sidewalks, people in heavy coats hurrying to parked cabs or building entrances of glass and concrete. He looked down again, the tape settled back on his lap. Yes, living that kind of life was enough to wilt any man's dick. Better to stick with the old woman who'd do anything for him. Even if she was as wrinkled and sour as a hundred-year-old lemon.

"We're here. I'll go in and talk us into a room," Victoria said.

André looked in the lobby. "You'd better let me. He may be a guy, but I'll bet you dinner he's not into women."

"All right," she said. "Just make sure you let him know we want a room with a VHS player. We brought our own movies, got it?"

André patted the back of her head like an old dog's, then got out of the stolen Chrysler, tugging his pants to give himself the best presentation.

The clerk watched as the most gorgeous hunk of man meat he'd ever seen climbed out of the silver-toned sedan, rearranging man parts that seemed to belong to a horse. "Oh, my…" he crooned, squirming as his fantasies began.

"Don't forget," Victoria called out, stepping out of the car to make sure the hotel clerk knew André was checking in with a woman.

"Good day, sir," the clerk said, his eyes blinking with excitement. "Do you need a suite for you and your mother?"

André couldn't help but laugh. "Yes, and if you would, make sure it has a VSH player in it. I'll put in an old movie and hopefully, she'll be asleep in minutes. I…um…like to play by myself to my own kind of movies. That is unless there's someone around to stimulate me."

"VSH? Oh, VHS players. Yes, yes. We have a few in back. Just fill this out and I'll go grab one. Or two. Sometimes it's fun to have two different *shows* going at the same time while…um…playing around."

The clerk went through the curtain. Thuds and thunks of boxes and shelves being moved around drifted out. "Just give me a minute or two. I know they're in here somewhere," he hollered.

André walked around the counter, looked down, and saw the cashbox. Unlocked. He popped it open, grabbed the large bills and left the ones and coins, then closed it and came back around.

"I found them!" the clerk sang out, then set two dusty boxes on the counter. "What time does your mother go to sleep?" he whispered.

André pursed his lips and nodded. "I have to feed her first so she'll be good and drowsy. You'd better give me at least an hour. Knock three times and if I don't answer, give it another five minutes. Just in case. Oh," André reached in his pocket and took out five twenties. "I'd rather keep this off the books if you don't mind. If I'm a little short, maybe we can make up the difference some other way."

The clerk glanced down at the bulge in André's pants. "Oh, this will be fine," he said, tucking it in his front pocket without counting it. "I'm sure you're not…ahem, short."

André kissed the tip of his index finger then placed it on the clerk's nose and winked at him. Mesmerized, the clerk handed him the room key. André accepted it and picked up the two boxes, letting his new friend open the door for him. "Later," he whispered.

"Um…" the man whimpered like a sad puppy, then walked back to the desk, sighing.

André opened the car door and set the tape players on the back seat. He looked at the number on the key and nodded to the end of the complex. "I got us a suite where we won't be disturbed. Oh, and two VSH players just in case one isn't working right. They look

82

new. Maybe we can make a few bucks selling them."

"I'm not a fence," Victoria said. "And that's VHS and that technology is so old, I'm surprised the players are even around."

When they pulled in front of the room, Victoria took the key from his overloaded hands and opened the room. "Pee-ew! This place smells of stale cigarettes, stinky feet, and B.O."

"Yeah, well, what did you expect?" André asked, setting their backpacks and the boxes on the bed. "It's not this easy to sneak into the Ritz."

"Ritz, Schmitz. Once we get this uploaded and advertised, we'll be rolling in it! That battering ram of yours and my squeals are sure to be the next rage of pay-for-porn."

"Only because of the story behind it, right? I mean, you and I could make a new one but it's not the same, huh?"

"Well, we did make this almost twenty years ago. I've aged a little bit..." Victoria saw André roll his eyes and changed her wording. "We've *both* aged a little bit. You're softer in the middle...but not where it counts."

"And you've lost a few pounds but you know what they say..."

Victoria giggled like a schoolgirl at a tickle-fest. "The closer the bone, the sweeter the meat. Oh, you big lunk. You are such a romantic!" She unzipped her jacket and threw it on the back of the chair. "Let me take a quick shower while you set up the player. I'll be right out."

André opened the box and took out the packing material and black and silver-toned machine. He turned it over, then heard a soft knock at the door just as the shower turned on.

Knock, knock, knock.

He set the box down and opened the door a crack. "She's in the shower. You're early."

"I know, but I thought you might need these cords. Just match the colors on the ends to the TV and tape player, then turn the TV to channel three. If you can't figure it out, we can wait until she's asleep..."

"André, would you bring me my conditioner, sweetheart."

"Sweetheart?" the clerk asked.

"Mothers," André huffed, then laughed. "Yeah, I'll ring you up as soon as the coast is clear." He repeated his coy fingertip kiss on the eager man's nose, then shut the door.

"Oh, yeah – conditioner." André dumped the contents of Victoria's backpack onto the bed and found the little purple bottle of thickening hair cream. He glanced at the label. 'For thinning hair or baldness.' "Maybe she'll share," he said, running one hand through his sparse locks.

"Was there someone at the door?" she asked when he handed it to her.

"Yeah, the manager or whatever he is brought me the cords to hook everything up. I'll see if I can get it going." He looked down at her body. Bonier than he remembered. Then up at her face. More wrinkled and spotted than ever without makeup.

"You like?" she asked seductively, her tongue covering the gap where her partial plate – now in a cup on the sink – would be.

"Oh, yeah," he said, his hand rubbing across his mouth to hide his lie. *That clerk just might be the diversion I need tonight. Give her a few snorts of wine and she'll be out until dawn.*

***

Fifteen minutes later, Victoria was still working on her 'quick' shower. André had all the cords routed and plugged into the holes on the TV and was studying the trash news magazine he had heisted from the convenience market earlier in the day. "Those can't be real," he said.

"What can't be?" Victoria asked, stepping out of the bathroom, fully painted with make-up, false tooth in place, hair styled, but only a hand towel held over her middle for clothing.

"Her boobs," he said, then looked up. "Wow! You look good, woman," he added, almost believing himself. She did look a whole hell of a lot better than she had in the shower. At least she had teeth and her hair didn't look like wet seaweed heaped on top of an ancient pier piling.

"Are you ready for a blast to the past? I know I was there when we made it, but I've never been the star of my own porn video. Would you like a little warmup or should we go straight to the main event?"

"There's nothing little about this warmup," André said, cupping his genitals. "But let's go check out the wayback machine. I've been in plenty of pornos, but never one with you. Plus, I've seen my classics so many times, they're boring. I'd like some new excitement."

"Oh, I like that. Maybe we'll see something we haven't done in a lo-ong time," she said, stroking him familiarly. "Let's get it on."

Already reclined and with his boots off, André unbuttoned his pants and started shoving them down his hips.

"I meant the movie. I mean, turn on the TV and tape player first. I want to make sure everything is working right."

"Well, we already know this is in fine shape…"

"André, please, just for once. Everything in this world isn't about your cock. Yes, it's big and beautiful but…" Victoria stopped. She'd lost him once before when she tried to stop him from being so self-centered, and it had taken her years to get him back. Imperfect or no, she needed him. "I'm sorry. Go ahead and get undressed. I'm sure you have it set up right already. I have the tape right here."

"She's just a bit out of sorts, Buddy," he said to his dick. "She said she was sorry, so don't hold it against her. Well, hold it against her maybe later, but for now, let's go back in time twenty years before either one of us had even one gray hair."

Victoria stifled a groan. He was talking to 'Buddy' again, having a conversation with his dick. Maybe he really was crazy. But whether he was or wasn't, he was manageable. She slid the VCR out and looked at the cords in the back. "He must be colorblind," she mumbled and plugged in the wires correctly. "Here we go."

She turned the TV and VCR on, stuck in the tape marked 'V and the Giant,' and slid next to André on the bed.

Black and gray crinkles came on the screen, then horizontal lines settled into a test pattern. "Is everybody ready?" a voice called out.

"Huh?" André asked.

"It's Dick and Dandy Doodle Time!"

"What the hell?" Victoria screeched.

Knock, knock, knock!

"Not now," André yelled at the door, then grabbed the remote from Victoria.

He fasted forwarded through grainy black and white images of marionette puppets and actors in gaudy costumes. He stopped and watched. "Who are you going to make happy with that big club?" the woman in Marie Antoinette garb asked the pasty-faced clown holding an oversized baseball bat. "It's not the size but how well you swing it that counts," she taunted.

Victoria reached for the remote but André pulled it close, knees on elbows as he bent forward to watch the underground parody of a kid's show from the fifties. "Was she talking about the guy's dick?" he asked.

She tossed her small towel at his head, hopped out of bed, and ejected the cassette. Grumbling in frustration, she held the tape up toward the lamp and looked at it.

"You can't see anything that way," André told her, repeating her earlier warning. "It's not like it's on real film or anything."

"Ergh!" She set it down and grabbed her backpack, pulling out her twice-worn but least filthy black jumpsuit. "I don't know which one I'll castrate, but I'll get either Hal or Silas." She paused, snorting in barely controlled rage. "Hell, I'll get them both. And I'll throw in Doc for free."

"Who's Doc? Oh, he's that other roommate, huh. Hey, are they gay?"

"What? No. Hell, who cares? I've spent every dollar I could steal on getting here just to get this tape, and then some idiot goes and switches it out on me!"

86

"Hey, Victoria. Sweetie. Isn't whoever did that like a genius or something? I mean, not to sound rude or nothing, but if the trick hadn't been on us, it would have been pretty funny. Hey, can I watch the rest of that show? I mean, we can't go anywhere or do anything anyhow. I mean, unless you want to get kinky. I think I know someone who might be interested in a three-way."

"What? Who? And how did you hook up with someone so fast? I've been with you twenty-four-seven for six weeks now. No, never mind. And no, I don't want to hook up with anyone right now. I'm too pissed to see straight. I need a drink. Damn! We don't have any money."

"If you leave me the remote, I'll give you some money so you can go out. Unless you need me to drive."

Victoria looked at André, his eyes cutting back to the TV as if by staring at it, the show would return. "Trade ya," she said, overthrowing the remote to the door. "Now, where's my drinking money."

André fumbled in his jeans pocket, pushing down a few bills so he wasn't giving her everything he had taken from the till. "Here. And take one of those menus with you. It has the hotel's name and address on it. If you're too drunk to drive back, at least you know where to tell the taxi to bring you." He looked at the TV. "You know what I'll be doing."

She took the money and was ready to put it in her pocket when she realized she was still naked. She picked up her outfit, sniffed it, and made a face. She took the bar of soap from the sink and rubbed it under the armpits, then put on her refreshened catsuit. Finally ready, she stepped into her boots, reached across André for the keys, and gave him a quick dispassionate kiss goodbye. "Don't laugh so hard you give yourself a hernia."

"Oh, I won't. Maybe after a wine cooler or two, you'll figure out where they could have hidden the real tape. And don't forget your coat," he said, handing it to her from the back of the chair.

"Thanks. Sometimes I don't know what I'd do without you."

And then she was gone, engine revving and tires squealing as she sped out of the parking lot, a loud long blast on someone's horn indicating she hadn't looked before pulling into traffic.

Knock, knock, knock.

"Come in. Oh, wait..." André said, still naked.

Click. "Don't worry. I brought my key," the clerk said, his hair slicked back and smile bright.

"Before you lie down," André said, offering him the cassette, "bring me that remote. You gotta see this movie."

"Okay, but just so you know, I can do two things at once."

André grinned broadly and patted the bed beside him. "Go for it."

Chapter 11: Clumsy

"When Tori gets back, you two finish up here," Julianna said, pulling off the work gloves Silas had offered her. "And don't forget to vacuum after you've swept twice…"

"And use the mop with the disposable cloths so there won't be any shards or tiny bits left behind," Oscar recited dispassionately. "I know, Mom. This isn't the first broken glass mess I've cleaned up."

"Well," she answered with a grin, "it's probably the first one you didn't create, though."

"Okay, that's it. I'm not protecting him anymore." Oscar set the broom against the wall and put his hands on his hips. "You know all those 'clumsy' messes I made? It wasn't me. Or at least, they weren't my fault. Dad may have been a great guy in many ways, but he had some major faults and one of them was his temper when it came to perfection. If I couldn't get a chess combination memorized or learn to throw a curve ball right away, he'd push me around. He wouldn't out and out slug me, but he'd shove me up against a wall or cabinet or door or whatever else was near. 'Oops!' he'd say. 'You sure are clumsy, kid.' Frankly, when he disappeared, I was glad."

"Wha…what?" Julianna gasped. "He struck you?"

"Yeah, well if by *struck me* you mean used the force of his body against mine, causing me to lose my balance, then yes, he struck me."

"Oh, Oscar… I had no idea! I mean, I knew he brow-beat the hell out of me, but I had no idea he'd harmed you. I'm so, so sorry. How can I ever make it up to you?"

"Mom, you don't have to make anything up to me. I realize now he's the reason you were in that nuthouse, strung out on that psycho-bullshit drug therapy. I mean, whether or not I agree with your belief in that time travel nonsense…"

Julianna interrupted, "And every time you call it nonsense, you're reinforcing your disbelief in it. Sorry, go on."

89

Oscar rolled his eyes. "Yeah, I'm sorry, too. The point is, he was manipulative. I can't tell you how many times I wanted to run away. I couldn't though. I had to protect you."

"Protect me?" Julianna gasped.

"Mom, did you ever notice how sometimes your research books would go missing, or your hard drive would suddenly crash? That was me. Didn't you think it was a bit odd, especially since it was always when you believed you were really onto something?"

"Yes, but I thought Hugh was the one sabotaging me. I figured he would do anything to stop me from finding a way..." Julianna took a deep breath and decided not to hide the truth from him any longer. "He wanted to stop me from finding a way home or to my sister...whenever she was."

She paused, reflecting on what he had just said. "Wait. How would you know when I was 'really onto something'?"

Oscar chuckled. "You'd glow. Not like a light bulb, but you were radiantly happy. He saw it, too. He'd start snooping into your reading material. I caught him once." He held up his left arm. "That's when I had my 'clumsy fall' and broke my arm."

Julianna's jaw clenched and her eyes widened in rage. "If he wasn't already dead, I'd kill him!"

"Yeah, well, that might not be the case, right? I mean, that suspicious note was all they had to declare him legally dead. A hastily written suicide note left before he took off to parts unknown. No body or data trail found. *Poof!* Just gone."

Julianna wobbled and put her hand on the counter to steady herself.

Oscar took a fresh cloth and wiped it across a bar stool. "Mom, come sit down a minute. It's 'fess up time on something else, too."

"I'm not sure if I'm proud you're telling me this or pissed that you took so long."

He shrugged off the comment. "It doesn't make a difference. No matter what you say, we can't change the past. Or at least, we can't change what we've already done."

"Now that I'll agree with, the operative words being 'we've done.' Go on."

"I left that note. Or rather, those notes. I planted lots of them over the last two years. I hoped he wouldn't find any of them, but I took a chance. I figured I'd deal with his wrath if he discovered it was me who had written them. Besides, I knew I was going to Oregon and figured I'd be out of striking range if he did find one. The only person he could hurt would be you. I knew you'd kick his butt if he laid a hand on you, so I wasn't worried there."

"Yeah, well, there are other ways of hurting a big person without using fists. So, he vanished on his own, or did you help him along there?"

"I had nothing to do with that part. I kind of hope he got himself a mean girlfriend in Timbuktu who won't let him communicate with the outside world. I don't wish him dead, but there's an uncomfortable portion of my brain that worries I have some superpowers and 'wished' him gone. You know, sent into an unknown portion of the universe."

"Purgatory?"

"Yeah, that's what it'd be. I just want him away and out of our lives. Is that wrong?"

"Nope," Julianna said tersely. "Me, too. So, you wrote that note…"

"Notes," Oscar interjected.

"Notes, so if he did disappear, at least one would be found. Then the police would think he committed suicide even if they couldn't find the body?"

"Yup. And when the cops called and said he was gone and you were *indisposed*," he grinned and shook his head at the word then proceeded, "I rushed back to the house, destroyed all the notes they hadn't found, then came and rescued my damsel in distress."

"I'm your mother and too old to be a damsel, but I was definitely in distress at that institution."

"So, you said you were wandering around the property earlier today? Still dealing with the insomnia the meds caused?"

"It was just the house but unfortunately, yes. However – and this is very important for you to believe – I am very happy with Silas. He was my true love when we were teenagers and we're picking up where we left off. Of course, it's a lot easier since we don't have to worry about college or money or …ahem… missions."

"I'll ignore the last part for now, Mom. Yes, he seems like a decent guy. I asked around about him and tried a little online research. Everyone who knows him, likes him. The last part came up nil, though, which means he's either a cyber genius who can manipulate data, or he's never done anything wrong. I mean, no matter how good a person is, if he's screwed up, there's going to be a record of it somewhere."

Julianna smiled nervously, not wanting to bring up that Hugh's public record probably portrayed him as a saint. An ideal man on paper wasn't necessarily one in practice.

The door burst open and Tori popped in, stomping her boots. "It's starting to snow again. Hey, do you want to build a snowman?"

"Let's finish up here first," Oscar said. "Maybe by then, there'll be enough to build a big one."

"Yeah, huh? There probably isn't enough for my Barbie doll. Well, when I get one."

Julianna smiled at her boisterous innocence then realized it would probably never leave. Silas had that same ability to find the good in any situation, and he'd lived forty years more than she had. "Didn't you ever have a Barbie doll?"

"Nope. I had stuffed animals and rag dolls that my mother made me. Except for a few weeks when I was in kindergarten, my parents homeschooled me. We lived off the grid. Well, sort of. We had electricity, but my life was pretty much just the three of us and books. No television or movies. They said there was too much garbage in the world. Still, I probably found out more about life than they wanted me to. Like about Barbie dolls."

"Gee, even my folks got me *action figures*," Oscar said. "My dad wouldn't call them dolls, but Mom wanted to stimulate my imagination."

"Yeah, well when I get a job and have my own money," Tori said, "I'm going to buy at least one. Or maybe three, so they can be sisters."

"Having sisters is good," Julianna said, giving Oscar a sidelong glance, reminding him they needed to continue their conversation.

"We'll talk more later," he told her softly then turned his attention back to Tori. "We can go shopping after we clean up this mess. That'll give it time for the snow to accumulate. Plus, we're going to be hanging out together for a few days. Using our imagination with *action figures* sounds like fun."

Tori giggled into her hand. "I know something else that sounds like fun," she said, blushing as she looked at Oscar with dreamy eyes.

"Granddaughter…" Silas said in a mock stern voice.

"Jeez! I didn't hear you come in," she squeaked.

"Yes, and you remember that. Just when you two think you're alone, getting ready to do something you shouldn't, be aware. I'm quiet and I'm sneaky." Silas looked at Oscar. "And I was a young man once, too."

"Yes…yes, sir," Oscar said, then caught Silas's wink and relaxed. Sort of.

"I'm taking your mother back to the house. We'll fix a big breakfast for us."

"And by 'we,' he means he'll cook and I'll hand him stuff," Julianna said, grinning at Oscar.

"That's a relief because I'm hungry and I'd like some real food."

***

"Damned cops," Victoria hissed at the patrol car parked in front of the house she and André had crashed in the day before. "So much for having a warm place for me to stay."

She came out from the bushes and looked up, pulling her jacket tight against the fresh onslaught of snow. "I'll be damned if I'll go back to that hotel until I have the real tape in hand. André will probably sleep all day anyhow."

She watched as a second cruiser pulled up to the first. She couldn't hear them, but suddenly the lights on both vehicles shone bright, rotating patriotic colors as they sped away. "Well, that's fortunate."

Threading her way back through the bushes, she retrieved the poorly hidden house key from the planter of plastic mums and let herself in. After cranking up the stove to warm up the kitchen, she rummaged through the pantry, coming out with a snack pack of tuna and crackers. She devoured the pungent feast, then realized it was the first solid food she'd had in almost a week. Wine coolers and bar mix didn't count.

Warmed and sated, she headed back outside to her portal through the properties. She sneaked through the gap and kept close to the bushes – and away from the fence. "What in the hell is he doing, having a party?" she asked. "And who are they? No, that can't be Grace…"

She watched as a woman with blonde flyaway hair tucked into a dark knit cap playfully threw a hastily formed snowball at a young man who couldn't be much more than twenty. The two tossed a few more, then gave up when he shouted out, "Let's do this later. There'll be a lot more snow after we get back from shopping."

"That can't be Grace. She's too young." Victoria realized she was talking to herself and stopped. Then she saw Silas and her jaw clenched.

"Come on, Tori," he said to the young blonde. "You don't want to get cold and wet now."

"Yeah!" the young dark-haired man with the Gregory Peck-deep voice hollered. "Save that for when we have enough snow to make it worth my while. I'll give you a pummeling you'll never forget."

And then the dark giantess came over, her hand settling on the young man's shoulder. "Now, Oscar, you be nice. You don't want to scare her away, do you?"

"No, Mom, I wasn't going to." He laughed then bent down, grabbed a fistful of snow, and made a hasty ball. "I was just going to terrorize her a little."

He threw the ball and the girl ducked, racing to the house as the group followed her to what looked like a family date.

"That has to be Grace's daughter, the one who just got married. No…Silas called her Tori. The invitation said the girl who got married was Vickie." A snarly grin split Victoria's craggy face. "Ah, Grace had twins…"

***

Julianna set the table while Silas prepared a huge breakfast casserole, stretching the meager amount of eggs, half-and-half, and ham with some of the vegetables he was going to use for dinner. "Looks like I'll have to do a little shopping," he said.

"*We* can do that," she said, looking up to give him a wink. "And speaking of we, do you have that itchy, crawly feeling like you're being watched?"

"Yes, I do. I was hoping it wasn't just suddenly having kids in the house after being alone with you and being…so…"

"So uninhibited?" she asked.

"That's a good way to put it. Why? I'm sorry. You wouldn't have brought it up if you felt uncomfortable. For what it's worth, I did send a text to my friend at the precinct. No one was at the neighbor's, but there were signs it had been recently occupied. They said they'd keep an eye on it. Does that make you feel better?"

He came to her side and gave her a peck on the cheek as she leaned over to set out the silverware.

She stood up, pulled him close, and gave him a lingering kiss, ending with a sigh.

"Ew, Mom," Oscar said.

"Ew, Grandpa," Tori followed, adding a giggle behind her hand.

"Yeah, how would you like it if you caught me kissing?" Oscar

95

asked.

"No problem," Julianna answered. "As long as it was someone you cared for."

"Like me," Tori popped in.

"And it was *only* kissing," Silas said.

"Yeah, well, that goes right back at ya, *Grandpa,*" Oscar said, his sarcasm heavy.

"We're adults," Julianna said.

"And so are we," Oscar answered, shoulders back.

"Well, as far as that goes," Silas said, "your mother and I are at least double, if not triple, adults. But don't worry. We'll be discreet. By the way, where are you two staying?"

"Oh, that's kind of complicated. I moved us out of the hotel, packed up everything, and put it in the car. Tori's folks said we could take a sightseeing tour if we wanted, too. They just wanted us to call in every night."

"Yeah," Tori added. "I don't know what got into them, but I'm not complaining. I guess they trust Oscar a *lot*."

Julianna and Silas looked at each other. No words were spoken, but he nodded in silent assent. "You two can stay in the guest house," he said. "No reason to run up a hotel bill."

"Plus, you can keep an eye on us, right?" Tori asked, giggling.

"Duh," Oscar mumbled.

"And you won't have to eat restaurant food," Julianna said, sniffing the savory aroma of the breakfast baking in the oven.

Oscar inhaled and grinned. "Well, what do you think, Tori?"

"I'm all for it."

"Brunch won't be ready for another half hour, so you can unpack now if you'd like," Silas said, handing Oscar the key.

"You know, it would be pretty hard *not* to like you," Oscar said, taking the key with his left hand, reaching out to shake Silas's with his right.

"Thanks. Back at ya."

Julianna put her arm around Silas as they watched the young

couple chase each other out the door, boisterous with teenage enthusiasm. "Yes, it's not hard to imagine us at that same age."

"So, while they're gone, I have a few questions. After we get the second coin, what then?"

"We can't go anywhere for a few months. It has to be the time of year my folks got their property. I know where the time portal near Woodstock is, but we'll have to drive from New York to North Carolina afterward."

"But we're leaving from 2010 to 2015. How are we going to get around? Do we pack a bunch of cash and buy a car? Or rent one? Or rely on public transportation?"

"Shoot, I just showed up. I forgot what a pain that was. Of course, being young and in the sixties and eighties, I didn't have too much trouble. I just held out my thumb."

"Weren't you afraid someone was going to attack you?"

Julianna snorted. "Me? As big as I am? Nope. I could give the 'I got separated from the rest of the basketball team' story and even claimed to be a New York model once, but no one ever tried to assault me."

She saw Silas raise an eyebrow and grin. "If you think I'm good looking, you should see my mother."

"I could easily believe you were a model," Silas said, his smile now wide and mischievous. "Do you want to come upstairs and pose for me?"

She looked around. "The kids might pop in," she whispered.

"We'll lock the door." Silas followed her gaze. "Not the back door, the bedroom door. Even better, how about the shower?"

"Only if we don't turn on the water. It takes a long time for this much hair to dry. Race you up there?"

"I'll hurry, but remember, you still have twenty years on me," Silas said, then winked and pushed his chair aside, scrambling toward the staircase.

"Cheater," she hollered and followed after him.

***

"I was sure it would be ready by now," Silas said as he put his sweatpants back on, "but I didn't hear the timer."

Knock, knock, knock.

Julianna looked to make sure Silas was finished dressing, then opened the door.

"Breakfast is served," Tori said, her eyes dancing with a smirk. "I saw it counting down to zero, so I shut it off and got the pan out of the oven. And I didn't even burn myself."

"Where's Oscar?" Julianna asked.

"Oh, he didn't think I could handle it and tried to help me."

"And he got burned?" Silas asked.

"Yup. One of these days, he's gonna learn he has to trust me."

Julianna leaned down and whispered, "Sometimes you have to let them help. A man needs to be needed."

"Oh," Tori said softly.

"We all need to be needed," Silas told her. "It doesn't make a difference if you're a man or a woman, young or old."

"And that's what being an adult times two or three means – picking up on life's lessons through experience," Julianna said. "Stick around. You might learn something."

Tori looked behind Julianna and saw Silas looking for his other shoe. "Does he believe you? I mean, about time travel?" she whispered.

Julianna nodded. "Very much so. We're going to take off, but it won't be for a few months. I'd really like it if you knew what was going on. I mean, I'm pretty sure you and Oscar will still be together. I don't think he could handle me just disappearing. That's what happened to his father, too."

"Was he a time traveler, too?" Tori asked.

Rather than reply that Oscar's biological father truly had been one, Julianna danced around the truth. "Hugh was Oscar's stepfather. We don't know what happened to him but according to the police report, he committed suicide. They found a note, but his body was never found. Please, don't ever bring it up to Oscar, though. He's very sensitive about it."

"Yeah," Tori answered, then whispered, "suicide sucks."

"Found it," Silas said, holding up his lost slipper. "Sometimes I think those darned things can walk on their own."

The trio joined Oscar at the breakfast nook, his hand wrapped in a damp paper towel. "No, I'm not *clumsy*," he said, looking at Silas with a scowl.

"I didn't say anything, but if I did, I'd say it was kind of you to help Tori." He opened the refrigerator and brought out a bowl. "How about some fresh salsa? I chopped up some tomatoes, onions, and peppers when I was prepping the casserole. The flavors should be blended by now."

Julianna took the container from him and set it on the lazy susan in the middle of the table. "Ah, home-cooked beats take-out anytime."

"No, it all depends on the chef," Oscar said, nodding to Silas with a half-smile of apology. "I tasted it. It's delicious. Sorry I've been such a sourpuss."

"We may not be related by DNA, but we both have the same low blood sugar issue," Julianna said, then set a big slice of casserole on her plate. "I don't know why I'm so hungry..." she began, then stopped.

"Yeah, waiting for breakfast to cook burned up a lot of calories, huh?" Oscar said, looking at her with a big grin.

Silas bent his head and blushed, rearranging the napkin on his lap.

"It's okay if you're tired and need a nap," Tori said. "We'll wash dishes for you."

"Nah, we got this," Silas said. "You two better hustle and get your shopping done after we eat. The main part of the storm is supposed to hit this afternoon. This little fluff coming down is just a warning."

***

"Damned snowflakes. Whoever said they were romantic?"

Victoria bent over at the waist and shook them out of her sparse hair, then pulled the jacket's hood over her head. "And when are they going to leave? I have to get that tape. This is taking a lot longer than I thought. If I don't get some income generated soon, André is going back to making money with his super salami some other way…and without me. Damn it."

It was an hour before Victoria saw activity at the main house. The boy – Oscar, they'd called him – and her granddaughter were leaving. "Ugh, I'm too young to be a grandmother. Well, at least to an adult. This Tori has to be nearly twenty years old by now. Has it really been that long?"

Victoria tried to count backward, remembering how old Grace was when she got pregnant and how many years she'd spent in Costa Rica, locked out of the United States by her ex-husband and the immigration service. Who cared if the attempted murder charges against her were true or not? She was still an American citizen and they should let her back.

The kids had left and the curtains to the room she'd found Silas and his iron-fisted girlfriend in earlier were closing. "Yeah, well, so what if you're still able to get it up, Silas? You keep popping those little blue pills and keep her away from me while I get that tape. It's a big place, but I'll find it."

She slumped back against the shrubbery, chilled and desperate, the canned tuna and cracker breakfast roiling in her gut, leaving a foul taste in her mouth. "I have to have a backup plan. He has to have some sort of valuables or jewelry in that house. He's too clever to fall for blackmail, and there's no way I could take his Amazon down, even with André's help." She rubbed her jaw and noticed the swelling from their first encounter had gone down with the winter chill.

"He'd have to have a lot of Rolexes to finance the kind of lifestyle I want, but maybe…"

"Boo!"

Victoria jumped at the shout and turned around to see André's grinning face.

"You were gone for a long time," he said. "I figured you'd be back here. I mean, you did say you were gonna find the right tape."

Still trying to slow her heart rate, she nodded her answer. After a moment, she asked, "How'd you get here?"

"Oh, that clerk fellow at the hotel's a real nice guy. He said anything we need, just let him know."

Victoria's stomach lurched but she held her food down. She knew that twinkle in André's eye and it wasn't from a free ride. Or maybe it was.

"Are you okay, Victoria? You look a little green around the jills."

"That's gills, and yes, I'll be fine. Fine as soon as I get that tape or figure out how to make money off Silas some other way."

"Hey, I got a good idea. Anyone who owns a house this big has to have lots of bucks."

"He doesn't own it. He's just the butler," she said. "That doesn't mean he doesn't have lots of stuff in there to steal, though." She looked down and saw André had brought both backpacks with him. "Dump out one of those. We're going shopping."

"I thought you didn't want to fence."

"Life changes and you have to be willing to make adjustments when it does."

André squatted down to unzip the bags. "Do you want me to throw your clothes in mine or mine in with yours?" he asked, looking up.

Victoria's eyes got huge. Four love bites colored his neck. And she never gave hickeys. "I. Don't. Care," she hissed, then turned aside and puked.

Chapter 12: The Photo Album

"Do you think she'll come back?" Julianna asked.

"I'm pretty sure she will. That is if she's not here already."

"Wait. What? I mean, we just can't sit around and wait for her, can we?"

"Have you ever hunted?" Silas asked, sitting down next to her. "It's not necessarily *hunting* as much as waiting. You have to wait for the prey to come to you."

"Then what? Shoot her? Throw a net over her?" Julianna pulled her robe closer as a chill of uncertainty covered her in goosebumps.

"I'm not sure, but I do know one thing. I won't let her out of our sight this time." He adjusted the pillows, kicked back, then patted the bed next to him. "Time to talk."

"Yeah, I hate to say it, but I agree. So, we wait?"

Silas nodded, his arm opened to cuddle her close.

"Didn't you tell me she tried to kill her daughter? Was it a gun? I mean, if she tried to shoot her own child, what would she do to the woman who not only stole her man but beat the stuffing out of her?"

Silas chuckled. "You didn't steal her man because I was never hers to begin with. As far as you proving you are the better woman, I figure if you don't want to take her on again, I'll have a go at her. I wouldn't hit a lady, but she's no lady. As soon as I – or we," he said, adding a wink, "have her incapacitated, I'll call the cops. She probably left prints if she was hanging out next door. Breaking and entering, plus the outstanding warrants ought to keep her busy with the legal system for a long time."

"Plus breaking in here and the guest house."

Silas shook his head. "Nope. I'm leaving the trespassing here off the books. They'll want to know why, where's the home's owner, all sorts of stuff. I'd rather clean up messes and board up windows and be able to maintain my very low profile: Silas the butler and caretaker who never gets in trouble."

"What about that goon of a boyfriend? Won't he be a problem?"

"He's a porno poster boy – a body without a brain. If she's not there to tell him what to do step by step, he'll find someone else. You see, he doesn't need a woman, he just needs a host, a warm body to sponsor his existence."

"Man, that's too bad."

Silas laughed.

"No, I'm serious. I kind of needed Hugh so we could adopt Oscar. Besides the fact we both loved the child, he wanted an heir, and I had made a promise to the birth mother. He was a decent guy and we worked well together, so we married. We did have a few good years at the beginning, but then he got so controlling." Julianna shuddered. "No, I was *stuck* with Hugh, but I didn't *need* him. My parents taught us better than that."

"So, about your parents and visiting them. I think we got distracted last time." Silas brought her hand to his mouth and kissed it. He noticed the faint narrowing of flesh on her third finger where a wedding ring had been worn for years, now bare. He'd have to fix that.

"You're getting distracted again," Julianna said, pulling her hand back.

"Rough draft of a plan – do you have one? I'm new at this."

"You don't know how good it feels to talk about this with someone who believes me. The only other one I feel comfortable with is Tori. To her, it's so logical."

"It is logical," Silas said, scooting up so he could talk with body language, too. "With the right device, challenges are simplified. Think big mountain, pickaxe, and dynamite. Do you realize how long it would take to move a mountain with a hand tool versus dynamite?"

"Can you imagine how many...everythings... there are in twenty years? How much food and sleep I skipped over? How many bills I didn't have to pay, and movies I missed?"

"How many emotions and life experiences?"

Julianna grunted. "Yes, I know. You truly are twenty years

wiser than I am."

"No, you're twenty years younger and less seasoned. Let's just say you missed twenty years of hay fever."

"Okay, so before the kids come home..." Julianna paused, smiling as she savored what she had just said. "That sounds so wonderful."

"Kids or coming home?"

"Both. Anyhow, I really think we need to bring Tori into this. I kinda, sorta let her in on this."

"What?"

"Hey, someone has to be our anchor. Plus, she outright asked if I had told you – and if I had, did you believe me – about time travel. I wasn't going to lie to her. You know, her parents may have isolated her from a lot of the world, but she has her head on straight with telling the truth and knowing right from wrong."

Silas inhaled sharply, holding back the pain of not knowing two of his three granddaughters because they had been adopted to strangers. He relaxed and breathed out. They were in his life now. Even if they moved to different parts of the planet, he'd be able to communicate with them. "Whoa. What's an anchor?"

"It's a focus point. If we left and wanted to come back to this time, we'd have to have someone here who we had a strong emotional bond with. Plus, I don't ever want to go a time where I don't have someone to connect to again. I must have been nuts to hop from '69 to '89 with nothing but historical data and a photograph to go to. Going back to my parents before I'm born is a gamble, but one I'm willing to take."

"A gamble?"

She smiled. "Remember I told you how much I look like my mother? Arriving as a stranger and trying to interact with family is chancey. But since my da is a veteran traveler, I think I can convince him who I am. He told us he and his grandfather looked to be the same age when he visited him as an adult. He knows the disparity is possible, so because he has experience with scrambled timelines, I think he'll accept me.

"However, on this end, I want Tori as an anchor. Then there's the other thing to consider. What are you going to do with this place? Just lock it up and be gone for five years without a trace? I'd suggest you put it in Tori's name or have her acknowledged as the caretaker. That way, if we go to the portal near Woodstock, jump forward to 2015, and hitch a ride back here, we'll have access to whatever goodies we need at this location."

"Like wheels?"

"You got it, Sherlock."

"Well, you're right except for one thing."

"What's that?"

"It's not *if* we go, but *when* we go. I'm more than happy to kick back with you here – in this time – getting to know you and my family better for as long as you'd like."

"Even if we have to watch out for the wicked witch of the west wall?"

Silas sat forward and lifted the edge of the pillow, exposing a gun.

"You'd shoot her?"

He whispered, "It's a paintball pistol. Looks like a real Walther PPQ. It'll sting and mark her – or him – but isn't lethal. I'm counting on the fear factor. But if I do have to shoot, the shock should be enough that I can back up the assault with a tackle."

Julianna bent down to look closer at the non-lethal weapon, then put the pillow back on it, tears brightening her eyes. "I don't know if I'm crying because I'm scared or because I'm so happy you wouldn't kill someone, even in self-defense."

"I'd duke it out first, even if I knew I'd break and bloody a few knuckles. Still, I'd rather fight with words and wits than bullets and blades. With the former, the only thing to get hurt would be feelings."

"And I don't even want to think about the latter," Julianna sighed and snuggled close.

"Are we going back to the little house or check out the big one?" André asked. "Because if you ask me, there's gotta be a whole lot more loot in that mansion."

Victoria glared at him, enraged at both his infidelity and stupidity. Suddenly, her ire subsided as the glimmer of a plan came into focus and her glower became a grin.

"Are you feeling better now?" André asked. "Because you're looking better. Hey, now that your stomach's settled down, do you wanna go over to that little house and pretend it was yesterday? That's was fun, sneaking around and having sex outside where we might get caught."

"Nah," she said with a fake smile, "we'll wait. How about we go check out the big house? That was a good idea you had. Maybe the front door's unlocked. Grab that empty backpack and you can play reverse Santa."

"Huh?"

"You take an empty bag inside and fill it with goodies for all the good boys and girls. Oh, and you and I are the only good boys and girls."

"Yeah, that'd be fun. Upstairs or down, first? 'Cause you know I always like going down…"

Victoria picked up the empty backpack and shoved it into his midsection with more force than necessary. "We're doing it my way. We'll start at the top and work our way down," she said, glaring at his hickeys.

André wrestled his way out of the shrubbery and onto the driveway, strutting toward the front door.

"What are you doing?" Victoria hissed.

"You said we were starting at the top. Isn't this the way?"

"Maybe for them, but we don't want to be seen. Look up there," she said, pointing to the flagpole in the middle of the roundabout driveway. "Those are security cameras up there. Silas is sure to see us if we go through the front. We'll go through the garage. Come on. You can give me a boost through my secret exit, then I'll unlock the side door from the inside."

"Why can't I go the same way as you?"

"Because you're too big."

André looked down at the front of his slacks, grinning. "Yeah, I am…"

"No, your shoulders are too broad for the chute. Besides, I couldn't lift you. Come this way. I'm getting cold out here."

***

Silas put his hand out for Julianna to pause her story. "Someone's here," he said. "Get dressed."

She slipped off the robe and picked up the sweatsuit she had bought earlier. By the time she pulled the hoodie over her head, Silas was already dressed. "That was fast," she whispered.

He grimaced, his intended grin skewed by knowing a confrontation was imminent. He reached under the pillow, grabbed the pistol, then stuck it in the back of his waistband, leaving it exposed and accessible. "Take a deep breath."

"I did," Julianna replied.

"I was talking to myself," he said and chuckled weakly. "We've got this."

From the second-story window overlooking the driveway, Silas saw an older pickup truck approach.

"Anyone you know?" Julianna asked.

"Nope. Just a sec. The door is opening. Someone's getting out."

Julianna clutched Silas's arm as they waited. Finally, a man – older by his cautious posture – made it out. He walked slowly, clutching the side of the truck bed as he moved gloved-hand over gloved-hand to the passenger door, wary of the new-fallen snow.

"I think those are Tori's parents," Julianna said. "Didn't she say they were checking out the east coast and that Massachusetts was their old stomping ground?"

"Something like that," Silas agreed. "Let's go say hi. Two to one, though, they're checking on the kids. I know that's what I'd be

107

doing if one of them was mine, that young and essentially by themselves."

"One of them is mine, and believe me, I'm glad they're staying here. As you said, we were their age once. I sure hope they had 'the talk' with Tori about getting pregnant."

"What about Oscar? It takes two, you know," Silas said, nodding to the stairs.

"Just bring it up to him if you want to see the brightest blush in the world." They walked side by side down to the front door. "Every time he'd even mention a girl around his father, Hugh would give him a lecture about respecting women and safe sex. I think he was eleven when he heard the talk the first time."

Ding, dong, ding.

"And here they are." Silas opened the door, Julianna at his side, both of them smiling wide. "Come in and warm up and dry off," he said.

"Here, let me take your coats, Leanne," Julianna offered. "You remember Silas Priest, I'm sure."

"Yes, yes," Luther said. "Tori's surprise grandfather. Looks like she got one of her wishes granted. She always wanted a grandparent. Both our folks passed a long time ago."

Julianna took the damp coats and hats and Silas hung them up. She glanced over to the parlor on the right. "In here?" she asked.

"Yes, that's a good idea. If you'd like, Luther, I can take your truck into the garage before it gets covered in snow. This is only the beginning of the storm. It's supposed to be a big one."

"Oh, we didn't want to impose," Luther said. "We just wanted to drop in and see how Tori was doing."

"The truth is," Leanne explained, looking down and then back up, trying to hide her guilt "I was missing my little girl so much, I pestered him until he said he was either going to tape my mouth shut, or he'd drive out here to make sure they were really with you and not out... Well, out and about."

"They're shopping right now," Silas said. "From what I see,

108

they're very responsible. And they are both of age. Now, whether that means they're adults…"

Luther laughed and turned to Leanne who was scowling.

"It's hard for me to imagine she's on her own," she said. "I mean, that we're not with her, under the same roof. She led such a sheltered life, but that's our fault. We wanted *some* control over her environment, but when she was old enough to interact with others, she didn't want real friends. She was always talking into mirrors." Leanne saw Silas and Julianna's confused looks and explained. "We had no idea she remembered them. She was only hours old when we got her, but she recalled having two sisters and would play with her imaginary versions of them.

"Anyway, she's always been a loner. She worked with Oscar last summer, but other than him, it wasn't until she met you, Julianna, that she spoke with a stranger. She," Leanne's clenched fist quickly opened and her arm moved out, indicating the vastness of the enormous sitting room and parlor, "suddenly blossomed."

"Sometimes it's fast and other times, you don't even notice they've changed until they're off to college or getting married."

"Married? Is that where they are?" she asked, tears and sniffles starting.

"No, I'm sure they're not," Silas said. "Actually, I believe they're buying Barbies and action figures to keep them entertained when they're not building snowmen and having snowball fights. They're not in any hurry to grow up from what I can see. They just enjoy each other's company."

"Oh, thank God!" Leanne said, wiping her nose, her eyes bright with relief.

Luther looked out the window and saw the truck already had a heavy white dusting. "Maybe I will take you up on that indoor parking. But I think I'd better drive. That ignition's a little finicky."

Silas handed Luther his coat and hat, then grabbed his own. "Ladies, we shall return," he said. "Make yourselves comfortable."

"It's an older truck," Luther said, apologizing, "but it's paid for and made it across the country without any problems." He paused then added. "At least, any problems I couldn't fix with duct tape or spray grease."

Silas took out his smartphone and clicked on the remote garage door opener. "I still have a few spots open. Why don't you take that one? Oscar and Tori can park at the other end. We old folks need to save our steps."

Luther paused to take off his fogged-up glasses, then drove in next to the Volkswagen microbus, blinking to keep his focus on parking and not staring at the vintage ride beside him. As soon as he stopped, he was out of the truck, eager as a teenager to investigate the VW.

"Is that yours?" he asked, his hand gliding over the curtained windows. "I'm sorry, of course, it is…isn't it?"

"Yes, it is. Reminds me of my youth, hitching a ride to Woodstock in one."

"Really?" Luther asked, wide-eyed. "That's how I got there, too. Only it wasn't like this. It was older and had brightly colored posies and peace signs all over it."

Silas chuckled. "Yeah, mine did, too. I think about half the vans there did."

"Oh, wait," Luther said. He opened the truck, reached behind the front seat, and brought out a tattered cardboard box. "When I was at my buddy's place this morning, his widow gave me this. I was trying to catch up with some old friends, and he was one of the few names I remembered. Anyhow, he died two years ago, God rest his soul. His wife said she wasn't at Woodstock and since I was, that she was sure John F. would want me to have it. Would you like to look through these together and see if we can find anyone we know? I'm pretty sure I'm in a few of them. I borrowed his thirty-five millimeter and shot a few rolls of film while he was… Well, he got pretty stoned. I figured if he wasn't going to remember the event, I'd show him what he missed."

Little flashes of recall popped like sparks from a grinder. That name – John F. Silas nodded his head minimally and grinned. "You know, I can't think of anything I'd rather do. Let's go show the ladies."

***

"What's that?" André asked.

"Shush!" Victoria hissed. She looked around and saw the quilt covering the bed in the van. "Lie down and hold still. I'll cover you."

"But…"

"That's the garage door opening, dummy! Someone's here."

"Don't call me dummy."

"Sorry. Now hush!"

Victoria tossed the quilt over André, then climbed under the tiny table, hugging the wall under the window of the VW as close as she could. She looked up and saw André move, then settle in. She stifled her urge to tell him to hold still and exhaled in frustration. Just a few more hours and they'd be in the clear. A vision of the hickeys on his neck popped into her mind. Just a few more hours and *she'd* be in the clear and he'd be framed.

***

"Guess what, Leanne?" Luther called out, toting the cardboard box, Silas following behind him with their coats and hats.

"What?"

"Silas was at Woodstock, too! We're going to look through these old photos and see if we can find him."

Julianna looked at Silas, mute but wide-eyed.

He grinned at her, then looked to Leanne and said, "Well, I hear there were five hundred thousand people at the event. What are the chances?"

Julianna's fear evaporated with the odds, then turned into excitement. Visions of the sea of people – all muddy but content – enveloped her as she recalled her first four days of teenage freedom. Then the sting of anxiety with not finding her sister popped in. "Five hundred thousand," she repeated softly, forgiving herself one more

111

time for not being able to locate Mali in a crowd that huge.

"Oh, and get this," Luther said, still as excited as a cat chasing a dragonfly. "He has a VW microbus down in the garage!"

"Like the one John F. had?" Leanne asked.

Julianna's face turned to Silas, her big brown eyes refilled with worry.

Silas winked at her and grinned, showing his confidence. "Luther says it's not the same as the one you rode in…Rapunzel."

"What? Where'd you hear that name?" Leanne asked. "Nobody but Luther's called me that in over forty years."

Silas looked at the bun on top of her head. "I'd say if you let those pinned-up locks down, they'd be to the back of your knees, at least."

"Oh, yes, I guess that's a logical deduction," she said. "I never thought anyone else would pick up on that."

"I guess that's why they call me Sherlock."

Julianna sat down with a thunk, unable to keep her emotions and fears from stealing the strength in her legs.

Leanne squinted at him as Luther put his glasses back on. "Nah, it couldn't be, could it?" she asked softly.

"Well, Luther," Silas said, clapping the still-stunned man on the shoulder, "how about we break open that book and go down memory lane."

Julianna watched them interact, the past forty years evaporating, the gray-haired crew suddenly young hippies again. Barely taking a breath, she kept mouth and body still – trying to be invisible but knowing it was impossible – while the three decided on the best place to look at the photo album.

"We can put it on the coffee table," Leanne suggested.

"But then Julianna couldn't see it," Luther protested. "Oh, maybe she's not interested. She's too young to have been there, right?" he asked, looking over at her.

Julianna blinked rapidly, coming out of her trance. "How about some drinks?" she asked, ignoring his question. "Hot or cold, soft or hard. Silas has everything from soda to liquor to sangrias and has been known to make a mean cup of cocoa." She looked at each person in turn, quickly bypassing Leanne who was studying her – unsure but still curious. "Or hot cider? All I have to do is heat it and pour it in a cup with a cinnamon stick. I think I can do that. You three get started and I'll join you in a few."

Leanne watched Julianna leave, then looked to Luther, trying to catch his eye. "Ahem...ahem..."

However, her husband was now absorbed in the big denim-covered photo album, faded denim fabric painted with peace signs and marijuana leaves. "Here we are getting ready to leave," he said, pointing to a group photo in front of the microbus. "When we started, there were only four of us."

In the kitchen, Julianna spilled the hot cider as she poured it into the last cup. "Damned fumble-fingered female," she said softly as she set the pan on the burner. She suddenly went weak-kneed. "Those were Hugh's words. Forget them. He's not here. And even if he was, Silas would escort him off the property. Stop beating yourself up, Jules. What's the worst..."

Standing behind her, Silas cleared his throat, rescuing her from her more self-flagellation. "Sweetheart, don't fuss over spilled cider. And don't ever feel guilty for looking young. You wouldn't feel bad for any of your other millions of assets, would you?"

"Millions of assets?" she asked, setting down the potholder and turning into his arms.

"How do I love thee, let me count the ways. Your eyes that sparkle when you see me in the morning, your softly curled cocoa-brown hair that springs to the touch, those long legs that reach from the floor all the way to heaven. Shall I continue or have you figured out what I mean?"

"I get the idea, but you're wrong. My eyes sparkle *every* time I see you."

"Come on," Silas said, setting aside the dishcloth. "I'll clean up the mess later. We have guests."

"Do you think they'll find out it was us?" she asked.

"If they don't, I'll tell them. In case I've never told you before, I'm proud of you. Every part of you, including our past, our right now, and what we'll have together when we're old and gray. Or rather, you're old and gray and I'm older and grayer." He ran his fingers through his short gray curls. "Or maybe bald. Who knows?"

Julianna moved in close and kissed him briefly, paused, then came back for a more thorough smooch. "Where is a tray, dear. I can carry them all at the same time, but I want to seem at least a little classy."

"Well, you're in trouble there. I can let you choose a tray, but you'll always be *a lot* classy. There's no little about you. And yes, that's a tall person joke."

"Gray-ate to know," she said, ruffling his hair. "Come on. They have to be wondering what happened to us by now."

Silas opened a cabinet, exposing a dozen serving trays. "*She* may be wondering, but he's absorbed in the pictures."

Julianna snorted as she arranged the cups and a bundle of napkins on the silver platter.

"What's the problem? All she can do is be jealous you aged so well. Be proud of yourself for eating all those greens and exercising regularly," he said and winked. "No one needs to know you managed to skip twenty years of life."

She chuckled and picked up the platter. "Care to bet who figures it out first?"

"Oh, hands down, she will."

"You're on."

Leanne was seated close to Luther when they walked in. Seeing them, she stood up. "I can look at this later. Why don't you two get on either side?" She paused and inhaled deeply. "That smells divine."

Julianna held out the tray and Leanne took a cup and a napkin. "I love hot cider," she said, then sipped it cautiously. "Oh, I'll bet that was pressed from local orchards. It tastes just that much different from Oregon apples."

"I've never been to Oregon," Julianna said, then walked over to Luther and bent down to offer him a drink.

Luther took one, then pointed to a picture of three glassy-eyed guys and a girl in a cloud of smoke, passing a marijuana joint between them. "Those were the days. Who would have thought it would be legal one day. At least, we grow medical marijuana in Oregon now. Mark my words, pretty soon, you'll be able to buy it anywhere in the US."

"I'm pretty sure you could do that in 1969," Silas said with a chuckle.

"Oh, I mean legally. If we can get every state in the union to follow Colorado's suit and legalize it for both medical and recreational, eventually they'll have to make it good to go on the federal level, too." Luther held out one arthritic hand. "My body is literally eating up the cartilage in my hands and feet. The only relief I can get is with a homemade cannabis cream and maybe a toke or two before I go to bed if it's been a rough day. I couldn't get the same effect with liquor without pickling my whole body."

"Or at least your liver," Leanne said. "I'm glad we have options."

Luther took an appreciative sip of the cider and was back into the album. He looked up at Silas and Julianna. "Come on and sit down. We might as well get used to each other. Looks like our kids are going to be friends – or more – for a long time."

"Yeah, it's the 'or more' part that terrifies me," Leanne said, then sat in the chair across the coffee table from the other three.

"Hey, look at that…" Luther pointed to a picture. "Unexploded grenade, huh?" he asked then stared deep into Silas's eyes, squinting to merge the image of the youth with long, dark hair in the photo with the gray-haired man beside him. His grin widened. Then he looked at Julianna and back at the young woman in the photo. He frowned, then slightly bent the edge of the picture and removed it from the album. He held it beside Julianna's face. "Dorothy?"

Julianna smiled with confidence. "I win!" she said, then reached around Luther to give Silas a playful pat on the back.

"Dorothy from Oz?" Leanne gasped. "Oh, my Lord. It is you! I want to know what moisturizer you use. You look great."

"Well, hooking up again after forty years was what, one in a million chance?" Luther asked.

"One in five-hundred-thousand," Julianna said, "but who's counting?"

Chapter 13: Proof Positive

"I never saw Silas again until the wedding," Julianna said, now confident and wanting to control the direction of the conversation.

"She recognized me first," Silas said. "Without a doubt, that was the happiest hour of my life. I found her and was able to acknowledge my daughter and granddaughters, all within a timeframe of less than sixty minutes."

"I wonder what your astrological chart looks like for that date and time," Leanne said. "I'm a little out of practice, but if you tell me your birthday – and Julianna's, too – I can work up a chart for you."

Julianna sputtered, conveniently choking on her cider to end the conversation. Her feigned health issue worked to awaken Leanne's maternal healing instincts, deflecting her attention and sending her plot to create supernatural astral charts to the trash bin. "Thanks, I'm fine," Julianna said a moment later. "And no, I don't want to cheat destiny or get a glimpse of the future with determining how much impact a planet will have when it's in whichever house or whatever."

Silas caught her gaze and rolled his eyes. *You already know too much about the future. How many times have you tried to mess with timelines already?*

Julianna frowned quickly in response, then looked up and smiled at the sound of someone coming in the front door. "The kids are home," she said brightly.

"Oh, I so want to show these photos to Tori," Leanne said. She turned to Silas and clutched his hand in hers. "When she was just an infant, we had a flood. We lost everything. Woosh! All gone. She's never seen me without gray hair or wrinkles. She's going to be so thrilled." She looked down and saw that in her excitement, she had brought Silas's hand to her bosom. "Oops. Sorry," she said and patted it, giving it back to him with a soft chuckle.

"And she's never seen her grandfather as a young man, either,"

Luther said. "And, Oscar," he shook his head in disbelief, "he's going to be amazed at how little you've changed, Julianna. He could only hope to have inherited those genes."

Julianna laughed. "He'd have to get them through genetic splicing. He's adopted, in case you didn't notice."

"Don't mind him," Leanne said. "He's special that way. He only sees the inner person. You could walk out of this room and he wouldn't be able to tell anyone what you looked like, whether you're short or tall, black or white."

"Yes, but I would remember if she was rude or polite," he said.

"The important stuff, right, Luther?" Silas asked.

"Amen to that." Luther stood up to greet the kids who had just walked in. "Tori, take off your boots and come see what your papa and mama looked like before you were born."

"Oscar, you come over here, too," Leanne said. "Did you know Silas and your mother were at Woodstock with us? Who could have guessed?"

Oscar stared at his mother, eyebrows pinched together. He opened his mouth to speak, then let it shut and closed his eyes, trying to remember the year. The media had made a big deal last summer about the fortieth anniversary of Woodstock. His eyes popped open and he stared at her.

"Doesn't seem possible, does it?" Julianna said and winked at her stunned son.

He stumbled backward against the door, smacking the door handle into his lower back. "I...I'm okay," he said.

"You'd better hold onto me while you take off those wet boots," Tori said aloud, then rushed up to help him. "Told ya," she whispered, then bent to work as his boot jack. She looked at the group, gathered around the big home-crafted photo album. "And it looks like they have proof, too."

Oscar emitted a low growl as Tori finished helping him. He took a deep calming breath, then patted her shoulder, letting her know to stand up so he could kick off the last one.

"Are you going to be okay?" she whispered.

"Hold me close, just in case. I have a lot to process already, and I haven't even seen the pictures yet."

Julianna stood up and offered Oscar her place next to Luther, sitting on his other side and taking over Tori's job as caregiver.

"I've heard you and Mama talk about Woodstock," Tori told her father, keeping her eyes on Oscar, "but why didn't you show me these pictures before?"

"These were given to us by the widow of a friend we visited earlier today. I thought you'd get a bang out of these. Look, that's me. See how long my hair was."

"Wow, you were good-looking, Papa. Where's Mama?"

"That's me. Back then, I went by Rapunzel."

"Because of your long hair?" Tori asked.

"Duh," Oscar said, then immediately apologized. "Sorry. That was rude." He bent over the album and asked, "Where's my mom?"

Silas turned a few pages and showed the picture of a handsome young man with long hair standing next to a sign that said 'Keep Back: Unexploded Grenade.' A tall dark-skinned woman stood at the edge of the shot, definitely Julianna. "There she is. And that's me with the sign," Silas said, bringing his hand up to his head. "Hard to believe I ever messed with having that much hair..." He looked at Oscar and winked.

Julianna was radiant as Oscar stared at her, his mouth agape. "It was such a wet, muddy mess, but the vibes were awesome," she said. "I want to see some of the other pictures. John Sebastian was wandering through the crowds. Did you get any of him?" she asked Luther.

The adults hovered over the book while Oscar leaned back into the couch, stunned. He stared at his mother, remembering how many times he'd crashed hard drives or hid her books on time travel, not just to protect her from his father's wrath if he discovered she was 'at it again,' but to stop her nonsense. Luther and Silas were of a similar age both then and now, although Silas was more fit and still handsome. Then he looked from is mother to Leanne, both the same age at Woodstock. Huge difference. Mom looked at least twenty years younger. The twenty years she had told him once, she'd 'lost' when time traveling to find her sister.

Silas brought out a magnifying glass and was sharing it back and forth, checking for celebrity faces. "Hey, I think I know him," Luther said. "Last I heard, he worked in the NYU Ag Department. Who could forget that nose? I bet he'd like to see these photos, too."

"Give him a call and see if he's still there," Leanne said. "We can go see him and you two can compare notes on your plant research."

"It's okay to say cannabis cultures, dear. We're all adults."

"Just some of us more so than others," Julianna whispered to Silas.

Luther thumped the photo album. "Other than The Nose from NYU, John F. was the only person I knew. I guess that guy who called himself Eros wound up a billionaire or something," Luther said. "I wish I had written down some of the names even a year later. How soon we forget."

"It probably wouldn't have made a difference," Silas said. "If you recall, I think you and John F. were the only ones using real names. If that *was* his name. Oh, and Eros wound up making his millions on inflated government contracts. You know, the million-dollar screwdrivers? He was one of them. A sly little sh...stinker."

"You can say it. We're all adults," Julianna said, "He was a sly little shit."

Silas looked up and saw the white glow of heavy snowfall through the window. "Well, Tori, it looks like you and Oscar will get to build your snowman today." He turned to Leanne and Luther. "Care to camp out here tonight?" He nodded toward the second floor. "We have plenty of room."

"Yeah, Papa," Tori said. "They even have a guest house. That's where Oscar and I are staying."

"A guest house?" Leanne asked, her smile rising quickly.

120

"Well, then, I think we'll just share that with you two." She looked at Luther, her head down like a bull ready to charge. "Right, Papa?"

Recognizing the tone, Luther set the magnifying glass down to give her his full attention. He noticed the smile of relief on Julianna's face. There would be two chaperones for the child-adults tonight. "Sounds like a good idea to me. Thanks for the offer. We'd be happy to accept."

***

"No, we have to stay hidden," Victoria said. "There's no telling when those two old fossils will be back to get their truck and leave."

"But I have to go pee real bad," André said, still lying in the van's bed, the quilt kicked off, his knees rocking back and forth in discomfort.

"Oh, all right. But make it quick."

André rushed out of the cramped van into the vast and immaculate garage, breathing in the fresh air. He and his very friendly clerk had showered together, but Victoria still stank of old-lady body odor and cheap hotel soap. He looked around for a bathroom but didn't see one, so he hustled to the outside door. He pushed it halfway open and saw it was snowing heavily. "Don't close the door. Don't close the door," he chanted to himself, remembering how many times he'd been locked out when an outside door shut.

A long minute later, he finished whizzing, spelling his name in the snow. "Well done, Buddy." He looked down to shake his member. "Oh, shit!" he said, seeing the hickeys. "That little asshole bit me." He sighed. "Well, I guess it was fun at the time, though, wasn't it big fella? I guess there won't be any blowjobs from her until the marks go away."

"Gotcha!" a playful young woman's voice sang from across the yard. A young man's laugh followed.

André quickly stepped back into the garage. He looked back at the van and saw Victoria leaned against it, puffing a cigarette. "Hey! I thought you gave those up."

"I did," she said.

He gasped. The ice in her voice was colder than the snowflakes on his exposed skin had been. "Um, I don't know if you heard, but there are people outside. I think we'd better lay low again."

"Who?" she asked, throwing the half-smoked butt to the polished concrete floor, grinding it out.

"I don't know. I didn't look. It sounded like a girl and a guy laughing. It's snowing, too. I think she just hit him with a snowball."

"My granddaughter," Victoria said, then huffed at the designation. "Tori," she said softly, rolling it around in her mind, tickled at her having the same name. Well, almost the same name.

"Are you okay?" André asked. "You got that funny look again."

"Yeah, I'm as fine as I can be, imprisoned in an old hippie van with a…a…man child."

"Hey, is that an insult? Because if it is, I'll just get up and leave. You can stay here by yourself. I'll slip into the big house tonight and haul out the loot without you. I'm just being nice to you, you know."

"Sorry," Victoria said sarcastically.

"Hey, say it like you mean it."

She took a rage-squelching breath, wishing she was anywhere but here, then remembered that if she played nice, she'd get everything she came for, and André would get the blame. "André, I'm sorry. I truly am. There, is that better?" she asked, giving him an ounce of sincerity.

"Yeah, I guess so."

"Fine, then. Why don't you take a nap? It'll make the time go faster."

"Yeah, okay." He lay down on the bed then turned to face her. "It's my second favorite thing to do in bed. Hey, do you want to guess what my first favorite is?"

"No, thanks. My brain is fried. Go ahead and sleep. I'll wake you when it's time to rob the place."

André rolled over and tried to get comfortable. Victoria stood up and adjusted the quilt over his shoulders. "Sweet dreams, ya big lug," she said under her breath.

***

"Let's see," Silas said, moving aside packages in his walk-in freezer. "This has been in here a while, but not too long. I only have a limited amount of fresh vegetables but do have a lot of frozen ones. Do you think they'd rather have surf or turf?"

"I don't know about anyone else, but I'd rather have both," Julianna said. "I'm sure Oscar feels the same. Go ahead and fix them all. I never have leftovers with Oscar."

"Are you sure they'll be okay in the guest house with the kids?"

"Absolutely. I know I'll feel a lot better with them just one bedroom away from a parent or two rather than fifty yards away from us."

"Ditto for them, I'm sure."

"If by them, you mean Leanne and Luther, I agree. Then again, there's a lot of pressure off the kids, too. Nobody wants to be the one to be bashful about saying no to the first time."

"Just in case, I tossed a three-pack of condoms in the bedside table. If they get carried away, believe me, a guy's going to look everywhere for one."

***

"That's it, I'm done," Oscar said, knocking the remains of the last snowball from his cheek. "Let's go to the little house and change into dry clothes. If I know my mom, she'll have food waiting for us. Now that Silas is in her life, though, I hope he takes over *all* the cooking. Having anything warm after a snow battle is appreciated, but packaged toaster pastries and instant cocoa from the microwave are pushing the limits of a hot snack."

"Let's go in through the garage," Tori said. "I don't want to make a mess in the front room like last time. That was kind of rude."

"Yeah, I didn't even think about it to tell you the truth. Did Silas give you the access code?"

"My *grandpa* didn't," she said the name with pride, "but I'll bet you your dessert tonight I can guess it. Come on, I'll race you."

123

First to the door was Oscar. "I just won back my dessert, but if you can't figure it out, I'll get yours, too."

Tori pulled her glove off with her teeth and punched in her birthdate. *Click.* "Told ya."

Oscar held the door open for her then stepped inside. "Ew, it stinks in here," Tori said. "Someone's been smoking."

"That's for sure," Oscar agreed. He sniffed again, then coughed. "Tobacco. I've never seen Silas smoke, but maybe he can't kick the habit and comes out here."

"Nope. I'd be able to smell it on his clothes or hair when I hug him. He just smells like a man."

"Okay," Oscar said tersely, then looked around. He heard something move then saw the VW bus shudder as if someone inside was moving around. He looked at Tori and put his finger to his lips and shook his head. "I guess it was just my imagination," he said a few decibels above normal. "Come on, we're done in here."

"But…" Tori started to protest but stopped when he put his hand on her mouth gently. She huffed, then quickly bent over and took off her boots, leaving her coat, hat, and scarf on.

Oscar took the boots and pushed her ahead of him into the house, not caring that he was trailing melted snow behind him.

As soon as they were inside, Tori opened her mouth to give him the dickens. "Not now, Tori. You can rip me a new one in two minutes. I have to talk to Silas first."

Once in the kitchen, he pulled Silas aside. "Someone broke into the garage. You can smell cigarette smoke and I saw the microbus bouncing around. Either you have a visitor or a very big rat."

"Both, I suspect," Silas said. He looked at Tori, now wide-eyed with a mix of fear and excitement. "No, you don't get to investigate, young lady. If it's who I think it is, she's attempted murder in the past. I don't want you in harm's way."

"Is it the person who has a line on my genealogy chart?"

"What? Oh, yes, I assume so. She and her…her…"

"Paramour?" Oscar asked with a strained laugh.

"Do you two make a game out of finding novel descriptions for common nouns?"

"Sure. You just did, too," Tori said. "See. It's a genetic tendency."

Julianna ignored the light banter, a scowl wrinkling her forehead. "Did you put it back under the pillow or hide it someplace else?"

"My Walther PPPQ?" Silas pulled open a kitchen drawer and shoved aside the spare dishtowels, exposing the pistol. "Its twin is back under our pillow."

"PPPQ? Is that for paintball PPQ?"

Silas kissed her on the cheek. "Yup. Now, if you'll set the table, I'll fire up the grill." He nodded to the large burner on the stovetop. "Flame-broiled lobster tail and prime rib aren't quite as good with propane as charcoal, but grilling inside is infinitely more convenient."

"I guess this means we're still playing the waiting version of hunting, right?" Julianna asked.

"You got it, Sherlock," he said and pulled her close to give her a real kiss.

"Ew! Are you two doing that again?" Tori asked, then giggled into her hand.

"Still," Julianna said and leaned over and whispered in Tori's ear. "And one of these days, you'll understand."

"I already do," Tori said back in the same soft voice. "It's just Oscar and I are more discreet. Especially since my parents are here. They still think I'm a six-year-old."

"And they probably always will." Julianna nodded to Oscar, searching the contents of the refrigerator for something to drink. "He's been through a lot in the last six months. I used to look at him as a child. Now I see him as my hero."

"Yeah, he told me how he rescued you from that in-sanitarium," she continued in the same hushed tone.

Julianna stood up and took a deep breath. She looked around the

125

room, so different than the ten by ten room she'd been kept in while in France. Her voice returned to normal volume. "I know you know it's not called an in-sanitarium, but it should be. For years, everyone thought I was nuts. Now, the three people I care about most are comfortable enough with my past and my present to make jokes about it with me. I think that's complete healing."

"Cheers, Mom, on your well-deserved emancipation," Oscar said, toasting her with a can of tomato juice. He came and stood next to her. "I'm just sorry I didn't understand sooner. Shoot, I still don't understand. But you know, I don't have to know how a car drives to know that it can. To accept it can go from point A to point B. I guess it's the same for you." He shook his head. "Actually, I think my brain would explode if I tried to figure it out, so no explanation is necessary, okay? Just don't go taking off anywhere – or any-when – without telling me, all right?"

Julianna pulled him close and kissed him on the top of his head, hiding her tears. "Deal."

***

"This meal makes me grateful I gave up being a vegan eighteen years ago," Leanne said.

"I've always been grateful for that," Luther commented. "This was the best steak and lobster I ever had."

"I'd ask if I could move in with you two just for the eats," Oscar said, "but I think I'll only be around for a day or two more. Tori and I are going on a tour."

"What?" Leanne gasped.

Julianna put her hand on top of hers and patted it gently, urging her to wait.

"Yup. We joined the Youth Advocates Council. We'll be traveling with an evangelical group reaching out to street kids and the homeless in need of guidance, job counseling, medical, you name it."

"Yup, we're the point people," Tori bragged. "You know, like if we were astronauts, we'd be the ones making first contact with the aliens."

"Now, that sounds pretty interesting," Luther said, nodding. He turned to Leanne who was dabbing her tears with a napkin. "Do a little time-tripping, sweetheart…"

Silas, Julianna, Oscar, and Tori all gasped and looked back and forth between each other, tight-lipped.

"Huh?" Leanne asked.

Luther continued. "If you and I had that opportunity when we were eighteen and nineteen, do you think we'd want to go on a project like that, or stay at home with our parents and go to college?"

"Already graduated," Oscar popped in, then sat back and grinned.

Leanne looked at him, eyebrow raised.

"Yes, he did," Julianna said, beaming with pride. "Top of his class, too. Go on, Luther."

"Leanne, I think this is great. Plus, they'll be supervised with some level-headed folks. I've heard about the group. Mark my words, these kids out there, giving up their comfort and video games to bring others out of despair and poverty, will be tomorrow's leaders. There's no way I'd want to deprive Tori of this opportunity."

"Well, when you say it like that. I mean, it's not as if they're getting in an old bus filled with pot-smoking hippies out to make love… I mean, out to make music and protest against war…" Leanne paused. "What were our parents thinking, letting us go…"

"They knew we had to grow up, too. I know my folks were more into the protest for peace part of the movement. Looks like our daughter will be going into the world to make a difference with others in a new way. See how much has changed in forty years? Shoot, who would have thought we'd be growing marijuana legally now?"

Julianna fought the urge to raise her hand and stifled a chuckle.

Oscar caught the reaction and smiled. *My mother, the time*

traveler.

Chapter 14: The Shootout

"It's a good thing you held still when I told you to," Victoria scolded.

"You know, I don't like the way you're treating me. I think I'm going to leave. Right now. I can pull this job on my own."

"André, you don't know how to get into the house."

"Yes, I do. I just follow those wet footprints left by that kid. Easy." André opened the door of the van and stepped into the garage. "Damn! It does smell like cigarettes out here. You know, you really should quit smoking."

"Wait, where are you going?"

André walked boldly to the door the young couple had left through, then looked back at Victoria. "Those prints won't stay wet forever. I'm going to see where they go first, then I'll come back and wait until night when everyone's asleep before I do the upside-down Santa. See, I'm no dummy."

"That's reverse Santa," Victoria said under her breath. She waited for him to return, thought about it twice, then gave in to the urge. "Screw it. I only have one left. I might as well smoke it and be done with it."

She dug into her backpack, found the lighter, then went to the door André went through for his piss break. "He won't smell it if I smoke out here."

She stepped outside and took three long, deep drags on the filtered smoke then tossed the butt into the bush. "Oh, crap," she said, twisting the doorknob. "Crap, shit, double damn…" She pulled and pulled, rattling the door, hoping.

"What's the matter?" André asked through the slightly opened door, a self-satisfied grin splitting his face. "Did the *dummy* lock herself out?"

"Shut up," she hissed, then ducked under his arm and pushed inside.

The two didn't speak to each other for hours. André passed the time twiddling his thumbs, humming the same tune over and over. Finally, Victoria blew up. "Would you stop singing that alphabet song?"

"It's Twinkle, Twinkle Little Star, and I'm not singing it. I'm humming it in all the languages of the world. Hmph! So there."

"If I ever get out of here…" Victoria mumbled then gritted her teeth until she felt a pop.

"Son of a bitch!" she screamed.

"Hey, Victoria, you'd better keep your voice down," André whispered. "Someone's gonna hear you. Hey, are you all right?"

"No…" she hissed, remembering not to call him a dummy. "I juth broke the wire on my parthial plate, damn it." She pulled it out of her mouth and threw it across the van, bouncing it off two cabinet doors before it landed in the mini sink.

André swallowed his chuckle and went back to humming his song, this time in Australian.

***

"Two-to-one they're waiting until they think everyone's asleep," Julianna whispered into the collar of Silas's t-shirt.

The two were lying down, cuddled together under a big synthetic fur spread. They had agreed to pass on the lovemaking for the night and to sleep in clothing they wouldn't be ashamed to face Luther and Leanne in.

"I think you're right. If they're in the VW bus like Oscar suspects, it shouldn't be too much longer until they come in."

"Do you think we should have told Luther and Leanne what's going on?"

"Nah. Tori and Oscar know. I doubt Victoria and the great ape will go back to the guest house. Thanks for telling them it was hurricane damage on the window and not a break-in."

"That was Oscar's idea." Julianna got up on her elbow. "He's really fond of you. It didn't take too long."

"I think it's because of Tori."

"Maybe a little bit, but he knows how I feel about you. He told

130

me tonight he's never seen me so happy."

Clunk!

"And there they are…" Silas whispered. He pulled out his smartphone and swiped across the screen, opening the security camera app. "They're coming from the garage through the kitchen. Look at that."

"Oh, good grief. He's looking in the refrigerator?"

"Well, there isn't anything to eat in the van. Unless they brought food… Hold on. Get out of the bed and hide."

Silas rolled out of bed, rushing to stand behind the door as Julianna dashed into the closet.

"Agh! Take that, you mitherable mutha…"

Silas grabbed Victoria from behind and tried to wrestle the cricket bat from her before she could inflict more damage to his faux polar-bear skin bedcover.

"Wha?" she screeched and turned around, shocked by his sneak attack from behind.

Seeing her gap-toothed gasp, Silas laughed, losing control just long enough for her to wriggle out of his clutch.

She grabbed the bat again, ready to swing it at his head. "Where ith thee?"

"Give it up," Oscar said, pointing the Walther paintball gun he had taken from the kitchen.

Startled, Victoria stepped back and eyed them both, wondering which man to strike first. "No way!" She repositioned the wooden club on her shoulder, her fingers flicking in and out as she clutched it tighter.

"That was rude," André bellowed, rubbing the back of his head with one hand as he strode into the room. He saw Oscar and grunted, shoving him in the back, pushing him into the window.

Oscar reached out to stop from going through the large pane of glass and the gun fired as he inadvertently squeezed the trigger. A bright blue paintball flew out, hitting Silas on the side of the head, the impact of the point-blank range knocking the older man to the floor.

Hearing the shot, Julianna burst out of the closet, hand raised high clutching one of Silas's shoes.

"Uh-oh," André said. He dropped his food-filled backpack and ran thunder-footed out of the room and down the stairs.

Tori remained hidden behind the decorative plant in the hallway, Oscar's smartphone in her hand, and video recorded the big man's exit. As soon as he was out of sight, she sidled toward the bedroom and the cacophony of chaos.

"You bitch!" Julianna yelled as she rushed across the room.

Tori stepped in just as Julianna was ready to bring her Florsheim weapon down on Victoria's head. She saw Tori in her peripheral vision and paused her assault. She backed up, took a deep and ragged breath, and composed herself. "You're lucky she came in, Victoria."

"Oh, don't stop on my account," Tori said, tapping an icon to stop recording. She stuck the phone in the pocket of her hoodie. "Go for it."

"No, no," Victoria begged, dropping to her knees awkwardly.

"Watch her," Oscar said, seeing the evil glint in her eye.

Tori looked over and saw Silas on the ground, a paisley mix of vibrant blue and blood-red sliding down the side of his head to pool beneath his face.

"Heh, heh. Thot by the kid," Victoria laughed.

Thwap!

Julianna's right hook sent the villainess to the ground, her lower jaw askew, the dark of her missing tooth stark against her remaining yellowed teeth and lolling pink tongue.

Dazed, Oscar cautiously stepped over the scrawny woman in black to get to Silas. "Is he alive?" he asked, hovering over his mother as she anxiously whispered words of hope and fear into the unconscious man's face.

Tori rushed to Silas's other side with a washcloth. She wiped the colorful smear from the point of impact, looking to see if anything had penetrated the skin. It hadn't. "No cuts," she said.

Julianna composed herself quickly at the good news and checked for a carotid pulse.

"It was just a paintball," she repeated, this time loud enough for the others to hear.

"Even blanks in guns can kill a person," Tori said without thinking. "I mean…"

She looked at Oscar, white-faced, now clutching the curtains for support, plump silent tears falling, stunned.

"There!" Julianna said, finding his pulse. "He's alive. He said he didn't want the police involved, but we have to get him to the hospital."

"What's going on…? Oh, my!" Leanne said, clutching her robe and coat around her tighter.

Luther gently moved his wife aside and knelt beside Julianna. "Let me check."

He rolled Silas's head to either side, looking for signs of bullet entry, then pulled both eyelids up. He looked at Julianna, fixing her fearful gaze with his calming one. "Why didn't he want the police involved?"

"That…that bitch was a liaison from almost forty years ago. He didn't want her or anyone else to know…" She paused and whispered in his ear, "To know he owns all this."

"Yeah, she's my biological grandmother," Tori said. "but I sure don't want to claim her. She must be some sort of genetic anomaly."

"She's an effin' freak of nature is what she is," Julianna said. "And wanted by the law. Silas said there are warrants out for her arrest and, for some reason, immigration wants her, too. How are we going to get Silas to the hospital and her… Get her out of here? Sorry, Luther, my brain's a scrambled mess right now."

"Don't worry about her for now," Leanne said. She rolled Victoria over and set her foot in the middle of her back. She pulled the tie from her robe and held it up as if it was a golden rope. "I've been tying knots since I was a Daisy Scout. She won't get out of this one. We can dump her at ICE or the police department, whichever is closest."

"What about the other guy?" Julianna asked.

"He's long gone," Tori said. She looked back at Oscar, ready to ask if André had hurt him, and saw he was still ashen. "Mama, I think we need to take Oscar to the hospital, too. I think he's in shock." She looked at Julianna. "And she's not too far behind."

Luther stood up. "All right, Leanne. You're in charge of the hospital run. I'll drag this bag of bones to the first place full of folks wearing shields. Son," Luther said to Oscar. "Son, son," he repeated, putting his hand on Oscar's cheek. "Clammy. You called it right, Tori. You help your mama."

"Oh, wait," she said. Tori pulled her phone out of her pocket, tapped a few times, then said, "Cop station two miles away. Turn right at the bottom of the hill. Can't miss it. I hope."

"Don't worry about me. I may be a male, but I'm not afraid to ask for directions."

"Julianna, I need you to carry Silas. Can you hoist him under your shoulder?" Leanne asked.

Julianna looked from her son to Tori, then to Leanne. "I'll be okay. The keys to the Caddie are on the hook by the back door. You drive, Leanne. Tori, you help her get Oscar to the car. From what I remember, the hospital is two blocks from the police station." Julianna put on her shoes, then squatted in front of Silas. "Come on. Let's go," she said and lifted him as if he was a child.

***

"You don't need my name, do you?" Luther asked the sergeant. "I don't mind bringing the trash to you, but if you don't put it on any documents, her buddies can't come after me. She's a real tool, I hear."

"Yes, she is, Mr. Doe," the detective said with a wink. "She tried to murder her own daughter." He shook his head, looking down at the printout of international crimes she had been involved with in the last ten years. "Here. Tell the missus or your girlfriend or whoever, thanks for restraining her."

Luther accepted the sash from Leanne's robe and stuffed it in his pocket. "Well, if we're done here, I have to go visit a friend in the hospital. Thanks for keeping her. Oh, and we certainly don't want her back."

"Yes, sir. Hope all goes well with your sick friend."

"Me, too," Luther said, not bothering to correct him and say he was injured, not ill. "Me, too."

***

André walked down the street, rubbing his arms, chilled in the late-night winter air without a coat or hat.

"Hey, there! Need a ride?"

A black Mercedes sedan pulled up alongside him, the back window rolled down. "You look like you could use some warming up, sweetie," the middle-aged man said.

André looked from the man calling out to him to the driver's window. A grim-faced driver was staring straight ahead, emotionless.

"Oh, don't worry about him, sweetie. We could do anything back here and he wouldn't mind."

"Buy me dinner first?" André asked.

"Dine in or take out?"

"I don't care as long as it's hot and I'm not paying for it," André said.

"Ooh, then we have a deal because it'll be hot and I'm paying for it."

***

"What's the patient's name?" the receptionist asked.

"Silas Priest," Julianna said.

She looked up at her. "Are you his wife?"

"Um, no. We're...dating."

"Practically engaged," Tori said, grinning. "Oh, and I'm not his wife either, but I'm his granddaughter. One of them. There are three of us. We're triplets..." She saw the woman frown, so pressed her

135

lips together, forcing herself to be still.

"Can we have someone look after him, too. He's my son," Julianna said, watching Luther try to urge a confused Oscar into a wheelchair.

"Oh, and I'm not his wife either, but we're dating," Tori said with pride, stepping over to put her hand on Oscar's shoulder, pushing him back down to a seated position.

"And what about you two?" the nurse asked Luther and Leanne.

"Oh, we're married," Leanne said. "But we consider it dating. She's our daughter." She patted Tori's shoulder, creating a link of diverse genders, ages, and ethnicities: tall, dark and concerned; blonde, bouncy, and chatty; seated, stunned and silent; a silly senior couple; plus one gray-haired man laid out in the back room with a triage nurse.

"But you didn't bring the other two?" the receptionist asked.

"Triplets? Oh, no. They were adopted to other families," Leanne said.

"Thank God," the dour-faced woman said. "Everyone but you," she said nodding to Julianna, "go sit down. I think I recognize the name Silas Priest. You," she handed Julianna the clipboard, "fill out this information on your...son?"

"Yes, he's my son," Julianna said. She exhaled in despair and added, "My only one."

"Thank God," the receptionist repeated, then looked up with embarrassment. "I'm sorry. It's been one of those nights. I'm sure he'll be okay. He's not on drugs, is he?"

"Absolutely not!" Julianna leaned down and got in the woman's face. "If you can't handle this job, then I suggest you find another one. And if I'm correct, you're a clerk. It isn't up to you to diagnose or evaluate patients, is it?"

"No, not my job. And yes, ma'am, I'm the receptionist."

"Fine. I'll do my best to be the polite parent and girlfriend involved with two of the hospital's patients, and you pass out clipboards and perform data entry. Deal?"

"Yes, ma'am."

"You sure told her," Tori whispered to Julianna when she sat next to her.

"Grr…"

"Sorry."

Julianna grunted and set the paperwork down. "There are only two men in this world I care about and they're both in the emergency room of a town I'm not familiar with. I have no one. I'm totally ungrounded, untethered…"

"You have me," Tori said, clasping the top of her arm. "And I'll stay with you and be your tether. I promise."

Julianna grimaced, picked up the paperwork, and tried to read it, her eyes glazing over. She set it back down. "Silas and I were just talking about that. If we were to go forward in time, we needed someone to come back to. The word I use is anchor, but tether is pretty much the same thing." She picked up the clipboard and tried again.

"You're wrong," Tori said, then squeezed Julianna's arm until she looked at her. "It's *when* you go forward in time, not *if*."

"You are so much like him."

"Yeah, I know. Ain't it great?"

She picked up Tori's hand, turned it over, and looked at it. "See this line up the middle? Not everyone has one. It's a fate line." Julianna opened her hand and pointed to the same spot. "And I have two. Weird, huh?"

"Weird as in cool," Tori said. "Now, finish those forms. I'm going to see what she meant about knowing the name Silas Priest."

Tori waited until the receptionist was finished with the police officer, then stepped forward. "Excuse me. Would you explain to me what you meant about recognizing the name Silas Priest?"

"You're the granddaughter, right? The triplet?"

Tori nodded, tight-lipped.

"You're the only blood relative here tonight, correct?"

She nodded again, her eyes starting to fill with moisture.

"He's been here before. He has a rare blood type. He donates on a regular basis. He's one of the hospital's unsung heroes. As that tall woman said, it's not my job to diagnose, but if he ever needs blood, there might be a problem."

"Because he's the one you'd be calling, right?"

She shrugged a shoulder. "Would you like to go back and see him? I'd like to let her back," nodding to Julianna, "but I can't legally."

"All right," Tori said, wiping under her eye with a knuckle to make sure a tear hadn't escaped. "But if you have any control when they send my boyfriend back, could you put him in a room right next to my grandpa? It wouldn't be illegal but would be mighty convenient."

She nodded and smiled. "I'll see what I can do. Here, put on this name tag and I'll take you back."

Tori hung the lanyard with the words Family, Visitor, Silas Priest around her neck, then followed the receptionist as she swiped her access card across the security card reader. When they got to the room, Tori clutched her escort's arm. Her grandfather was laid out in a pale hospital gown, the faint green tinge of the cotton drape accentuating his own poor coloring.

"Is he going to be okay?"

"Probably. Most people who come here do go home eventually. The ones who don't get to the hospital are the ones who don't make it." She pointed to the white plastic bag on the chair with his name on it. "Those are his personal belongings. You might want to take any valuables home with you."

Tori nodded then stood by him, holding his hand as the monitors blinked and beeped on a steady basis. A butterfly bandage covered the end of one eyebrow, a huge orange and rose-colored lump beneath it. "You're going to be okay. I promise."

"Not your call," he mumbled.

"Oh, of course it is! I'm your granddaughter. You have a whole lifetime of promises and parties and piggyback rides you owe me."

"Don't know about the piggybacks…"

And then he was out again. Tori looked up. The line on the graph had gone up when he spoke but was now back in the lower range, bouncing on a steady basis.

"Up and down is good, straight is bad," a man's voice said.

"Who are you?" Tori asked then looked at the badge. "Jarryd?"

"That's my name. I'm just the nurse. The doctor will be here soon. They're going to look for clots or aneurysms or little black ants…"

Tori giggled despite her fear. "How long?"

Jarryd snorted. "Have you ever heard of the phrase 'hospital time'?" She shook her head. "Probably because they're still trying to figure it out."

She laughed again, still weak but feeling better to have someone in the room with her.

"You're the granddaughter, right?" She nodded. "Make sure you take any of his valuables with you. Not that we have gangs of bandits roving the corridors…"

This time, she laughed out loud. "Okay, I promise. I'll do that while I'm trying to find a constant variable for hospital time."

Jarryd patted her on the shoulder. "I'll be back shortly. Keep him company. Talk to him. I don't know what just went on, but you got his vitals going in the right direction. Keep 'em up."

"Will do, Jarryd."

Tori waited until the nurse was gone, then set the bag of clothing and other personal items on the table. "Well, he said talk to you." She paused, tongue-tied, and looked around the room for inspiration. "I don't know why that's suddenly a problem," she said, her speech stilted. "I guess it's because I have to carry on both sides of the conversation. Then again, I'll just pretend you're my ventriloquist dummy. Do you like that idea, Silas?"

She laughed nervously and asked. "Do you want me to stick my hand up your shirt and make your mouth work?" She dropped her voice an octave lower, pretending to be him. "No, your hands are cold. How about you be the dummy and I'll be the puppet master?"

Tori frowned, her little theatrics falling flat. "I guess not this time. Well, they want me to check and see if you were carrying a million dollars in your pajama pockets, Grandpa." She dumped the contents of the bag on the chair then picked them up and rummaged the pockets before folding his clothes and setting them in a neat pile. "Who carries a wallet in their pajamas? See, nothing."

She had replaced everything into the bag when she looked up and saw his jacket on the coat hook. "Now, let's see if you have any treasures in there."

Silas's eyes fluttered but Tori didn't see them. He was unconscious but aware, in a sleep state so deep he couldn't move or talk but could breathe. He pulled in a deep breath and tried to snort with the exhale, but didn't have the strength.

"Well, look what I found, Grandpa. Your wallet. Do I have your permission to look through here? I know I'm your next of kin, but I want to make sure you don't keep one of those 'In Case of Emergency' cards…"

Huff!

"Grandpa? You heard me?" She stared at his face, then realized his chest was rising more than a usual breath would require.

Huff!

"Okay, okay. That takes a lot of energy. Let's do like the movies. One blink for yes, two for no. Or is it the other way around? No, no. Let's keep it one for yes, two for no. Now, do you understand me?"

Blink.

"Cool. Now, right now, all I want to know is should I look in your wallet?"

Blink.

"Gotcha." Tori carefully pulled all the cards from his wallet, looked at them, then put them in a neat pile on his belly. "How about that, Grandpa. Our first card game."

Silas's belly went in and out rapidly.

"You're laughing, I know you are," she said, then looked at his eyes.

Blink.

"Is this our special man, Silas Priest?" the very short man in a clean but tattered dingy-white lab coat asked.

"Yes…" Tori answered, frowning as she checked the non-official looking man over.

The man was at least a head shorter than she was, clean-shaven but wearing his hair long, drifting over his worn collar in oily strands. Tori sniffed, wondering if he was a vagrant who hadn't bathed or someone emulating men from centuries ago. He had an earthy smell that was intriguing but in no way foul or disgusting.

"Ah, that will do," he said, taking the bag of belongings from the plastic chair and setting it in the corner. He looked at her and nodded, his mouth pulling aside as if to smile but not quite bringing sincerity to the gesture.

"Who are you?" she asked.

"I'm Mast…um…you may call me Doctor Simon. I'm a specialist here."

Tori's eyes widened as she recognized the near slip on his name. "I think you're Master Simon…" she said accusingly, her eyes squinted, fixed on his for his reaction.

She couldn't have made a stronger impact with an eight-pound sledgehammer. His mouth opened, gasping for words that wouldn't come, then he felt for the chair and sat down.

Tori smirked and set her hand on his shoulder. "It's okay. I'm a friend," she whispered.

He quickly shrugged out of the familiar touch and scowled at her – suspicious but not wanting to leave the room.

"Oh, and I'm also his granddaughter. I'm one of triplets!" she bragged. She realized she was no longer whispering. "Can you fix him? My boyfriend accidentally shot him with a paintball gun. I mean, at the time he was trying to protect his mother and someone shoved him and it went off. It wasn't on purpose. He feels really,

really bad about it. Can you maybe erase his memory or something?"

Simon pursed his lips together thoughtfully, then patted the pocket of his jacket. "Whose memory? Your grandfather or your beau?"

"Can you do both?"

He opened his lab coat and verified the contents of his jacket pocket. "Only one. You do know he can hear you right now, don't you?"

Tori nodded. "One blink for yes, two for no." She grinned. "And he just breathes real fast for laughing. He understands funny, too."

"That's good to know. Now, if you'll let me check him out…"

"Here, I'll move the chair around for you. I want to help."

Simon started to tell her he didn't care to have assistants, but her wide blue eyes of concern warmed his ancient time-traveler's heart. Not many of Silas's bloodline were left. She might be special, too. It was better to keep her as a friend.

The two worked together with limited chatter, Tori intentionally biting her lower lip to keep from asking him what he was doing or telling him she was friends with another time traveler, too.

"Now, I have one question for you and then I'll have to ask you to leave the room."

Tori inhaled deeply, ready to beg to stay, then blew out the breath. Sometimes it was best to be quiet and observe. She nodded without a word but kept the pout.

"What's the boyfriend's name?"

"Oscar."

"All right. Go ahead and leave." Simon saw she was reluctant to go and tears were ready to fall. "My dear, I'm going to use a little – shall we call it, medicinal powder? – and say a few *encouraging* words to Silas. I don't want you near either of them."

"Fairy dust and charms?" she asked, wiping under her eyes and nose with the back of her hand.

He canted his head to the side, lifted one shoulder, and softly grunted an affirmative.

She leaned down and gave him a long, hard kiss on the cheek, then scurried out of the room, pulling the door shut behind her.

Simon reached up and rubbed the side of his face. He blinked rapidly, trying to figure out what felt odd. "So that's what a kiss feels like. How soon we forget."

***

"Tori," Julianna called out. "We're over here."

Tori looked from where she had been to where Julianna was. Opposite sides of the emergency rooms.

Julianna recognized her glare of scorn as she walked toward her. "The receptionist apologized all over herself. She said she tried to get us close so I could check on Silas, too, but it wasn't possible. How's he doing?"

Tori nodded and shared a weak smile. "And Oscar?" she asked.

"They gave him some anti-anxiety medication and said to keep him away from any excitement for a few weeks. Oh, and that means no snowball fights for a year. At least. Airborne projectiles are a no-no."

"Got it. Can I see him?"

"Tori, what aren't you telling me? I've never heard you so quiet in my life. Well, even if I've only known you for a couple of days."

Tori held her hand up for her to wait, then stepped into Oscar's room. He was asleep. She pointed to the chairs across from the nurses' station and Julianna followed her there.

"Remember when you were talking about fairies and Master Simon?"

Julianna nodded, her eyebrows crowded in concern.

"He's the one seeing to my grandpa right now."

"Wait. What?" Julianna pulled Tori's chin up then looked in her eyes, checking the dilation for any signs of drugs or insanity. "Are you okay? I think maybe you need a doctor, too."

"No, I'm fine. I kind of recognized him. I asked him to erase

143

Grandpa's memory of Oscar accidentally shooting him..."

"You what?" Julianna screeched, then looked around, offering a weak smile of apology to the only person – a janitor – who appeared to have heard her. "He can do that?"

"He said he's going to try. He could only do one, though. Oscar will know he accidentally shot him but Silas won't. I figured since he was already kind of konked out, it would be easier than messing with Oscar. He's going to be okay, isn't he?"

"Oscar? Yes, I wish you'd chosen the other way. I think the only problem Oscar's going to have is leftover guilt. Silas won't care. He's already one of the most forgiving people who've ever walked the earth."

"I'm sorry. I didn't know," Tori said.

Julianna wrapped her arm around her and pulled her close. "I'm sorry I said anything. It was a flip of the coin decision to make. I'm feeling a little anxious and unsettled, too. If you had chosen the other way, I probably would have found a reason for it to be wrong, too." She pulled out of the hug and looked at Tori. "You know, you're the closest person I've ever had to a daughter." She squeezed her close again. "And it sure feels great."

"You're not the only mother I've ever had, but even having three feels great, too."

***

"A triplet, eh?" Simon said as he looked over Silas. "I guess if there was any doubt that your rare blood type was a fluke, producing triplets even a generation down the line should be another mark in your favor. Or disfavor."

Simon took a small piece of folded paper out of his pocket, opened Silas's mouth, and put a twist of flower stamen under his tongue. "Remember nothing of Oscar, my friend. Nothing."

Chapter 15: Recovery

Tori jumped up and tried to get the short man's attention, frantically waving goodbye. "There he goes," she whispered hoarsely to Julianna.

"That's Master Simon?" she asked, standing to get a better look.

Simon turned around to offer a silent farewell to the granddaughter of Silas Priest, then looked beside her and saw Jane. He blinked twice. No, not her. Tall enough, the same features, but too fair. This one must be her daughter.

He raised his hand in a brief salute and left, waddling behind a male nurse, making use of the other man's access privileges to leave the secure section of the hospital.

"He looked like he recognized you, Julianna."

"I thought he did at first, too. Did you see that little shudder, though? I think he's seen my mother and thought I was her. We look a lot alike."

"Yeah, I look like my birth mother, too," Tori said. "Oh, and they told me to take home Grandpa's personal, I mean, his valuable stuff. They didn't want to be responsible in case bandits came through. This is all he had."

Tori handed Julianna the wallet, studying her face. "He had a few hundred dollars in cash, but I think the most precious item was this." She held out her hand, showing her the ancient Greek drachma drilled with two holes.

"Oh, yeah... It is," she said, adding a soft chuckle of approval and a nod.

"Is this what you need to travel?"

"Yup, and we need another one – one for each of us. That's what we're up to as soon as he gets healthy, a coin hunt." Julianna looked Tori in the eye. "Still willing to be my anchor, Little Miss Tether?"

"Yup."

"And look after Oscar?"

"My pleasure. Oh, and where are you going?"

"We're going forward five years to 2015. I think I know where to find my mom and da. I…um…have to tell them I'm sorry." She held Tori's hand. "I don't care if it's a parent, a friend, a teacher, or someone you accidentally bumped into, never wait to apologize. You never know what tomorrow will bring."

"Like today?"

Julianna looked toward the room Silas was in. "Like today."

"Miss Priest?" a woman asked impatiently as if it was a second or third time.

Tori looked up and saw the name tag read Doctor Johnson and the pinched-face crone was staring at her. "Priest? No, I'm Tori Greene, but my grandfather is Silas Priest. Are you looking to speak with me? I'm his next of kin." Tori almost made an introduction to Julianna, but by the dour look at the professional's face, she didn't want to be bothered.

"Would you like to chat in a private room? I'm here to discuss your grandfather's release orders and plan of care."

"No, here is fine. Actually, my friend will be helping me, so it's good if she hears it firsthand. Proceed."

Julianna chewed back her laugh as Tori gently putting the medico in place then sobered up and listened.

"There is a blood clot right behind the point of impact. Normally, this doesn't happen with paintball injuries. However, if the balls have been stored for a long period of time, it's possible the contents solidified. The projectiles are denser, more like a real bullet. We want to take him in for an MRI to confirm what we saw on the x-ray. I have to tell you, it's a little dicey."

Tori looked over at Julianna and mouthed, 'Dicey?' then turned back. "So, you took x-rays as soon as he got here?"

"Yes, before he even got a room. If there's any internal bleeding, we have a baseline. We can see exactly how much worse it is."

"Or better," Tori offered, leaning forward. "I mean, because it is

146

possible to get better, not worse, right?"

"I suppose…"

"Look, lady," Tori said, standing up and towering over the seated doctor, "I don't know where you studied medicine, but you should get a refund. Anyone with any brains at all knows in healing the body, you never underestimate the power of hope or the destructive force of despair. And you can quote me on that."

"And you just said release orders and plan of care. Is he going home with a potential aneurysm or are you keeping him here for observation?" Julianna asked, hands on hips.

"Oh, wrong papers." The doctor looked at Tori, ignoring the dark angry woman, hoping to intimidate the younger, blonde female in front of her. She pulled her clipboard close and rattled off generic instructions off the top of her head. "Either way, he is to rest, but if he can't be wakened, call an ambulance right away and we'll readmit him."

"I think he'll stay right where he is until we get the MRI results back," Julianna said, rising. "And if anyone has a problem with that, we'll call his lawyer."

The doctor's neck craned back to take in Julianna's height, her stern words suddenly registering as the second blow of a one-two punch. "Right," she said and got up and left.

Jarryd the nurse walked up to Tori. "Thanks. It's about time someone put her in her place. She's about one season shy of retirement and making all of us miserable. She upsets the families who take it out on us."

"What do you do?" Tori asked.

"Tell them we understand and ask them to please file a complaint and let the administration know. We can't do anything."

"Yes, you can," Tori said. "And you're doing it right now. You're taking care of the sick and injured and giving the families hope."

"Thanks," Jarryd said. "Oh, and cool beans on that quote you came up with. I think I'll make it into a label and paste it on all the status whiteboards. We all need to remember that about hope and despair. If you two want to grab a bite, I'll call you when they're done with the MRI and have the results."

Julianna nodded to Oscar's room. "My son is in there. I think he'll be ready to leave soon. At least, I hope so."

"Yup," Tori said, "there's that wonderful four-letter word again. Hope."

Bzz. Bzz.

Tori looked down at her phone and saw the text message. 'How's it going?'

'Good. Be right there.'

"I'm going to let my folks know what's going on. Coming?" she asked Julianna. "I think he has us covered. Oh, and I wrote my cell number on the board in Grandpa's room. Just in case he wakes up."

The women stopped and turned back when they heard Silas roar from across the hall.

"No, I do not want an MRI. I don't need my head examined!"

"Oh, my," Julianna said, leading the way to his room.

Despite her head start and long legs, Tori beat her. "Grandpa, you be nice to these people," she scolded mockingly, her face shiny with tears of joy and a wide smile.

"Tori?" he asked, confused. "Why am I here?" He looked up and saw Julianna, her eyes wide with fear and uncertainty. "Are you sure you shouldn't be the one in bed, sweetheart? You look like you're ready to be sick."

"You remember me?"

"Of course, I do. Both of you. What?" he asked and smiled mischievously, "did I fly in a tornado and land in Oz, Dorothy?"

Tori looked at both of them, unsure about what he had said. The smile on Julianna's face, though, showed it was an inside joke and his mind was clear.

"So, if I know who both of you are, then it's okay to put on some clothes and go home?" He grabbed the back of his hospital gown. "What they put me in is a *little* breezy on the south end."

Julianna laughed and cried at the same time. "All right, but I have to stay here a little longer. You and Tori go on back. Luther and Leanne are in the waiting room."

"Luther and Leanne?" he asked, then blinked, thinking. "Oh, yeah. Your parents, Tori. I'm so glad they dropped in on their way to visit old friends on the east coast."

Tori stole a glance at Julianna. She was as confused as she was. Evidently, there were a few side effects with Master Simon's fairy dust cure.

***

Two days later

"I haven't felt this great in years," Silas said, bouncing around the kitchen, flipping bacon, slicing potatoes and dicing onions. "I hope everyone's hungry because we're having a breakfast feast!"

"Mom, are you sure he's going to be okay?" Oscar asked. "He keeps asking me who I am."

"I think it's selective amnesia. It has nothing to do with you."

"If you don't tell him, I will," Tori said.

"Tell me what?" Oscar asked, looking from her to his mother.

Julianna huffed. "The doctor didn't want you to get excited so I wasn't going to tell you anything."

"Yeah, but not saying anything is more upsetting," Tori said. "So spill."

"I don't want you to get mad because it has to do with time travel and you always get wound up..."

"Mom, just tell me, all right?"

"When that paintball pistol accidentally discharged..."

"When I shot Silas, you mean," Oscar said.

"Accidentally discharged," Julianna repeated firmly, "it seems the paint in the ball had solidified. It inflicted more damage than normal. Brain trauma."

"Yeah, I remember the blood and you carrying him like a child to the car."

149

"It didn't look so good. Well, it just so happens an old…as in very old…"

"Ancient time traveler," Tori spit out. "Speed it up or my folks will be here and we'll have an audience."

"Tori, you tell me," Oscar said.

"This Master Simon did some mumbo jumbo and fairy dust and made Grandpa forget you ever shot him. Except I think he did a little too much mumbo or dust or something because he keeps forgetting who you are. The good part is, Grandpa will never know you hurt him. Can you deal with that?"

"God, I love you, Tori," he said and pulled her close. "Yes, I can. Mom, you try to protect me too much."

"Well, I suppose that's why the Lord made both mothers and wives. Or girlfriends."

"You had it right the first time. Tori and I are getting married soon. Very soon."

"Yup, and we don't want anything fancy. Just legal. And our family. Especially my sisters. And…"

"Everything good over here?" Luther asked, carrying a tray of drinks in his hand.

"Nothing's plain around here, is it?" Oscar asked, taking a crystal goblet of orange juice with a wedge of sliced strawberry on the side.

Luther grinned then frowned at Julianna. "Are you sure he's going to be okay? Whatever it is they gave him in that hospital, I'd like a drop or two."

"Maybe they gave him some Fountain of Youth water," Tori said, then giggled into her hand.

"If they did, I'm all for it. He's like a puppy with that boundless energy."

"Tell me about it," Julianna whispered into her goblet, smiling.

Luther sat down beside his daughter. "Drink up, Tori. It has lots of vitamin C."

Tori took a glass, ready to salute. "Grab a cup, Grandpa. I'm toasting."

Silas took his goblet and lifted it. "Go for it."

"Here's to friends and family and all the good memories we'll make from this day forward."

"Here, here!" everyone toasted.

"Here, here," Oscar said softly and put the strawberry in his mouth. "As long as he doesn't forget Mom and Tori, that's good enough for me."

Chapter 16: Trial Run

Later that day

"Mom, we've been back from the hospital for less than six hours and he's already asked me four times who I am. I'm sorry, I thought I'd be fine, but I can't take it."

"Oscar, it might take a while. He has head trauma."

"I know, and it's all my fault. I talked with Luther and Leanne. They're both cool with Tori and me leaving with them. I made a call to the Youth Advocate Council. They said we can start our volunteer work any time we're ready." Oscar took a deep breath. "And believe me, I'm more than ready."

"You were ready a long time ago. Yes, go ahead and pack. If you need anything, you still have the credit card. Make sure you pay for gas and a few meals for everyone along the way."

"I'd ask if you're sure you'll be okay without me, but by that dreamy-eyed look you have, I can tell you're still in honeymoon mode."

Julianna felt her face warm but grinned in pride rather than feel embarrassed. "Do you know how good it feels to have an open relationship with you?"

"Yes, I do; it goes both ways. I'll be fine. I don't know if you've noticed or not, but I think Luther thinks of me like a son. He's even called me that a few times. We got along great working together in Oregon last summer, but this just feels…different."

"Mutual respect goes a long way. Will you all be staying for dinner?"

"Sorry. Luther and I talked about it. He's fine with leaving right away to beat the traffic."

"You'll hit it no matter when you leave."

"I know, Mom. And so does he. Luther's just considerate that way."

Julianna pulled Oscar close and rocked him back and forth like a baby. "I'm going to miss you."

"Hey, I'll always be in your heart. Besides, you have a new life ahead of you. Young love, even if it is about twenty – or forty – years late."

She kissed him on top of the head. "Having no secrets feels so great."

"Yes, it does. If you don't mind, I'm going to skip saying goodbye to Silas. It just hurts too bad, seeing him ditzy like that."

"Well, thank God he's only that way with you. Here's hoping it's temporary."

"Speaking of keeping secrets, Mom, Tori said you sort of had a plan... Were you going to tell me about it?"

"Yes, but I thought I had a few months, or at least weeks, to get the details worked out. Since you're leaving for I don't know how long, I'll give you the outline now. Tori knows the basics, but sometimes she goes off on a tangent and misses the main point when explaining it to others."

"That's for sure." Oscar double-checked his chair for broken glass shards and sat down near the boarded-up window. He looked up. "I'm ready – shoot," he said, then squeezed his eyes shut in embarrassment. "I mean, let me have it."

"See, your sense of humor is already covering for your insecurities. The big plan is Silas and I will go to 2015 to see my parents. We might make a test hop for a few hours, but I'll let you or Tori know. Before we do anything, he'll have legal paperwork drawn up so Tori's designated as the caretaker. She'll have power of attorney for everything he owns. He'd like it if when we're gone, you two stay here."

"Two? You don't think he'll have a problem with me, a stranger?"

"I'm sure he won't. Doesn't. Before the accident, he liked you. I don't plan on leaving his side, so I'll remind him that you're Tori's beau if he forgets. Or when he does."

"Good, because I won't be going anywhere without her."

"It sounds like you plan on spending the rest of your life with her?"

Bottom lip stuck out in determination, Oscar nodded. "As soon as we can, we're getting married. I mean, we have to establish residency here in Massachusetts, I think. So, you plan to leave from now, 2010, and you'll skip forward to 2015?"

"Yup. We'll only age a few seconds in the time you and Tori and everyone else will have aged five years."

"Wow. A lot can happen in that much time. Just think of where we were five years ago?"

"Thanks, but I'd rather not," Julianna said dryly.

"Yeah, come to think of it, me neither. So, what do Tori and I have to do?"

"Don't change the locks or access codes to the garage and keep the tags on the Cadillac current. Oh, and you might want to take it for a spin once a month or so just to make sure all systems are go. Silas and I will pop in, say hi and tell you how it went, then grab the Caddie and drive to North Carolina to see my parents. Simple, right?"

"So, if you're going to stop by and say hi, why do you want to make sure the locks aren't changed? Won't we still be here?"

"I hope so! Look, I know what date we're aiming for, but if we're off by a month, or even a few years, we don't want to be stranded. Cash we can take, but it's a lot easier if we already have wheels and a home to come back to. Besides, if we miss by even a few hours, you might be out shopping or something."

"Sounds good." Oscar stilled and looked into his mother's eyes, not saying a word.

"What?"

"I want to remember you as you are right now, Mom. And say how sorry I am for not believing you. Man, life must have been miserable, knowing what you do and not being able to tell anyone."

"Meh. I had you to keep me busy for most of that time. Now you have a life and I have the companion I've always craved."

"Well, that much is obvious." He patted her hand. "Take good care of him. He's a great guy….even if he can't remember who I am."

"Yes, he's the greatest. Well, at least next to you."

***

One week later

"There! That's exactly what we need," Silas said, pointing to the picture.

Julianna enlarged the image on the computer screen. "Except for the holes, but you can drill those." She sat back, lips pursed, her arms crossed under her breasts, a scowl covering her face.

"What's wrong. I thought you wanted to do this."

"I do. But obviously something's bothering me. Silas, how much do you remember about last week?"

"It snowed?" He shook his head. "I'm sorry. I don't know what you're referring to."

"Do you remember seeing Luther and his family?"

"Of course, I do. They came to Vickie's wedding. Tori let everyone know I was her grandfather and therefore Grace's father. I got to see Ria and her family again…"

Silas stopped talking when he saw all emotion drain from her face. "That's not what you wanted to hear, is it? I mean, did I miss something important?"

"Yes and no. Let's not worry about it now." She sat up straight and pushed her hair back in frustration. "Go ahead and make arrangements to inspect the coin. I want to make sure this isn't some scam."

"Are you sure you're okay? You ask me a variation of that same question every day. I'm about ready to print it out and just hand it to you."

"Nah. Don't worry about it. I guess I'm insecure and want to make sure you healed completely."

Silas rubbed his fingers over the spot near his eyebrow. "It's just barely tender. When Victoria or André grabbed my paintball gun and popped me in the noggin with it, I was more worried about

155

you. But you and Tori doctored me up and I was good to go."

"Whoa. You never said that before."

"What?"

"You don't know who shot you then?"

Silas took the strand hair she had moved behind her ear and twirled it around his forefinger, then leaned in and kissed her full bottom lip, slack with shock. "What difference does it make? We're here, together, with a plan. Those two scum are gone out of our lives forever."

"Where?" Julianna asked, a smile growing, her eyes now bright with curiosity.

"Don't know, don't care," he said. "Do you want to go upstairs and celebrate finding a coin?" He took the original drachma out of his pocket. "I'll flip you for who gets to be on top."

She took the proffered coin with a grin, happy that he'd remembered more of the events from the week before. Maybe he *was* getting his memory back. Now *that* was worth celebrating.

***

One week later

"That's it?" Silas asked, looking around at the budding trees. "Are you sure it worked? Everything looks the same."

"Did you drop your coin or lose focus?" Julianna asked.

Silas shook his head, looking in his hand to verify he still had the drachma.

"Then it should have worked. Grab a newspaper and check the date. Hey, I wonder if cell phones grab the info automatically like when you fly to a new time zone?" She looked at her phone and laughed. "Mine says critical system update needed to connect to the network."

Silas checked his. "Mine does, too. But hey, look on the bright side. These batteries lasted a year without a charge."

"Now that should be a world record. All we need is to find a paper to verify the date, then pop back home. No one will even know we left."

Silas hemmed and hawed for a moment then said, "Well, except for Tori…" He turned and looked around. "Where's a newsstand when you want one?"

"We may be in New York, but we're on the outskirts of Bethel, and you won't find so much as a convenience store to buy one."

"Let's start walking and see if someone offers us a ride." Silas looked up and saw the sunrise peeking over the hill. "This way. Walk away from the sun until noon and then let it warm your back until it sets."

"Maybe next time. I don't want to be gone that long. I only want to verify we can travel – make a safe round trip – then go home and get ready to see my parents."

"Good idea. Hey, look over there! Come on." Julianna and Silas jogged up the road a few hundred feet to a cluster of mailboxes in varied shapes and colors. He looked inside a long narrow red container placed next to them and took out a rolled-up newspaper. "March 21, 2011. We made it a year. I can't see a reason we can't make it to five, can you?"

"Sounds doable. Let me see that for a minute, please."

She opened it up. "Japan earthquake toll continues to rise," she read aloud. "Crap. Another disaster."

"Are you thinking your sister's ex-boyfriend has something to do with it?"

She shook her head. "Catastrophes have been happening since… Well, that's pretty much how the world began, isn't it? With a big bang? Much as I'd like to blame Storm for everything, I can't. Still want to, and now I'm more determined than ever to stop him."

"Whoa, wait, Jules. I thought we were going to see your parent so you could apologize. Do you have a hidden agenda?"

"Well, yes and no. Yes, to hidden, but it's not really an agenda. Rumor is there's a bag of coins stashed at my folks' new place."

"Coins, as in drilled ancient silver drachmas?" Silas asked, re-rolling the newspaper and returning it to its weatherproof housing.

She nodded. "Yup. That's another reason I chose the date. I

want to retrieve them before he shows up and starts looking. With that many coins, he could equip a whole army of mischief-making minions…and I don't mean the cute little yellow guys who talk funny."

"Little yellow guys?"

"Believe me, you'll know who they are soon enough. Now, let's go home."

"Stop for breakfast first? You know, I'd like to celebrate my first time travel experience with at least a cup of coffee and a pastry."

"We're only halfway there. We have to make a safe return for it to be considered successful."

"Do we have to go back to the exact time? Couldn't we skip over all the mud and slush of spring break up?"

"Well, since I wanted to go to September tenth, 2015 for the 'big trip,' we might as well try a smaller increment in date deviation. How about a month – April sixteenth? That way, we can skip tax day."

"Sounds good to me. I sent my return in the first week in January, so I'm good."

***

One month later by the calendar
One hour later by biological clocks

"Well that worked out well," Silas said. "We're home." He rubbed his chin. "And we weren't even gone long enough for my whiskers to grow."

Julianna looked around and saw the cherry trees were blooming, all the ice and snow was gone, and a fresh flush of green grass was overtaking the golden-brown carpet of a dormant lawn.

Silas looked at Julianna, standing frozen as a Greek statue at the end of the driveway. "Was it that ridesharing car? I mean, we could have chanced it with hitching a ride but…"

"No, I'm just scared." She looked at the post that housed the security keypad. "They changed it."

Silas ran his fingers over the bricks. "Nice job of covering up the old bullet holes." He felt the side of the structure and noticed his override system was still there. Would it still work if a new mechanism had been installed? "Try the code. You do remember it, don't you?"

Julianna snorted a quick laugh. "It's only been a day, sweetheart. Dementia usually takes a while," she said then gasped, remembering how quickly Silas had lost his memory of Oscar. "Well, it usually does."

"Does that mean you're not going to ask me about yesterday again?" Silas asked, one eyebrow raised. "I mean, you haven't so far today."

"Actually, I'm not. Nothing but looking forward today. Oh, and just a suggestion. When we get a chance, we might look up the news highlights for the last month on the internet so we're current. I haven't lived in this era before. Who knows? Maybe something big happened?"

"Go for it," Silas said, pointing to the keypad.

She keyed in Tori's birthday and the gate swung open.

"Home again," Silas sighed. "Let's go see if the walls inside are still standing."

Before they got to the porch, Tori and Oscar were running down the drive to welcome them home, arms open, Tori squealing like the winner of a Miss America pageant.

"We were worried about you," Oscar said. "We went out there every day for two weeks, but Tori told me to chill out. If it was her, she'd wait until spring to come back."

Silas and Julianna looked at each other with suppressed grins of guilt. "Well, obviously it was a great idea, or she wouldn't have had it, too," Julianna said. "That's my girl."

"Oh, and speaking of your girl, how about legally gaining a daughter?" Oscar asked. "We want to get married soon. Like as soon as possible."

"What about your youth corps group?" Julianna asked, then

raised her hand to stop his answer. She looked at Tori again, this time carefully. "Let me guess, there's a reason you want it right away and part of it has to do with her taking it easy for the next what…eight or nine months?"

"See," Tori said, "I told you we wouldn't have to tell her, that she'd guess right away."

"Well, I always knew he wanted to marry you. I think I figured that out the first time I saw him beaming when he talked about you on the phone. You're positively brilliant with that pregnancy glow." Julianna looked at Oscar. "You are too, but yours is marred by a gray smear of doubt about how you'll do as a father."

"How…how did you know? I mean, I don't know if all guys feel like the same way, but I didn't exactly have the best role model in the world."

"Hey, I'm your mother, aren't I? I know everything about you. You'll be fantastic."

Silas watched the back and forth banter, content to be an observer, impressed by how a month had been spanned in less than a minute. Tori's boyfriend was going to be her husband. He was glad she had found someone. The young man…

'I'm your mother, aren't' I?' she had said.

He's Julianna's son? Silas's knees started to buckle. *That's why she keeps asking me about yesterdays.*

He took out his phone and opened up his calendar app. He quickly typed in 'Oscar is Julianna's son' and hit 'repeat as daily reminder.' Something was wrong with his memory, but not with his brain. He'd fix it right now, one way or another.

"Hey, Grandpa, isn't your birthday next week?" Tori asked.

"Um…"

"Today's April sixteenth," she whispered.

Silas took a breath and answered, "Then, yes. Well, a few more days than a week. It's April twenty-fifth."

"Cool. Let's have a party. And before you can say anything about getting older or whatever lame excuse you can scrounge up for not having a celebration, remember, it's the perfect way to get all our families together."

"I'll say okay to the party, but let's announce the wedding at the same time," Silas said.

"How about a compromise. Can we just tell *some* of them?" Tori asked. "Our *condition* is still a secret. I think my papa threatened to emasculate Oscar if he bedded me without being married first."

"Okay. I'll leave the wedding announcement part to you two." Silas sniffed under his arm and shook his head. "If you don't mind, I think I'll go freshen up. It's been a month since I've had a shower."

Julianna copied the movement. "Nope, it's not us. I think that car we came in had one too many air freshener trees in it."

***

"It's okay, Mama," Tori said. "We'll all be here, and that's all Oscar and I care about. White weddings are overrated. I think they're for the mothers of the brides, not the brides." She looked at the pile of bridal magazines her sisters had given her, leftover from their weddings. "Well, maybe some brides, but not me."

"I'm fine with it, too," Oscar said. "Everyone we care about is already here for Silas's birthday. Tori and I got the license and he's an ordained minister. Shoot, he already performed the ceremony for his other two granddaughters. Might as well make it all three sisters."

Leanne wiped her face again. "It's just you've always been my baby."

"And I always *will* be. That's not going to change. I wasn't going to say anything, but you're going to be a grandmother. You'll have babies to play with before you know it."

"Babies? You're having twins? Triplets?"

"I don't think so. I mean, I'm just a little bit pregnant..."

"No such thing," Luther said. "I'm glad I overheard it. It's the easiest way to find out." He looked over at Oscar and huffed. "I guess my threat can go out the window since you planned on marrying her anyway."

"We would have been married six weeks ago if we hadn't been waiting to make sure Silas was going to be okay. That seems to be his new bad habit, scaring the dickens out of us. First, the head injury and then a week later, disappearing just like that." Oscar snapped his fingers. "*Poof!* He and Mom, gone without a trace for a month."

"But they're back now," Tori said firmly, "so on with the show."

"Oh, and my mom wanted to add a little color to the event." Oscar handed a package to Luther and a bag to Leanne. "I guess you could say this is a costume wedding. No tuxes allowed, though."

Leanne looked in the oversized sack he had given her. "Oh, my! This looks just like my old hippie uniform!"

"She had them made based on what she remembered and the old photographs. Go ahead and change." Oscar looked at his watch. "Show starts in an hour."

Luther clutched his box close but didn't open it. "Come on, Rapunzel. I'll help you fix your hair. Here's hoping Julianna allowed for the few inches that forty years of your homecooked meals added on."

***

"Vickie! Ria! Grace! Oh, my God! Where's a camera. We need to get pictures of us," Tori said, squealing. "I haven't seen you in…in…"

"Since two months ago at Vickie's wedding," Grace said, "but to me, that's about fifty-nine days too long."

"Hey, Other Mom," Vickie said, "We all live within a couple of hours drive from each other. You pick the day of the month, and we can fill the calendar with rolling mothers-and-daughters reunions."

"Are you sure your moms won't mind?" Grace asked. "I mean, they brought you up…" She looked at Ria and grinned. "Well, except Ria. Chuck had help for a few years, so I guess I'm your only mother, even if I never changed a diaper or bandaged a scraped knee."

"Okay, Other Mom," Tori said sternly but with a smile, "I'm going to blame your moodiness on my pregnancy hormones. Knock it off, already. We all turned out fine."

"Yes, you did," Grace said, "but I have a few of my own lady-hormones kicking in. We're pregnant. Dusty and I are having twins…at least."

"No way…" Vickie said. "At your age? But you're going to be a grandmother in eight months."

"And you're getting little brothers and or sisters in seven. And hey, I'm only thirty-seven. I'm still plenty young enough to have at least one more pregnancy after this one."

"Depending on whether we want to go through more in vitro," Dusty said. "Hey, girls. Looking good in your sixties retro gear. How do I look?"

The girls' biological father, Dusty, a handsome brown-haired man, turned around in place, hippie beads dangling around his neck, full-sleeved pink paisley shirt, and hip-hugger bell-bottom pants covering his sockless sandals.

"Anyone up for a love-in?" Luther asked, announcing his presence. "Look at this." When he twisted back and forth, the fringe on his vest swung out nearly a foot. "I feel so groovy, man…" he drawled.

"Mama?" Tori gasped, seeing her mother standing in the doorway. "Your hair! It's so beautiful. Shoot, you could go as Lady Godiva and not get arrested for indecency. It's like a blanket over you."

"Her silver shield," Luther said softly. "Leanne, you're as gorgeous today as you ever were. No, wait. Even more so."

"Oh, you really should have that cataract surgery, Luther."

"No, my eyes are fine. The cloudiness is the gilding from loving you all these years, gold and silver streams of love, sparkling with memories of passion, joy, and tenderness. Of moments shared together, of everyday events made special by your nearness."

"Wow, Luther. You just kicked up the standard of saying sweet nothings to the ladies about fifty feet higher," Oscar said, Dusty and the other men mumbling agreement.

Luther looked at Oscar and winked. "You can call me Dad, Son."

"Thanks, Dad. I'll do that."

Chapter 17: A Woodstock Wedding

"Dearly beloved, we are gathered here today to witness the marriage of these two fine young people, my granddaughter, Tori Lynn Greene, and Oscar Rickman Shaw..."

A loud wail interrupted Silas. He paused to let Leanne compose herself. Luther was beside her, sniffling into a bright red bandana, patting her back with his free hand. His gentle reassurances, though, had gone astray. Leanne's knee-length hair – and the flowers and ribbons weaved into it – were now snarled with the beaded fringes of his vest. Grace, wiping her own tears on the puffy shoulder of her granny dress, was on Leanne's other side, trying to unknot the elderly couple. Her hands, though, were heavily bejeweled with costume jewelry. She was like Brer Rabbit and the Tar-Baby, now tangled in the mess as much as Luther.

Dusty had promised himself he would keep it together, letting the attention go to Luther and Leanne, the couple who had adopted Tori. His emotions had rejected the memo, though, and his lower lip was trembling, tears slipping through his lashes. To wipe them away would prove their existence. He sniffed and realized no one at the wedding cared whose blood ran through whom or which names were shared. They were all family. His family. He wiped his face on his pink calico shirt and hollered, "You go, Tori and Oscar!" hoping to give Grace time to straighten out Leanne and Luther.

"Tori! Oscar! Tori! Oscar!" the small clan joined in. Silas watched from his impromptu podium of a barstool seat stacked high with journals draped with a vibrant tie-dyed length of fabric. Pride bloomed warm in his chest. From over fifty years as an acknowledged bachelor to a member of such a diverse and passionate family. He took in the brilliance of Julianna, his special lady friend. Nearly a head taller than those around her, her long hair was accentuated with colorfully beaded braids, her grin showing she was as content with her collection of oddball relatives of choice as he was.

Silas turned back to Grace, Leanne, and Luther. When he saw they were no longer tied together, he raised his hands to silence the chanting. "As I was saying, my lovely granddaughter, Tori Lynn Greene, the daughter of Leanne and Luther Greene and a person most special to Grace and Dusty Rhodes; and Oscar Rickman Shaw, the son of Julianna MacKay Shaw, a person most special to me..."

Julianna's eyes sparkled as she clutched Dusty's other arm. "You tell 'em, Silas," she whispered.

"...to honor and respect each other, through good times and bad, whenever and wherever life takes you?"

"I do," Tori said.

"And do you..."

Did he just say whenever? Julianna looked at Grace and Dusty, then Luther and Leanne, then across the aisle to Tori's triplet sisters and their husbands. If anyone had heard Luther's unusual variation of the wedding vows, their faces didn't show it.

"I do," Oscar said.

"Then by the power invested in me by the Commonwealth of Massachusetts, I now pronounce you husband and wife."

The hugs, kisses, and crying overwhelmed the room, but it was Tori who called it back to order. "I have an announcement to make," she said, stealing a glance at Oscar, then fixing her gaze on Silas.

Oscar paled. He wasn't ready to announce his impending fatherhood yet. Tori's two sisters had already been married a few months and they weren't pregnant. He didn't want this to be a race.

"I just want to say a special thank you to my grandfather, Silas Priest, ninth-generation Mayflower descendent of Degory Priest. For those who know him, he's a man of many talents. But being clever or a great cook or exceedingly handsome..."

Tori paused, waiting for the anticipated laughs and applause to finish, then continued. "All these assets are pale in the rainbow of life when it comes to class. Oscar and I asked for a short ceremony. We wanted the service to be fun, with family and close friends, but legal. The way we figured it, the shorter the ceremony, the more

166

time for celebrating. But what he did in less than one hundred words was to acknowledge the two people who gave me and my two sisters life. And he did it without lessening the importance of the parents who brought us up. Who thought that something which started so grim could come together so beautifully? Thank you, Mama, Papa, Other Mom, Other Dad, and all my other biological and emotional family members."

Oscar looked at her with pride at her generous words, sighing in relief that she hadn't spilled the beans.

"Oh, and thanks, Grandpa," she said, interrupting the applause, "for giving my husband, me, and the rest of our family…" Tori patted her flat belly, "a home to stay in while you and Julianna go on your grand tour."

The group clapped, hollered, and whistled as Oscar turned beet-red, suffering the backslapping from his sisters-in-law's husbands.

"Don't worry about it, cousin," Rick said. "Vickie and I were waiting until after the hubbub of your wedding to announce our new addition."

"Um…" Evan interjected.

Rick and Oscar looked at the other newlywed husband who was now a sickly shade of puce. "I guess I can say something now, then," he said reluctantly. "Ria's pregnant. Surprise!" he added softly with a weak smile. "Oh, and I hope you guys don't get morning sickness, too."

"Is that what's wrong with you?" Rick asked.

"Uh-huh. Ria's fine, it's only me who's miserable. Our wives may not have known each other growing up or done things together then, but they're sure making up for it now."

"No kidding," Oscar said. "Oh, in case you haven't heard, Grace is pregnant, too. Silas is getting two – at least – grandchildren from her and Dusty, and then at least one each from his granddaughters."

"Yeah," Rick huffed. "All within a few months of each other. That's a lot of messy diapers."

Oscar started laughing, then shook his head and grinned broadly, recalling an earlier conversation with his mother.

"What's so funny about messy diapers?" Rick asked.

"Not that. I keep finding packs of condoms all over the house. I asked Mom if Silas was giving me hints or something. She blushed scarlet – which is hard to do when you're as dark as she is – and said they were for her and Silas. They…um…liked to be spontaneous and she is still fertile."

All three men burst out laughing, then turned to find Silas. He was still at the podium, speaking with Dusty. The three young men all gave him a thumbs up. "You're next, old man," Oscar shouted across the room.

Silas paled, knowing they were teasing him about becoming a father. He feigned a wide-eyed look of confusion. "Who are you?" he asked, then laughed before Oscar could reply. *"Que sera, sera,"* he added, not caring if his glimmer of anticipation shone through.

"What will be, will be," he said softly and smiled at Julianna. *Sometimes being careful doesn't work when you're a Fertile Ferdinand.*

Chapter 18: The Real Deal

Two weeks later

"Are you sure you don't want to wait a month?" Tori asked.

"Why? We already discovered we could play around with the calendar," Julianna said. "Besides, you don't want us running around this place, bumping into each other at, ahem, inopportune moments. There's no reason to confine yourselves to the guest house. If you're here all the time, you're just a few rooms away from work. I still think it would be easier if you converted one of the bedrooms into a second office. You don't need to share the same one."

"It feels more like a business this way," Oscar said. "You don't know how much paperwork is involved with getting people off the streets and settled into jobs and homes, finding medical services, and such. I can look up and ask her a question rather than sending an email."

Oscar stopped when he saw his mother look down her nose at him. "Hey, what can I say? I like being around my wife. I get the idea you and Silas enjoy each other's company a lot, too."

"Hmph. Just a little bit..." she admitted with an embarrassed grin.

Tori rose from her desk and moved into Julianna's arms. "I'm going to miss you, but I'm glad you have the opportunity to get closure. Who knows, when you go back to see your folks, maybe your sister will be there? You'll get two wishes for one."

"Three," Oscar corrected, coming to stand on his mother's other side. "She has two parents."

"Yes, she does," Tori said. "And I have..." she paused to count on her fingers, smirking at Julianna. "Even if I had a dozen mothers, I'm still going to miss you when you're gone."

"I'll miss you, too," Julianna replied. "Silas and I are leaving in the morning. He's getting the Caddie checked over and fueled up right now. Oh, and he's packing a few clothes and such in the trunk.

I don't think they'll get too stinky, sitting in a car for five years."

"Don't worry, Mom," Oscar said. "I'm sure Silas has already planned for that and has everything in an airtight container. I can't believe how selfless that man is. I swear everything he does is for someone else. Be sure to make time for something you know he wants to do, okay?"

"Absolutely."

***

Silas awoke at five-thirty as he always did. He looked over and saw Julianna, her eye twitching as she smiled in her sleep. He took his smartphone from the bedside table and opened up the calendar. Two items showed. 'Oscar is Julianna's son' and 'Departure Day.' *Her son? She has a son?* He noticed the little icon. At some point, he had set this as a daily reminder. *Crap! Am I getting senile?* Then he looked at the other event: Departure Day. *Now that, I remember. There has to be a reason for setting 'Oscar is Julianna's son' as a daily repeat. Best to trust myself and not delete that reminder.*

He put the phone back and snuggled into Julianna. As always, her arms pulled him close. "Mine," she whispered. He felt her tense then relax.

"Are you okay?"

"Oh, yeah. I just remembered what day it was," she answered, her smile growing as she sighed in satisfaction. "D-Day."

***

The ride to Bethel was an emotional patchwork of pained, awkward silences, giddy recollections of joyous past events, and soft-spoken words of hope. Once they were at the copse of oak trees – the site of the portal – their farewells began.

"I'm glad you let us bring you here rather than get a rideshare," Oscar said. "I knew where the site was because Tori and I came here looking for you when you didn't come back right away the first time." He shifted in his seat, took a deep breath, and looked at his mother. "Don't think I'm being weird or anything, but I want to see what it looks like when you *go*."

170

"Me, too," Tori said. "But what I really want to see is you coming back. Can you take a quick trip in and out – or is that back and forth? – for me? I mean, for us?"

"Tori, I don't know how many times I can do this," Julianna said. "It doesn't hurt, but what if it deteriorates the body somehow? You know, like wearing out your favorite shirt by washing it too many times? I want to be respectful of it. Just remember, today isn't a final good-bye but more of a 'see ya' later' farewell."

Silas reached out and put his arm around Oscar. "Make sure you take care of that great-granddaughter of mine and her aunts and cousins, too."

"You sound pretty sure we're having a girl."

"And my sisters and Other Mother, too?" Tori asked.

"Family tradition," Silas said. "You're all alpha females. From my experience with strong women, they only beget more strong women. I don't think you two could build a boy if you tried."

Oscar chuckled. "Oh, we'll try all right. Not to have a son, but to have a big family. We were both only children..."

Tori raised her hand and interjected, "Brought up as an only child. Sorry, Oscar. Go ahead."

"And as long as we can give our children what they need emotionally and physically, we want plenty."

"That's all well and good," Julianna said. "Just remember there are literally thousands of children out there without families. You can always bring a few of them into your lives. I know my parents did. I can tell you from my own experience, all of us – siblings, parents, and the foster and adopted kids – were happy with the arrangement."

Oscar looked at Tori. "Well, we'll save room for another build-it-yourself baby, just in case we get a second surprise."

Tori patted her belly. "Yes, she's a surprise, but not unwanted. You just chose your own time, didn't you, darling," she said looking down.

"They always do," Julianna said.

171

"One more hug and squeeze and then we're out of here. If I stay any longer, I'll want to go back to the house with you two," Silas said.

"Ah, Grandpa. You and I know you wouldn't let Julianna go anywhere without you."

"Oh, he would," Julianna said. "But not for long. One way or another, we'd find each other...even if it took twenty years or more."

***

"That's it? They're gone. They just walked through and disappeared?" Oscar asked.

"No, they didn't 'just' do anything. They had their coins and their focus. No wonder your mother wanted to keep them out of the hands of others. Someone with an evil agenda could create all sorts of chaos."

"Hey, Tori, did you ever wonder why they never found JFK's shooter? Someone could pull a disappearing act like that if there was a portal near Dallas."

Tori paled at the thought. She shook her head, stunned at the concept. "I don't even want to go there," she said. "I'm ready to leave. This place is sad."

"Only because they just left," Oscar said, holding her close, his hand stroking her back as if she was a skittish foal. "It'll be the happiest place on earth when they come back. Let's go home. Immersing ourselves in work and pasta should bring us out of this funk."

"I hope so," she said.

"Ah, there's your favorite four-letter word again, hope. Come on. We'll get an ice cream cone on the way home – drop-in or drive-through, your choice. That's better and faster than pasta."

"Deal."

***

"Um, since the leaves on the trees look a lot drier than they did when we started walking through them, I'd say we did it. At least for

172

a few months. Try the phones again?" Silas asked.

Julianna wiped sweat from her brow, then reached in her pocket and grabbed her cell phone. This trip through was different. She felt queasy. Here's hoping it was nerves and not some weird cellular breakdown. "Mine says, 'Multiple updates required,'" she said, stingy with her words in case her voice was as shaky as she felt.

"Twenty-three updates required before this phone is functional," Silas recited. "Hmm. I wonder if those folks still get the newspaper." He looked up the road. "They do. Race you there!"

"Nah, I'll save my energy," Julianna said, then looked for a boulder or barricade to sit on.

Silas pulled the newspaper out of the now faded red tube. "September seventh, twenty-fifteen." He folded it back up and returned it, chuckling. "Ah, five birthdays have passed, and I don't feel a day older."

"Just as sweet and sassy as ever," Julianna said, hoping she sounded brighter than she felt.

Silas jogged over to the guardrail and sat down beside her. "Tired?" he asked and reached out to hold her hand, surreptitiously checking her pulse rate. It was weak, but not dangerous. Her hands cool but not clammy.

"Do I pass the physical, Doc?" she asked, a smile in her voice.

"With a strong C, maybe a B minus. Bad case of nerves?" he asked.

"Yes, I'm pretty sure that's what it is," she answered, looking away so he couldn't check her eyes for signs of fibbing, or at least stretching the truth soap-bubble thin.

"Well, you sit there, and I'll see if I can get someone's attention." Silas tried mussing his hair, then realized it was too short to make a difference. He frowned and stuck out his bottom lip with an exaggerated pout, then looked at her, hoping to elicit an honest smile. "How's this? Do I look pathetic enough?"

She chuckled as much from his silly expression as from appreciating his effort. "Yeah, that'll steal a second look and get somebody's sympathy engaged. If you don't mind, I'll stay here. My height isn't so intimidating if I'm sitting down."

Several dozen cars and transport trucks later, a gold-colored minivan pulled over for them. Silas waved heartily, then grabbed Julianna's hand to help her up. The driver saw her struggle and put the vehicle in reverse, cutting the distance by half.

"Where to?" the dark-haired young man asked Silas. "Oh, and Mac doesn't take up much room. I can easily fit two more, even with his mega diaper bag."

"Destination Plymouth, Massachusetts, but anywhere east of here is a good start."

"He's adorable," Julianna said, letting the redheaded toddler grasp her finger.

The driver stomped on the brakes at hearing her voice, halting his access onto the highway. He looked in the rearview mirror, for the first time seeing the face of the tall woman. "Jane?" he asked.

Julianna's eyes opened to maximum width and her jaw dropped. She stared at the man. "Do I know you?"

A sly grin crossed his face. "I've never met you, but I might know your parents."

Julianna felt a warm glow of recognition begin. "Is that why you asked if I was Jane?"

He nodded. "Maybe I shouldn't say anything…"

"Um, do you two know each other?" Silas asked, his stomach turning flip flops with their sudden change from strangers to old buddies.

"He's never met me, but..." Julianna looked at Billy in the mirror again, then winked at Silas. "Did you say this little boy's name is Mac?"

"Nicknamed for his godfather," Billy said, smiling as bright as the rising sun on a clear summer day.

"Silas, our driver is Billy Burke Melbourne. Oh, and I'd like to introduce you to my older brother, Wee Mac." Jane bent and kissed him on the top of his head. "My da's surprise."

"Hold on, folks," Billy said, watching the traffic for another break. "This van's fueled up and we're heading to Plymouth! We're taking a detour, Mac."

Silas sat dumbfounded for a moment, the casual chatter between Billy and Julianna completely going over his head. "Can I interrupt you two for a minute? Julianna, would you give me just a mote of background, so I know what's going on?"

"I've known Billy since I was a child, probably younger than Wee Mac. They haven't met me because technically, I haven't been born yet. I'm still about two years from conception. Anyhow, my da and mom and Billy are old friends. When Da bought Mom from the eighteenth century through the portal near Greensboro... That was what, two years ago, Billy?"

"Only one," he said. "What a trip, your mother riding in an automobile for the first time. It was this one, too. But I'm hogging the story. Go ahead."

Julianna took a deep breath, happy to be able to speak freely of time travel, comfortable with the company she was with. "There's some big secret – which I really don't want to know about – of how Wee Mac came about, but his birth mother died just after he was born. They had already agreed to put Billy's name on the birth certificate as the father: no blood test required. Billy and his husband adopted Wee Mac without a problem. When all this happened, Da was in the eighteenth century, meeting Mom and catching up with his grandparents. He didn't even know he'd sired a child."

"Surprise," Silas said softly, then blushed at his lame joke.

"Yeah, well, when he and Mom came back, they worked everything out with Billy. Da is officially Wee Mac's godfather. I saw Billy and Wee Mac every year until I left..."

Now it was Julianna's turn to be uncomfortable, her words and excitement stilled with the memory.

Trying to spare her, Silas turned the topic of conversation sideways and the focus on the boy. "So, this is your half-brother?

He's a cute little fart."

"Fart," Wee Mac said, giggling at the new word.

"Pass gas," Billy corrected, then laughed. "Oh, what the heck. He's going to hear it plenty by the time he gets to school."

"And that's how come *you* know Billy," Silas said to Julianna, "but *he's* never met you. Wow. This is strange. No wonder you didn't want to say too much to each other at first."

"I just want to ask one thing. It's Julianna, right?" Billy asked, waiting for her nod. "Do I go bald?"

She chuckled. "No, you don't. In about eighteen years, you'll have the most intriguing silver streak running through your hair. And Wee Mac here…"

"Yes, yes…" Billy asked.

"He's going to be tall and smart, not necessarily in that order. And he'll have the most mischievous sense of humor. All I'm going to say about that is always look before you sit down. Peanut butter looks like something else when it's on the outside of your pants."

They all laughed out loud. Wee Mac repeated, "Pants," then stuck his thumb in his mouth and snuggled into his car seat, already worn out from the drive.

"Is Plymouth your final destination?" Billy asked, looking at Silas.

"That's where I live. We're picking up my car there and dropping in on the kids for a couple of days. That leaves us three to get to North Carolina. Julianna wants to be there by the tenth."

Silas noticed Billy frown, glance at his watch, then look up again.

"I hate to tell you, but today's the eighth," Billy said. "If you want to be in North Carolina, you're going to have to shave some time somewhere. We're about five hours out of Plymouth now. It's a long day or day and a half drive south from there to Greensboro. Even with two drivers, you'll have to take a few breaks. You'll have to make it a quick visit with the kids."

Silas took out his phone. Still no signal. "Damn," he hissed, then gasped in embarrassment and looked at the baby to see if he'd heard. The young mimic's eyes were shut, fluttering with dreams.

"Time travel mess up your apps?" Billy asked, nodding to Silas's phone.

"Yeah…"

"Here, use mine. The map function is already open. Go ahead and plug in your destination. I can reset it easy enough."

"So, Uncle Billy, what were you doing out here?"

Billy chuckled warmly at the designation. "I wanted to see where the original Woodstock Festival was before Mac and I started our first annual tour of Revolutionary War sites. His grandfather – yours, too – fought in the war, but I figured I'd just say he had ancestors involved in helping create the United States. Or something like that. In the last two years, I've found that no matter how hard you prepare, most of parenting is winging it."

"Ain't that the truth," Julianna said.

"Do you two have children?" Billy asked, looking from one to the other. He saw Julianna's face go blank, then quickly added, "Oh, wait. Don't tell me. If I'm going to see you sometime in the future, I don't want to know *anything*." He paused and added. "Well, except for the important stuff like whether I keep my hair or not."

She and Silas shared a grin, both relieved at not having to explain the complicated arrangement of Silas's daughter, granddaughters, and all those adopted parents and their spouses who made up their large but loving family.

Julianna brightened. She knew Silas had been on the sidelines of Grace's life, very much like her da's godfather relationship with Mac Melbourne. She ran her fingers through the sleeping boy's ginger hair. Strange but wonderful how things worked out. Her da's surprise, her half-brother.

"Benji and Jane's little girl," Billy sighed, then looked up at her in the rearview mirror.

Julianna heard him and caught his gaze. "Uncle Billy," she said. "Nice meeting you."

Chapter 19: Arrivals

September 8, 2015

"It doesn't look like anyone's here," Julianna said.

"You're being paranoid. I mean, cars aren't usually in the driveway when we get home." Silas got out of the van and walked around to the access panel and punched in the code. The gate swung open and he got back in.

"Go ahead and pull up to that side, if you will, Billy," he said. "We can go through the garage."

Billy glanced in the rearview mirror to see how Julianna was faring. She looked scared, nervous, *and* paranoid.

"Ow, JuJu," Wee Mac said, pulling up on her index finger to loosen her grip on his wrist.

"Oh, sorry, honey," she said and let go, gently patting his hand in apology.

"It feels like we're in an old sixties black and white TV series," Billy said. "All that's missing is the eerie music."

"Doo de doo doo…" Silas sang then got out again and reentered the code at the door.

"Do you want to come in and meet everyone?" Silas asked brightly.

"Um…maybe not," Billy said, glancing back at his son. "I don't know how to explain this to him. He's young but seems to pick up on a lot of what's going on."

"Do you think he'll want to be a detective like his daddy?" Julianna asked, her funk disappearing as she talked about her favorite 'kin,' as she always called Wee Mac.

Billy's chest puffed in pride. "I don't care what he does as long as he's honorable and does it because he wants to, not has to."

"Ah, spoken like the world's best dad." Julianna leaned in and whispered, "That's what he always called you."

He grinned, then his face fell. "What about Peter?" he asked

179

softly. "He's still around, right?"

Julianna's voice returned to normal. "Oh, he calls Uncle Peter 'the world's best pop.'"

He sighed in relief. "Thank you. I don't think I want to know even a little bit more. Too much room for misinterpretation. You have it from here, right?"

She looked around to make sure. "Silas. Silas? Where are you?"

The throaty hum of the Cadillac turning over let them know where he'd gone. "We're all set to go after we say hi to the kids," he shouted, standing beside his car.

"Then this is goodbye for at least two years," Julianna said. "Do me a favor, remind me of this when I'm about six or seven...or whenever you think I can handle it."

"How about four or five? I'll bet you're a bright little girl," he said, stepping out of the van to give a proper farewell.

She reached around and gave him a hug that ended with a hard kiss on the cheek. "You've just met me, but I haven't seen you in over twenty years. Weird how I miss you and yet I'm a stranger to you."

"Not weird at all," Billy said, giving her a hearty squeeze back. "I'm just grateful for the preview of what a wonderful woman you become. Take care of that man of yours. Something tells me he's a keeper."

"We met at Woodstock," she whispered. "But don't worry. It has nothing to do with you and your trip there. Oh," she gave him a firm kiss on the other cheek. "Give that one to Uncle Peter next time you see him. You don't have to tell him it's from me, though. I know when I'm sixteen, he still doesn't know about us and time travel. He suspects something's odd about our family but always shakes off hearing any details."

"So, I guess this means you're heading for your tour of historical sites with the young man, then," Silas said, offering his hand to Billy.

Billy shook it heartily. "Never too early," he said. "I figure if I start now, maybe it will make it more personal to him later."

"Just like giving skis to a two-year-old," Silas said.

"Yup, that's on the list of winter activities in a few months," Billy said. "Take care of this woman. I probably won't see her as an adult again."

"Yes, but you'll love me as a little girl."

Billy reached up and wiped at his new-sprung tears. "I have to go. I don't want to even think about telling Mac why I'm crying. It's going to be hard enough to tell him who you are."

"Just tell him we were nice hitchhikers," Silas said. "Nice meeting you, and thanks for the ride."

Billy nodded, then got back in the van. "Come on, sport. Time for American History 101, the Pilgrims and the Mayflower. The Revolutionary War will have to wait a while."

Julianna waved goodbye, surprised she wasn't crying but Billy was.

"Are you all right?" Silas asked.

"Yeah. Seeing him is like a vibrant dream, the kind where you have to pinch yourself to find out if you're awake or not. He was here, but he wasn't."

"But you'll see him again, right?"

"Yeah. Hey, let's go scout around and find out where Tori and Oscar are. I want to see if I have a granddaughter or a grandson."

Ten minutes of calling out plus a thorough investigation of the garage and guest house revealed a large playroom with lots of children's toys plus three single beds and a crib distributed between three bedrooms.

"Five years and four children?" Julianna asked. "My boy's been busy."

"Your boy?" Silas asked. "You have a son? I thought we were here for Tori and her husband, Oscar. Didn't I just marry them just a few days ago? I mean, a few days before we left?"

Julianna groaned deep in her throat, holding back the scream of frustration. *I thought that 'forget Oscar' crap Simon had brainwashed and fairy-dusted him with had worn off. Is time travel screwing him up again?*

"Silas, I'm going to tell you again," she said slowly and deliberately, "Oscar is my son. Okay? Please don't forget. Again."

"You said again twice. Does that mean I forget all the time? Sorry, I'm sure it does. Do I forget anything else or just that? I'd hate to think I have dementia."

"No, just that," she said, easing up on her severe tone. "Excuse me, that sounded rude. Let's leave a note for them then go. It's really sad being here in an empty house. I'm sure there's a good reason, though."

"Well, dear," Silas said, "from what I see, I bet they're having another baby. The nursery is stacked with newborn-sized diapers and clothing, and the other three bedrooms look like the children's maid hasn't been here for a while."

"They'd never have a maid."

"Exactly. If *your son,* Oscar, has been busy tending to three youngsters and a very pregnant wife, I doubt he'd care if the older children made their beds or not. He'd be more concerned if they were clean and well-fed."

Julianna chuckled, remembering her mother when the twin boys were born, dealing with her and Mali at the same time. "Semi-clean and at least fed cereal with milk," she said. "Don't forget to leave a note."

Silas stepped into the playroom filled with building blocks, toy cars, and a shelf unit of art supplies. He shuffled through that and found a tablet with paper pre-printed with picture-framed edges. He tore a piece from it then set the pad back. He wrote on the back of the page in blue ballpoint pen, 'Sorry we missed you. Grandpa'

Silas chewed on the end of his pen as he stared at the note, trying to remember what else he was supposed to say. He saw a picture on the table drawn by a child. It was a red-crayon rendition of a person with sticks for arms and legs, lots of straight-lined fingers, and a big circle for a belly. 'MOM' was written at the top of it.

"Oh, yeah," he whispered and added 'and Mom' after Grandpa. "Don't forget again. Oscar is her son, Oscar is her son," he repeated then wrote it on the inside of his wrist. He turned to leave and saw Julianna, standing in the hallway.

"Check it out." He picked up the picture from the table and handed it to her.

"Mom," she read. "Oh, my God! Her child drew a picture of Mommy. Tori's pregnant again."

"And that's why they're gone. I'd say they've been *very* busy."

She handed it back. "Leave the note somewhere you know they'll find it and let's go." She sniffed back tears. "I'll meet you in the car."

Silas went to the kitchen. A young family always seemed to visit the fridge more than any other place. He looked at the refrigerator door, already covered with children's art. He resisted the urge to take the drawing of a blue dog – or horse or hippo – for himself but did use one of the fruit-shaped magnets to affix his note to the door. As he was leaving, he saw it. A plate of brownies.

"Bet you can't eat just one," he said, lifting the plastic cover and taking a piece. He popped it in his mouth, then grabbed two more. "One for my Jules and one for the road. Thanks!"

***

At that same moment, across town

"Just one more push and she's outta there," Oscar urged. He turned back and looked into the hall. "Okay, kids. Do you want to see your sister come out?"

"Nah, we're good," Hope said. "Hey, boys, I'll trade you this doll for one of those cars."

Huff, huff, huff, huff. "Leave-them-out-there," Tori blurted as one word, then pushed. "Catch!"

The midwife was ready but had to nudge Oscar out of the way when he leaned in at the last minute. "Excuse me, Dad," she said.

"Oh, sorry." He stepped back, then looked over her shoulder,

183

biting his lip with a mixture of fear, eagerness, and excitement.

"One more push…" the midwife said.

"I-know-I-know," Tori grunted.

"And there she is." The midwife pulled the baby out the rest of the way. "Well done, Mom. Another perfect little girl." She suctioned the birth fluids from the baby's nose and mouth then set her on Tori's belly and bent to finish her work.

Two minutes later, the baby was cleaned up and swaddled in flannel, ready to meet the rest of the family. "Here you are, Dad," the doula said.

Oscar sniffed, unbidden tears dribbling down his cheeks just like when he'd held Hope for the first time. "Do we want to name her now or later?" he asked, then handed her to Tori.

"Ah, she's so cute," Tori answered, ignoring his question. One hand on her new daughter's back, Tori leaned to one side and looked out the door. "Let's get me cleaned up a bit more before bringing them in. As long as they're not *too* quiet, they're good."

"It's okay to be sad. I miss my mom and Silas, too," Oscar said. "They'll be back. You just have to have faith."

Tori grunted, partly from an afterbirth pang, mostly from hormone-enhanced anger. "We have other things to consider. Did you hear from my dad today?"

Oscar shook his head and bit his bottom lip. "He said there wasn't any cell service out there. Next time he was in a town, he'd call. If he knew this one was coming early, they never would have started the tour."

"Yeah, well, I told them to go ahead. The baby would come with or without them. Dammit." Tori saw his wide-eyed but silent admonishment. "Dammit because I told them to go when I should have asked them to wait. I love you and the kids, but for once, I'd like a grandparent here when a baby was born."

***

Two hours later

"Okay, kids, I'm fixing dinner again. Do you want chicken

184

salad, scrambled eggs with veggies, or tuna surprise?"

"What's tuna surprise?" three-year-old Andrew asked.

"Yeah, huh?" his twin added.

"It's canned tuna with mayonnaise and the same vegetables I'd use for the chicken salad or eggs. You just get to choose your protein."

"Rock, paper, scissors," Hope said. "One, two, three."

Hope's open-handed paper gesture covered Jamison's and Andrew's rocks. "Okay, Dad. Let's go with the chicken tonight. Need help?" the perpetually helpful girl offered.

"Nah, I got this. Why don't you take the boys in the playroom and build something?" Oscar asked.

"Sure thing." She pulled the new piece of paper off the fridge with one deft tug. She'd color the back of it so she wouldn't have to bother Dad to get the tablet down from the top shelf. "Come on, guys. You build the castle and I'll be the princess in the tower."

***

"I'm sure this is the way," Silas said, rubbernecking to get a better glimpse at the street signs whizzing past.

"It doesn't look the same," Julianna said. "I think we should have taken a left at that exit in Trenton this morning. Why don't you pull over and ask at the gas station?" She looked over his shoulder at the gas gauge. Seeing it was still half full, she changed her tactic. "I need to make a pit stop, anyhow."

"Can you wait just a little bit longer..."

"No. I'm uncomfortable. Please, just let me take three minutes to pee and for you to ask the way to Lynchburg. From there, I know it's pretty much due south without any interchanges."

"I'm sorry. Look, I'll pull in here and check the map again. Would you get me a big cup of coffee when you're done?"

Julianna huffed then changed it into a cough. "Sure. Black?"

"Add a little cream and a lot of sugar, if you would. I don't want to take the time to stop for lunch." Silas looked up, realizing he had unintentionally made another decision without asking her.

185

"Unless you'd like to?"

"I'll grab something when I get the coffee."

Julianna splashed water on her face after she'd used the bathroom and washed her hands, hoping to perk herself up. She was tired but had dozed just outside of Plymouth. Poor Silas had been driving for over twelve hours. He'd been up for at least thirty-six.

She grabbed the first sandwich she saw from the shelf and fixed a tall super-sweet coffee with extra cream in it for him. If he wasn't going to eat, at least he'd have calories to run on. "Excuse me, sir," she said to the convenience store clerk. "Can you tell me how far we are from Lynchburg?"

"Quite a ways, ma'am. Once you get to Richmond, you can follow the signs and take Highway Sixty right to Lynchburg."

"Whoa, wait. Richmond?"

"Yes, ma'am," he said. He took out the oft-refolded map from under the counter and pointed to the red circle. "We're here. Richmond's just a few miles south, and then you take Sixty over to Lynchburg."

She unfolded the map one more section. "Or we can keep going south on Eighty-five and hit Greensboro without taking any exits. Thanks," she said, handing him a twenty-dollar bill. "Keep the change. You just made my day."

"Back at ya, lady," he said, pushing up his Dallas Cowboys ball cap. "You made mine, too."

Julianna walked up to Silas's side of the car, handed him the coffee, then came around and got in. "Good news and bad news. We took the wrong exit way back around Trenton. Good news is if we stay on this road, we'll wind up in Greensboro. From there, I could find my way blindfolded. Let's not worry about that yet, though. Drink up. I don't know if my stomach's burning from excitement or fear, but I have tuna on wheat and a box of milk. I'm ready to roll."

"Me, too," Silas said, then put the Caddie in drive. "Me, too."

186

Chapter 20: The MacKay Manse

Outside of Greensboro

Silas slowed as he approached the destination. "It's up ahead. You can see the roof from here."

"Stop, stop, stop," she said. "I know where we are now, for sure. I'm not ready yet. Pull in under those trees. That's where the state stockpiled rock for road repair."

"By the looks of it, they still do. Do you need a moment?"

"Yes. I want to take it all in. I mean, you know how a surgeon steadies himself, sort of prepares before he goes into to do an appendectomy or whatever?"

"I know the principle. Priests and preachers pray, actors meditate, athletes stretch…"

"Okay, okay. You got it. Roll down all the windows and turn off the engine. I want to hear the sounds of this place."

Silas did as she asked, then listened with her. The gentle squawks and chirps of birds, the rustling of grasshoppers in the weeds, and the wind blowing through the dried bamboo peppered the otherwise stillness. "Not so quiet, eh?" Silas whispered.

Julianna turned in the seat, the squeaks of the cushion against her clothing suddenly seeming loud. "Amazing, isn't it?" he added.

"You see that stand of bamboo? Da's going to transplant it to our place as a windbreak. I think he did it so he could watch us from the house and make sure he knew where we were. Not that he needed line of sight. All Mom had to do was listen for us. That woman could hear a cockroach fart."

Silas chuckled. "I'd sure like to meet that woman."

"You will…if all goes right. Okay. I'm ready. Let's go."

Silas started the Cadillac and pulled back onto the two-lane road. "And there it is."

"Oh, my God," Julianna gasped in horror. She looked at the shabby, weather-beaten building then at the phone's map again.

"That's it? I mean, it has to be, but really? That's the MacKay Manse?"

Silas glanced at his map, then up at the number scrawled on the paint can lid wired to the fence. "Indeed, it is. You did say your father bought this place as a fixer-upper, right?"

"Yeah, but... Wow, I have a new respect for all the work he put in. I never saw pictures of the original place. Man, what a dump!"

"Meh," Silas mumbled. "Nice big chunk of land. Looks like there's some water down that way, too."

"A creek that runs all year. How'd you know?"

Silas grinned. "The green trees. Everything else is parched. I'd say by the dry vegetation that it's quite verdant in the spring and summer."

"What?"

"By the height and density of these weeds, the water had to come from somewhere. Since I didn't see irrigation equipment or ditches and furrows, I'd say it was from natural rainfall."

"I'm always amazed at how much you see and how little most people do. Hey! There's a car out front. I don't know who that is, but I'll bet it isn't my parents. Keep going up to the next driveway and park about halfway down. That's commercial acreage and no one's ever there except when it's time to seed or harvest."

Silas pulled in and shut off the engine. "Stay put. I'll go see who it is." Not hearing a reply, he looked and saw her eyes were wide in fear. "Hey, I got this, okay?"

Julianna nodded, dozens of scenarios going through her head, none of them good.

The noise of the idling muscle car parked out front covered the sounds of Silas wading through the tall grass and weeds toward the house.

From the edge of the overgrown field, he watched as a red-haired man – even taller than Julianna – pulled the rickety screen door off its hinges and stepped inside. Now more curious, Silas ran to the house and stood beneath the window, listening. The man was

188

angry, cursing in Swedish or Norwegian. He caught a word. Norwegian. The intruder's heavy footfalls headed for another part of the house. Silas stuck his head through the glass-less window and peeked inside.

He was in the kitchen now, looking up. *Whoosh!* Silas watched as the man jumped into the attic – no stairs or ladder required. *Thump!* More curse words, boxes and or furniture being kicked around, and then running steps. Silas moved back into the brush and watched as the man leaped out of a window at the back of the house, as agile as a cat jumping off a three-foot fence. The man dusted off his hands, strode back to his bright-yellow Camaro without so much as a backward glance, and sped off.

Silas stood up, looked inside again, then headed back to Julianna and the car. This had to be Mali's ex-beau Storm, looking for coins. If it was, Julianna might be in danger.

Julianna and the car were gone! Returning to the house – hoping she had driven around to pick him up – Silas heard a vehicle approach. It wasn't his Cadillac or the Camaro, though. It sounded like a truck.

Two tall men got out of the huge late-model pickup, both redheads. *What is it with all these giant red-haired men?* The one with fairer skin was leaning through the truck's open window. "…Just hit the horn if ye need me."

Silas moved aside, hoping for a better look. *Yes! With that accent, it must be Benji. And he's speaking to Jane. Yes! Yes! Julianna's parents are both here. She's going to be ecstatic… Oh, shit! Where'd she go?*

He backtracked to where he had parked. She still hadn't returned nor had she moved the car further up the driveway. *She'll come here eventually, I know she will. I hope she will.* He looked up again and saw Jane, sitting by herself in the truck, fanning herself with a magazine. Time to make an introduction.

Silas wiped his face with the shoulder of his shirt, ran his fingers through his hair, then took a deep breath. *Like a Priest before a sermon.* He chuckled at the play on names, then walked up to the side of the truck.

"Hi, I'm…" he began, then stopped when he saw how scared she was. Jane scooted away from the window, her eyes wide, little gulps confirming her fear. She reached out and smacked the steering wheel, pounding it everywhere, finally finding the horn button.

"I'm sorry I frightened you," Silas said, then moved away.

"Step away from my wife!" Benji bellowed as he strode towards him.

"I'm sorry. I'm truly very sorry," Silas said, taking two more steps back. "She looks so much like my fiancée. I mean, my friend," he stammered. "Well, I was going to ask her to marry me soon. Very soon. Maybe even this evening." He paused and took a deep breath, oblivious to the rage in the fairer man's eyes. He squinted at the other man again, wondering who he could be, then shook his head. *Sleep deprivation. Are there really two Benjis or am I hallucinating?*

Trying to compose himself and restart the conversation on neutral ground at the same time, Silas looked up at the dilapidated house in awe. "She said this was the place."

"Who did?" the darker Benji without the Scottish accent asked.

Silas looked from him to the man he was certain was the real Benji, verifying they were two different people. Their physical forms were very similar. Other than the accent, they even sounded alike. One had African heritage, though, and the other did not. Or not enough to show.

"Just a sec," the man without the accent said. He stepped between Silas and Benji and opened the truck door for Jane.

"I've never met anyone who looks like me," she said, her hand on second man's arm as she gracefully straightened to her full six-foot-four inches.

Silas half-smiled, half-grimaced in return. "Your children look like you," he said sheepishly, shrugging a shoulder.

Jane's legs buckled, but the second man was ready and reached out for her, pulling her close so she could compose herself.

"My mother?" the man asked softly, his eyes bright with excitement.

Silas watched confusion overtake the second man's features but was unsure of what to do or say, so stayed mum.

"My mother was here?" he asked again, shaking his head. Then his indignation and voice exploded. "You know my mother?" he shouted at Silas.

Silas's mouth opened and shut, fatigue and uncertainty slowing his explanation.

The man snorted, frustrated at not getting an immediate reply. "Well?" he bellowed.

Silas looked at Benji to see his reaction.

Previously angry, Benji's rage had now been replaced with a mixture of puzzlement and fascination. Now it was his turn to shrug. "What he asked," he said, nodding to the other man. "Answer him."

"Let me back up a little. Or a lot, depending on how we're measuring *time*," Silas said.

Jane and the men looked back and forth between each other with an identical curiosity.

"*When* did you come from?" the non-Benji male asked.

"2010. Just a short five-year hop forward. Oh, forgive me for not introducing myself. I'm Silas Priest from Massachusetts."

"What are you doing here?" the man asked, continuing the interrogation.

"Now, before I answer a lot of questions – and I will answer them all," Silas said in his most congenial but no-nonsense tone, "may I have the pleasure of knowing your names?"

"Mac MacKay. This is Benji MacKay and..."

Mac paused his introduction and stared as Silas went ga ga, back gazing at Jane.

Silas felt himself grinning as if he'd just met a movie star. "So, it is you, isn't it?" he asked. "I mean, do I have the pleasure of meeting Jane MacKay?" He picked up her hand, not sure whether to shake it or kiss it.

"Am I supposed to know you?" she asked and stepped back, holding her hands behind her.

"I never had the honor," Silas said, "although I've heard what a charming and beautiful woman you are. Yes, your beauty is beyond description…"

Benji stepped between Mac and Jane, mumbling an 'excuse me' to Mac. "Ye'd better not be makin' a pass at my wife, especially with me standin' right here," he said, his arm around her protectively.

"Oh, I'm so sorry. I think that came out wrong. I haven't slept in nearly forty-eight hours. Julianna and I drove all night and day from New England." Silas looked back to the porch. "If you don't mind, I'm a bit light-headed, sleep-deprived, dehydrated… What I'm trying to say, is can we sit on the porch? A bit of shade would be welcome."

Mac came up to Silas and helped him to the porch as Benji moved some barrels around to serve as seats. "Hush about Julianna for now, all right?" Mac whispered.

Silas took a deep breath and nodded. "Who are you? I feel like I'm in a dream."

"You're not. I'm Mali's son, Julianna's nephew. Benji and Jane are my grandparents, and yes, I'm from your future. Kick back and chill for a bit. The show is about to begin."

Silas leaned against the wall. Jane was next to him, a stoic look on her face as she watched a small sports car come up to the house. Soon, Mac and Benji were speaking to a short man with a toupee, discussing the purchase price of the property. Words flowed in and around Silas, dreams stumbling over reality, events and conversations distorted by lack of sleep and too much sugary caffeine. His head jerked up from a slumped over position several times, then the scent of Julianna brought him about.

"Do you smell that, too?" he asked Jane.

"I do," she said. "It smells like flowers."

Benji sniffed, turning his head to follow the scent carried on the gentle breeze. "It's coming from down there," he said.

Mac jumped over the steps and picked up a pink floral scarf. He sniffed it. "It smells like lilies of the valley."

"Actually, it's a perfume called Lily of Lourdes," Silas said, accepting the piece from him. "Put your hands out," he said.

Mac gave him a quizzical look but did as he was told.

"I don't have a worktable," Silas said. "If something's in here, it will fall into your hands, not onto the ground."

"Sounds like you've done fieldwork before," Mac said.

"My nickname's Sherlock. I guess it's considered a hobby since I've never charged for my services," he said and carefully unwound the fabric.

Benji and Jane watched the proceedings. "There!" Jane said. "Look, there's something written on it."

"Coins 4 J," Silas read. He folded it in half and shook it over Mac's hands, hoping a scrap of evidence would drop. "There! Grab it before the wind catches it."

Mac held onto one long curly dark-brown hair. "Do you recognize the scarf?" he asked, looking at Silas.

"It's Julianna's. So is the hair, I believe. It must have flown out when the window was rolled down."

"Let's put this whole conversation on pause fer a moment," Benji said, looking between Silas and Mac, then back at Jane to make sure she understood his reference. She nodded that she did. "I asked ye before and we were interrupted by me makin' the agreement to buy this place, so I'm asking ye again: who is Julianna to me and my wife?"

Silas turned to Mac, one eyebrow raised, asking, 'Which one of us should answer?' Mac shrugged, so Silas replied. "She's your daughter. And also my fiancée or girlfriend, depending on her answer…when I get a chance to ask her."

"I thought Mali was our daughter," Jane said, her hand gently touching her lower belly.

"They both are," Mac said.

"Julianna's your second born," Silas added. "By the clock, I met her six months ago. By the calendar, it was five years. She came back from 2032 to 1989, looking for Mali. She's never found her as far as I know. I mean, I re-met her at a wedding. We recognized each other from Woodstock in 1969."

"But you just said she went to 1989, not 1969," Benji said.

"She took a detour, looking for Mali. It didn't pan out," Silas said. He looked at Mac, his new associate detective. "Does 'Cash 4 J' mean anything to you?"

"You really need to get some sleep, Silas," Mac replied. "It says coins, not cash. Big difference."

"Especially when it comes to time travelers, aye?" Benji said.

Silas groaned softly and shook his head.

"What?" Mac and Benji asked at the same time.

"Julianna and I had a drachma for each of us. She said she had hidden a bag of them here at the MacKay Manse a long time ago. That's the other reason we were coming here – to get them."

"Well, where are they hidden?" Benji asked. "We'll give him those and get her back."

"It's not that easy," Silas said. "Even as ditzy as I'm feeling right now, I don't believe he really has her. I think this is a fake ransom note, meant to make us retrieve the coins for him."

"If he doesn't have her, where could she be?" Benji asked.

"Maybe they're still here. Where did the girls hang out when they were younger?" Mac asked Jane, then winced in embarrassment. "Shoot! I'm sorry. They haven't even been born yet. You wouldn't know, would you?"

"Well, maybe I would," Jane said with a sly grin. "If I lived here as a child – and I did over two hundred years ago – I'd be out there at the trees, playing in whatever water was available, enjoying the shade."

"Now that's some clever thinking," Silas said. "Let's go find Julianna."

Benji paused and mused, "Julianna."

194

"I've never heard that name before," Jane said, "but I like it."

"It reminds me of a dear friend, my Uncle Wallace's stepfather," Benji said. "Julian Hart. Yes, even if ye hadna told me about it, I'd lean toward choosing the name Julianna fer a second daughter."

"Then let's get moving and see what we find at those trees," Silas said. "And if Julianna's there, the second thing I'm going to do is ask her to marry me."

"What's the first thing?" Mac asked.

"Make sure she's all right and not in danger."

Twenty feet from the trees, they all heard it. Giggles from two females coming from up high in the branches, and then a 'shush' admonition. "Someone might hear us," one voice whispered.

"Julianna!" Silas hollered, running to the source, ignoring Mac's warning to be discreet.

Thump!

Julianna dropped out of the trees. "Shush!" she repeated. "He might still be here."

"Who?" Silas whispered.

She looked around to see if he was alone, then saw three people come forward slowly, each one staring at her as if she had a purple horn sticking out of her forehead. "Mom? Da? And who are you?"

Thump!

Another woman dropped from the branches, also agile despite her forty-something years. Mali.

Silas inspected Julianna, patting her shoulders, pausing his wellness check to cup her cheeks, and ask, "Are you sure you're all right?"

Benji held Jane close as they watched, stunned. They were seeing their daughters for the first time as adults, completely passing – and missing – their infant through teen years.

Silas was down on one knee. "You're sure you wouldn't mind being married to an old man with gray hair?"

Julianna squealed again and this time, grabbed him by the

195

elbows and pulled him to his feet. "Gray hair, blue hair, or no hair – yes! I want to marry you."

Silas heard Mali and Mac bickering. Something about Storm and a legend or a curse pertaining to a son. He didn't care. From what he understood, Mac was Storm's son. It was his and Mali's problem. Julianna was here with her parents and they could reconcile. Mali was safe and – after a few days or hours of reconnecting and apologizing or whatever time traveling families did at reunions – he and Julianna could return to good old 2010, Grace, Tori, her sisters, and all those babies that were due before summer of 2011.

"Excuse me," Silas said, putting on his peacekeeper's shawl. "If I may offer an observation. If the legend is true, I would think that this Storm person would try to eradicate all of his progeny, not just Mac. Julianna, how do you know he has another heir?"

"Because he's my son."

"You have a child?" Silas asked, his voice ending on a high note of surprise.

"Not again!" Julianna hissed. Her eyebrows narrowed and she bent to look him in the eye, determined once and for all to permanently impress the fact somewhere in his pickle-loaf brain. "You know him. A few months ago, you performed his wedding ceremony. Remember Oscar, your granddaughter Tori's husband?"

"Oscar, yes. But he's white..."

"Ergh!"

Silas put up his hand, hoping to calm her, then noticed the inside of his wrist. 'Oscar is J's son' was written so only he'd see it. "Do I have dementia?" he asked.

"No. It's complicated," Julianna said, resigned to a life of constant reminders. "Let's just say you had some selective hypnotism and I can't seem to reverse it."

"Oh, that's easy enough. Maybe I should get this tattooed, then?" he asked, showing her his penned crib note.

Julianna laughed. "No. How about if I just stick around and try not to get bitchy when you forget? Oh, and maybe update your phone so it'll show up on your daily calendar. Worked before."

Chapter 21: Homecoming

Twenty-four hours later

"Are you sure you don't want to go back to 2010? You're positive about staying in 2015?" Silas asked. "I mean, it is the only way you can catch up with everyone. Storm's neutralized. Benji and Jane have a plan. Mali and Mac are sticking around to help them build the MacKay Manse. I guess we could return to the time you left, but I'd be totally lost. At least, for a while. It would be pretty odd arriving in 2032, though. You left as a sixteen-year-old and if you suddenly showed up…"

Julianna cleared her throat and said, "Older?"

"That's a good way to put it."

"I'm positive. True, we'll miss Tori and Oscar's first years of parenthood, but I'm sure they took lots of pictures. I don't care how we explain being gone. Maybe we can tell everyone else we got stranded on a desert island."

Silas shook his head. "You look too good. I think we'd either be emaciated or wrinkled from too much sun, rather than looking like it was only yesterday – not five years ago – since we'd left."

"This should be easy then. All we have to do is drive north to get on with our lives. No trip through any time portal trees required," she said.

"Just a few hours of drive time and a couple of tanks of this era's high-dollar unleaded gasoline. Oh, and a new driver's license next month for you."

"Expired already? That I can handle."

"Especially since you'll need a new one anyhow."

"Why?"

"Because you told me you'd marry me. I was sort of hoping you'd take my name."

"Julianna Priest. Sounds good to me."

"Me, too. Come on. One more round of farewell hugs and kisses, and we'll hit the road. Our next MacKay family reunion should be a lot easier to manage."

"And I'll get to see Uncle Billy again!"

***

The next day

"Hey, I know who you are," Hope said. "You're my other grandma." She looked at Silas. "And you're my other grandpa! Hey, guys, our other grandma and grandpa are here."

Two little boys, their skin as dark as obsidian, their faces identical except for the odd shapes of their heads, bounded into the room. "Hi, Other Grandma and Other Grandpa," they said, chattering over each other.

"Go ahead and give them a hug," Hope directed. She saw their reluctance and huffed. "Like this, guys." She reached around Julianna's knees and squeezed tight, almost toppling her. Silas saw what was coming, and as soon as the young girl neared him, held onto Julianna to steady himself.

"When we dropped in a while back, I saw something with Hope written on it. Is that your name?" Silas asked, now squatted down to her level.

"You were here?" she asked. "We didn't see you. Were you playing hide and seek and forgot to tell us?"

"No, I left a note and put it on the refrigerator. Oh, and I took a few of those brownies," Silas said. "They were delicious," he whispered.

Hope heard her father come into the room. "See! I told you I didn't eat them," she said.

"Mom? Silas?" Oscar said, tears welling. "Oh, thank God you made it. I was afraid you were going to stay and we'd never see you again."

"Stay? We're all in the same time now," Julianna said. "We were in North Carolina, visiting my family there."

"So, you had a chance to catch up with your parents?" he asked, sniffing and patting his pockets for a handkerchief.

"Here, Daddy," Hope said, handing him a box of tissues.

"And my sister," Julianna said, stepping around the little boys to hug Oscar. "Oh, how I missed you and it was less than a week for us." She looked down at the children, wide-eyed with wonder at the new people who were making Daddy cry.

"Oh, and no doubt you've already met Hope. You were right about little alpha females. She runs the house if Mom and Dad are busy."

"You're always busy," Hope said. "But that's okay. At least you're always here," she added, looking up at Silas with a scowl of reprimand that quickly turned into a giggle that sounded just like Tori's.

"Oh, and here are the boys, Jamison and Andrew," Oscar said, putting a hand on each of their shoulders.

"Yeah, look at this," Hope said. "Do it, guys."

The boys stood side by side then bent their necks toward each other, matching the tops of their heads. The odd shapes meshed almost perfectly.

Oscar shrugged and grinned sheepishly. "They were conjoined twins. Abandoned at a hospital in Haiti. We sponsored them as foster parents for about..." Oscar paused and nodded to Hope, giving her the go-ahead to finish the story.

"About two minutes and then I said we should keep them forever." She put her hands on her hips. "It might be the only way I'd get brothers. But even if my baby sister had been a boy, I wouldn't give them back for nothin'!"

"You have a baby sister?" Julianna asked.

Hope dashed to the refrigerator and took the yellow magnet with googly eyes off her masterpiece. "See, there's six of us now," she proclaimed. "And I can write my whole name now, too."

She gave him her crayon-created picture of a stick figure family. There were three children, a dad, and a mom holding a baby, all standing under a rainbow of at least ten colors and signed Hope Priest.

"That's you?" Silas asked. "Your name?"

"Uh-huh."

Silas looked at Oscar, one eyebrow raised.

"Hey, now you can't forget who I am, right, Dad?"

"Is he Dad or Other Dad?" Hope asked.

"Doesn't make a difference," Silas said, "as long as Dad's in there somewhere."

"Just made it easier with this place and all," Oscar whispered. He looked up and saw his mother's sterned-face silent admonition and grinned sheepishly. "Well, as long as we're all being honest, Tori and I both wanted to honor you. And thank you for all you've done for us. Plus, I never really had an emotional bond with Hugh's heritage. He was constantly scolding and belittling me for not being man enough to carry on the Shaw last name. And so I'm not."

"Well, I can tell you now, I'm highly honored," Silas said, pulling Oscar close and patting him on the back, sniffing back tears.

"Oh, and check out the back of this masterpiece," Silas said, turning over Hope's family portrait.

Oscar gasped. "Why didn't I see this? 'Sorry we missed you. Grandpa and Mom.'"

"Oops," Hope said.

Oscar ruffled her hair. "Don't worry about it. Just ask before using paper with writing on it, okay?"

Silas grinned at the gentle parenting. "So, where are your mother and sister?" he asked Hope.

"We're right here," Tori said.

A bedraggled woman, barely recognizable, was leaning against the bottom of the stairwell. Wrapped in an oversized pink terrycloth bathrobe, a small flannel-wrapped bundle over her shoulder, she looked like she'd had a rough time, her face puffy from crying.

Silas enveloped her with a cautious hug, gently kissing the top of her unkempt hair as if he'd found a long-lost treasure.

"Okay," she said to Oscar, wiping her face on the sleeve of her robe. "Her name is Faith."

"Did we miss something?" Julianna asked. "I mean, I know we

missed a lot but…" She turned to look at Oscar, now holding one boy in each arm. Hope had come over and was holding onto Silas's leg.

"This time's been rough," Oscar said. "Crazy hormones, her folks out of town and unreachable…"

"Her grandfather and mother-in-law God only knows where…" Silas said, sniffing.

Ding, dong, ding.

Hope and the boys raced to the front door. "My turn," Jamison said. Hope held onto Andrew's shoulder and waited for a split second, then helped her other brother tug the door open.

"Grandma! Grandpa!" all three shouted, bouncing over each other to find a leg or hand to grab onto.

"Mom?" Tori called, walking toward them, Oscar at her side, baby Faith now in his arms. "I thought you were in China looking for ancient strains of citrus or something."

Leanne took the baby from Oscar. She pulled the blanket down to see her sleeping face, ooh and ahhed, then kissed the top of her little blonde head. She showed her to Luther, then cuddled her close.

"Meh, those plants have been around for centuries," Leanne said. "Another few months won't make a difference. It was a bit of a tussle, convincing the tour leader to drop two from his manifest and let us fly back, but at the last minute, two Americans came up, waving cash in the air."

"Yeah, some rich old fart with the buffest boy-toy I've ever seen," Luther said.

"I couldn't believe it," Leanne whispered to Tori. "The old guy kept calling him sweetie, saying how Buddy was going to like China, too, then giggling."

"Don't tell me," Silas said, "the big guy's name was André?"

"Yeah, as a matter of fact, it was," Leanne said. "The old man kept going on and on about André and Buddy, but we never did see Buddy."

"Well, that's a good thing," Julianna said.

"And how was your trip? Did you bring back some good news for us?"

"It was fine," Julianna said "The good news is we won't be going anywhere for a while."

"Except," Silas said boldly, his single word getting everyone's attention, even the four and younger crowd. "Except to the altar. I asked her to marry me and she said yes."

"Hmph," Luther huffed. "Took you long enough. Five years and a world tour of coffee plantations to make up your mind? With someone like Julianna, it shouldn't have taken you even a month."

"I'm not complaining," Julianna said. "Silas and I have our own calendar, don't we dear?"

"From Woodstock in '69 to today, it seems like days, not decades."

Silas looked around the room and saw everyone had settled into little family groups. Content. Mostly. He was ready for complete contentment. "Hey, new grandma." Both Julianna and Leanne looked up. "The one whose name starts with J."

Julianna patted Leanne's back and stood up. "Yes, dear?"

"A porch chat if you don't mind."

"Okay." Julianna went outside while he told the little boys he'd be right back. She stepped down onto the first step and waited.

He came up to her and saw something was different. "Huh?"

"I just wanted to see what it was like with you taller than me," she said. "So, what's going on that you don't want the others to hear about?"

"That obvious?" he asked softly, nuzzling her nose to nose. Before she could answer, his lips brushed hers. "Mmm. A whole different set of nerve endings are getting stimulated."

"Well, don't let them get too happy. We have a lot of hours before bedtime," she said, then leaned in for another kiss.

After their kisses became more arousing, Silas forced himself to stop. He pulled away just enough to break contact. "When were you going to tell me you're pregnant?" he whispered.

"Hmph. How'd you know?"

"They call me Sherlock for a reason."

***

Hugo the thug snickered into the phone line. He put his hand over the mic. "Hey, Vinnie, it's the Killer Queen's baby sister. She's in a bind. Do you think we ought to help her?"

"Hell, no. I've heard about little Icky Vicky. KQ cut her off years ago. Tell her big sister hit the road." Vinnie laughed. "You know, hit the road like in 'got run over by a big rig' after shooting a cop?"

Victoria pulled the phone away from her ear and hit end. Another dead end contact.

She handed the borrowed cell back to the buxom guard. The dour-faced woman's foot was tapping threateningly, her other hand open, waiting to be paid.

"Do you think we can work something out?" Victoria asked. "I…um…smoked my last cigarette."

The guard pulled Victoria's chin up and looked at her, assessing her potential as a lover. "Maybe…"

***

Backwoods, North Carolina
Spring, 1681

"I know I had that coin. Where did it go?" Hugh said, sticking his hand in his pocket again. This time, his middle finger poked through. "Shit!" He bent over, picked up a fallen twig, and threw it into the bushes, startling a covey of quail.

"Damn! Damn! Damn!" He turned around in circles, looking for the stand of tall trees he had walked through. They were gone. All that was there were three scrawny saplings and wispy little twigs, all leafless. He crossed his arms in front of himself and rubbed the sleeves of his Yankees sweatshirt, trying to keep warm.

"How in the hell did I lose the road? It has to be here somewhere." He walked toward the edge of the forest, then back again. "Keep your bearings, Hugh. You must have hit your head or

204

something, and you're still in the park. Time travel isn't real." He swept the ground with his cross-trainers again, looking down for the drilled silver drachma he had ordered online, just to prove to Julianna that it wasn't a magic token.

"Hmph!"

Hugh looked up.

An Indian in buckskins and beads was standing in front of him, his pony piled high with the gutted remains of an elk, a travois loaded with beaver skins behind it.

"Ya ta hey?" Hugh squeaked.

Just when you need help to prepare the meat and furs, the Great Spirit sends a slave. It's a good day. A very good day.

The End

Thank you and more

Thanks for reading *They Call Me Sherlock*. In case you didn't notice, this is the fifth book in the **Triplets: Three Aren't One** series. It also incorporates characters from The Fairies Saga and a brief drop in from Hugo and Vinnie from THAT TWIN THING.

If you want to know more about Mac, Mali, Storm, Benji, and Jane, and what transpired while Silas was fighting sleep and confusion, check out BIG MAC.

To read the fascinating tale of Jane coming from the 18th century to the 21st, her story is in THE GREAT BIG FAIRY.

If you could take a moment, I'd appreciate a short review on Amazon, Goodreads, and/or BookBub. Other readers love knowing what to expect before picking up a book. Let them know how you felt about this one.

Thanks again!

Dani Haviland

Afterword

Would you like to know more about Chuck, Grace and Dusty, and all those wannabe grandpas? I intentionally went back in time to late 1991 and early 1992 to begin this saga. Here's a quick overview of the upcoming stories:

Grace – Surviving an evil mother was just the first of her challenges. A gritty women's fiction story. *The Set Up*

Vickie – Gloria and Roger's daughter – is dealing with lifestyles of the rich and famous – and devious – in *Diamonds Aren't for Everyone*

Ria – Brought up in the backwoods by a single father dedicated to helping those less fortunate, she also has *That Magic Touch.* Is there more to life than healing and living on the edge? Would Evan be the one to show her what made life bright and enjoyable?

Tori – An independent free thinker brought up by hippie parents who grow wine grapes and pot, Tori tries not to fall in love with the new hand with the sexy voice in *How Love Grows.*

Silas – Everyone's friend, confidant, and go-to guy in this series, has his own story. The young woman he met at Woodstock in 1969 has shown up in his life again. Will they make a go of it? Will her secret ruin their possibility of a second-chance romance? Find out more about him in *They Call Me Sherlock.*

Thanks for reading, and remember, authors love to get honest reviews!

About the Author

 Author Dani Haviland started writing late in life and has been making up for lost time with a flood of works from sports, rom-coms, historicals, time travel, and Sweet and Sassy romances to Unforgettable romantic suspense and cozy mystery tales – with a few short stories thrown in to round out the reading experience.

Dani is also the owner of Chill Out! Books, one of the publishers for The Authors' Billboard. Follow her on Amazon and BookBub to make sure you get her latest stories.

Contact information:

Website: www.danihaviland.com

Facebook: Dani Haviland Author and Dani Haviland & Friends

Readers Group: http://bit.ly/2DaniStTeam

BookBub: http://bit.ly/BBDani

Goodreads: http://bit.ly/2DHgdrds

Email: dani@danihaviland.com

Twitter: @dani_haviland and @gr8authors

I love to hear from readers!

Sign up for my newsletter to get the latest information on new releases, free stuff, and contests at: http://bit.ly/2DHnews

Other Books by Dani Haviland

ARLIE UNDERCOVER SERIES
(romantic suspense based in Alaska and Arizona)

A Stingray Christmas: (Book One) Anchorage detective on medical leave travels from Alaska to Arizona to see for the first time the son he'd fathered as an anonymous sperm donor. Great and rotten surprises await the cop with the smartest smartphone around.

The Biggest Heart Ever: (Book Two) When would Arlie learn that trying to do everything by himself could be deadly—and make Charlene a widow before they were married?

Always a Bigger Fish: (Book Three) Back in Alaska, Arlie finds out he's a target. Will vacationing detective Billy Burke (from THE FAIRIES SAGA) have information to help nab the scalper?

How to Fix a Broken Life: (Book Four) When Arlie's very pregnant wife is kidnapped by pseudo terrorists, will he be the one to rescue her or will a surprise hero come in to save the day?

Because You Said So: (Book Five) Something's amiss at the Port of Anchorage. Will Arlie be able to solve it and still be back in time to wear the Santa suit?

Heaven and Heartbreak: (Book Six) How will Louie handle being a daddy? And what about that baby momma?

TRIPLETS: THREE AREN'T ONE

The Set Up: (Book One) Grace's story. How it all began with the mother from hell.

Diamonds Aren't for Everyone: (Book Two) Vickie's story – Growing up a billionaire.

That Magic Touch: (Book Three) Ria's story – Doctoring in the backwoods with secrets.

How Love Grows: (Book Four) Tori's story – Growing up in vineyards and marijuana farms.

They Call Me Sherlock: (Book Five) – Back to Woodstock with a friend.

THE FAIRIES SAGA SERIES
(historical fiction/time travel, listed in order):

Kibbles and Bits: FREE ebook: Sample the first stories in the series before you buy. The Fairies Saga stories. Find out how the first five books got their crazy names, too.

Naked in the Winter Wind: (Book One) How does an older woman wind up as a young hottie in Revolutionary War era North Carolina? First book in the time travel series.

Ha'Penny Jenny: (Book Two) More about the naïve and psychic young girl who was adopted into a time traveling family. Will her past catch up to her?

Aye, I am a Fairy: (Book Three) Young British lord finds himself entwined with a time traveling family and must decide if he should go back in time, too.

Dances Naked: (Book Four) Directionally challenged time traveler is rescued by Cherokee in 18th century. What must he do before the chief will show him to The Trees, the portal through time?

Chasing Christmas: (Book Five) A young Cherokee is rescued from an abusive man and changes the lives of many in this 18th century America family.

The Great Big Fairy: (Book Six) Very tall Benji grew up in the 20th century but was born in the 18th. When he finds a way to return to his grandparents in the distant past, he goes for it. Once there, he realizes he can't stay, but must return to the future.

Little Bear and the Ladies: (Book Seven) What's a bachelor trapper to do with all the females he rescues from the Hessian mercenaries? He'd better hurry and figure something!

Little Drummer Boy: (Book Eight) Young Scout works to earn money for a home in post-Revolutionary War America but runs up against prejudices and snowstorms.

Never Too Young: (Book Nine) Scout and Ha'Penny Jenny have grown up, but will they be able to spend their life together, or will the past and ruffians get in their way?

Time in a Little Blue Bottle: (Book Ten) Elvis, Mark Twain, and the prime vampire are racing to get the bottle of Fountain of Youth water before sweet Bella and the youthful pickpocket. So why are time travelers Marty Melbourne and Master Simon interested?

Kidnapped!: (Book Eleven) Benji's sister has been abducted and he and his Scottish police officer brother-in-law will do anything to get her back...even trust the mysterious letter sent by an ancestor, a convict on The First Fleet into Australia!

Big Mac: (Book Twelve) Can Big Mac stop his sire, the errant Viking time traveler, from starting a pandemic?

BENJI, THE LOST YEARS
(contemporary novellas about a young Benji MacKay)

Pool Boy Wanted: No Experience Preferred: (rather racy) Young Benji has been a hostage and slave, but life gets worse when an older woman decides she wants him as her own.

Luke the Unexpected: Love of classic motorcycles brought them together, but Luke and Holly have other challenges to face. Find out how their friend Benji got his stripes here.

STAND ALONE NOVELLAS
(contemporary romances)

Kit Kringle: An Alaskan Tale: Kay moved to Alaska for the wrong reasons, then decided to stay and start her own business. What she hadn't planned on were prejudices and falling in love.

Be My Angel: Wyatt's dream to help save the wild mustangs began with the purchase of a rundown ranch in western Oregon. What he hadn't anticipated was being mesmerized by a sassy woman in a wheelchair.

Three Are One: The post chaplain tried to help the young widow adjust, but would his feelings for her and the search for his lost sister cause problems?

One Arctic Summer: That unforgettable summer of 1994 in Barrow, Alaska, and the touch she never forgot…If she goes back, will he remember her?

The Polar Xpress: Will the California chiropractor get a first chance at romance with the owner of Second Chance Kennels when he is stranded in Alaska?

Too Fast For You: Ten years after Little League, two talented professional baseball players wind up on the same minor league team. Will she remember him? And will their friendship be ruined if she does?